She wouldn't leave her home, no matter what he said.

"You see," Matthew said, "the poachers are hard-hearted men. And hard-hearted men are a threat to a woman and child alone. If you or your little girl get in the way of what they want, even by accident, you could be hurt . . . or killed."

Alexis finished half her coffee before she spoke. "What makes you think they'll be back?"

"You border the park. If the koalas are leaving, they're moving through your land. I imagine I could lead you on a tour of this property and turn up half a dozen."

"Then the poachers *will* be back."

"Precisely. So you see why you should leave, too, at least until the poachers are jailed?"

"Oh, no, Matthew. I'm not leaving. If they come back and no one is here they can kill the koalas without any trouble. I'm going to be here to scare them away. I can't leave. You see, I know what it's like to be hunted."

Dear Reader,

When two people fall in love, the world is suddenly new and exciting, and it's that same excitement we bring to you in Silhouette Intimate Moments. These are stories with scope and grandeur. The characters lead lives we all dream of, and everything they do reflects the wonder of being in love.

Longer and more sensuous than most romances, Silhouette Intimate Moments novels take you away from everyday life and let you share the magic of love. Adventure, glamour, drama, even suspense—these are the passwords that let you into a world where love has a power beyond the ordinary, where the best authors in the field today create stories of love and commitment that will stay with you always.

In coming months look for novels by your favorite authors: Kathleen Creighton, Heather Graham Pozzessere, Nora Roberts and Marilyn Pappano, to name just a few. And whenever you buy books, look for all the Silhouette Intimate Moments, love stories *for* today's woman *by* today's woman.

Leslie J. Wainger
Senior Editor
Silhouette Books

Emilie Richards
Out of the Ashes

Silhouette Intimate Moments

Published by Silhouette Books New York

America's Publisher of Contemporary Romance

SILHOUETTE BOOKS
300 East 42nd St., New York, N.Y. 10017

ISBN: 0-373-07285-6

First Silhouette Books printing May 1989

Printed in the U.S.A.

EMILIE RICHARDS

believes that opposites attract, and her marriage is vivid proof. "When we met," the author says, "the *only* thing my husband and I could agree on was that we were very much in love. Fortunately, we haven't changed our minds about that in all the years we've been together."

The couple lives in Ohio with their four children, who range from toddler to teenager. Emilie has put her master's degree in family development to good use—raising her own brood, working for Head Start, counseling in a mental health clinic and serving with VISTA.

Though her first book was written in snatches with an infant on her lap, Emilie now writes five hours a day and "rejoices in the opportunity to create, to grow and to have such a good time."

Author's Note

Nurunderi was a man of great size and power who lived in the Dreamtime, the long-ago past when all the earth's features were created. Nurunderi expanded the River Murray to its present width and length, and created the very fish who live in its boundaries and the trees along its banks.

Despite his great powers, Nurunderi was a man filled with anger. His two wives, who were sisters, could not live with his angry ways, so they ran away from him, fleeing south.

Nurunderi followed, and on the way, his anger grew. He changed a group of shy, fearful people whom he encountered into small blue birds who still live along the shore of Lake Alexandrina near Victor Harbor in South Australia. At the bay of Pultana, where he saw the tracks of his wives, he threw three spears into the water, turning each spear into a rocky island.

Nurunderi could not see his wives, but he could hear their laughter. He climbed to a high cliff, where he saw them crossing Backstairs Passage to Kangaroo Island, for in those days, the passage was dotted with partially submerged rocks. The women were leaping from stone to stone, laughing as they went.

Nurunderi was filled with rage. When his wives were halfway across, he caused a flood to pour into the passage. They were swept out to sea. Terrified, they fought the waves to swim back to the mainland, but instead they were trapped forever in the passage, where they were transformed into two islands.

The islands, known as the Pages, are still there today.

(This is a retelling of a legend of the Australian aborigines who dwell along the shores of the River Murray. Unfortunately my research did not uncover what happened to Nurunderi. Perhaps he dwells in the hearts of all men who turn their strength and power against the women they marry.)

Chapter 1

The child's scream shattered the early morning stillness. When it ended, silence washed into the space where it had lingered, smothering all traces of its existence.

By then Alexis Whitham had already left her warm bed and raced barefoot to the front porch of the small farmhouse. By then she had already had time to name her fear. The man she and her daughter had crossed the world to escape had found them anyway. Charles had found them.

"Jody!"

As if to assist in Alexis's search, the still-hidden sun began to streak the purple horizon with fire.

"Jody!" Alexis took the porch steps in one frantic leap, nearly tripping over the hem of her nightgown. "Where are you?"

There was a cry from behind the spiny bushes rimming the small patch of grass that passed for a front yard. Alexis could just make out the outline of Jody's thin body, bent as if she were searching the ground. She was alone. "Mommy! Quick!"

Alexis swallowed a sob of relief. Jody was still here. Charles hadn't come and taken her, stolen her so he could hold her until he could get the prize he really sought. He hadn't found them yet. Perhaps he never would.

But something else was wrong. Alexis ignored the sharp rocks stinging her feet as she ran along the path. "I'm coming." In seconds she parted the bushes, heading for the nine-year-old sprite who was her whole world.

"Over here." Jody didn't even turn at her mother's approach. She was bending between bushes, just visible in the dim light. "It's a koala bear."

Like a disqualified runner halfway to the finish line, Alexis abruptly halted her frenzied flight. She took a deep breath and willed the overload of adrenaline in her system to evaporate. She didn't trust herself to speak, but Jody didn't notice.

"He's been hurt, Mommy. I was out looking for the wallabies. I left some carrots on the steps last night. They were gone this morning, but I saw a wallaby near the porch, and it hopped over to the bushes. Then I heard this crying, like a baby, and I came over here to see what it was, and it was a koala. And he's bleeding!"

Alexis found her voice. She forced herself to sound calm. Jody mustn't know what she had feared. The child had lived in fear of her father for too long already. "Move away from it now, Jody."

Jody grunted, a universal signal conveying disgust with adults who dared to issue orders. "But he's hurt."

"Now."

The little girl grunted again, then did as she'd been told.

Alexis stepped around her and peered down at the ground. She averted her eyes after she saw that Jody wasn't just exercising her fertile imagination. The koala lay almost hidden by the bushes, its huge eyes open as if in censure. A child's slaughtered teddy bear.

"He's still breathing," Jody said when her mother didn't speak. "I felt his chest."

Alexis was struck with new fear. This wilderness they lived in was filled with menaces as dangerous as her ex-husband. "Jody, never, never touch a wild animal!" Alexis faced her daughter, moving her a safe distance away.

"He's not wild. He's hurt. I'm going to make him better. Then he can be my pet. You said I could have a pet!"

"I said you could have a cat."

"A cat would disturb the ecological balance."

Not for the first time Alexis silently wished that she could lop twenty points off Jody's IQ. The points wouldn't be missed, and Jody would be so much easier to parent. She gathered the resisting little girl in her arms, nightgown to nightgown. "Now look, neither of us has the faintest idea how to take care of the poor thing. We don't even know what's wrong with him. It could be something like rabies." She held Jody tighter as she realized what that could mean.

"Rabies is not a problem in Australia," Jody informed her. "I've been reading."

Alexis didn't question her daughter's facts. She'd learned long ago to trust the total recall capacities of the brain that resided under Jody's brown pigtails. "We still don't know what the problem could be. We're going to have to find someone who does." She felt Jody relax a little.

"Then you aren't just going to leave him here?"

"Of course not."

Jody peered around her mother's shoulder. "He knows me already. He knows I'm his friend. You've got to think of somebody who can rescue him!"

Alexis was already trying to think of someone who might be able to help. She was living on a remote island, halfway across the world from her home. She had been here just a month. She knew no one, had no resources other than her own two hands and her bank book. And she couldn't draw attention to herself. If she did, her own life could be worth less than the dying koala's.

"Go get dressed," she told Jody as an idea formed. "We'll both get dressed, then we'll go over to Flinders Chase Park. Somebody there should know what to do. They won't be answering their phones yet, but maybe somebody will be up."

Jody took one last look at the koala, then, with a sniff, turned and ran up the path. Alexis hurried after her, the animal's huge eyes haunting her steps. She knew what it was like to lie injured with no hope of rescue. She had recognized the grim acceptance of death, and it had stirred something painfully familiar inside her.

She would find a way to help. And if she had to wake everyone at the rangers' station to do it, she didn't care.

Matthew Haley was having his second cup of tea. He had drunk the first an hour before dawn. That was always the time when the memories took over his dreams, forcing him into a sweating awareness that he was alive and the two people he loved were not. The tea was a ritual cleansing of dreams, a cup of reality, a passage into daylight.

It always took two cups to produce the desired effect. He drank it steaming hot and as dark as the sky when he awakened. He sweetened the first cup with Kangaroo Island's own honey, a honey that was known nationwide. He never drank that first cup without thinking of the way Jeannie had always sneaked an extra spoonful into her morning tea when she thought he wasn't looking.

But Matthew had always been looking, because everything Jeannie had done delighted him.

Invariably he drank the second cup plain as he stood at the cabin window and watched the sun climb past the tree-shadowed horizon. And each time the sun cleared the tree-tops, he put all thoughts of the past out of his head and concentrated on that day alone.

He had no reason to believe that today would be any different. He stood at the window wearing little except the expression that had become as much a part of his face as his long, straight nose or the dark brows that sheltered his cold blue eyes. The expression said, "Don't touch me. I know you mean well, but I don't want you in my life." It was an expression that had chilled the heart of every man and woman who had tried to get close to him in the three years since his wife and son had died on a ferry plane to the South Australian coast.

The sun had scarcely peeked through the straight, tall trunks of the park's sugar gum trees when Matthew heard a banging at his door. He set his half-finished tea on a

wooden table and, cursing softly, climbed the stairs to pull
on a pair of khaki walking shorts before he responded.
There was no need for anything more. He knew who would
be waiting patiently on the steps. Harry Arnold, another
Flinders Chase ranger, was checking on him. Harry checked
on Matthew each morning, just as he checked on the park's
kangaroos, emus and koalas. No one else could have gotten away with such a blatant show of concern. Harry did
simply because he was Harry.

"A bit early, even for you," Matthew said as he opened
the door.

Harry wasn't on the stoop. A woman with cornsilk hair
and china-doll features stood blinking at him, a music box
figurine come to life. Beside her stood a pigtailed pixie who
was investigating the hair on his chest with curious eyes.

"I'm so sorry," the woman began.

Matthew crisply cut her off. "The park is closed. If you're
campers, the ranger station opens at—"

Alexis didn't move. "I'm not here to see the park, Mr...."
She waited for him to give his name. When he didn't, she
stepped back to look at the brass plate beside the door.
"Haley?"

He nodded, frowning. "I don't mean to be rude, but as I
said, the park isn't open. I'm not on duty yet."

"That's okay," Jody said before Alexis could speak
again. "We don't care if you're official. We just want you
to come take care of my koala."

Alexis silenced Jody with a look. She had the distinct
feeling that the scowling brown-haired ranger was about to
close the door in their faces. "I'm Alexis Whitham, and this
is my daughter Jody. We live on the Bartow farm, at the
park border. There's a koala in our front yard, and he's sick
or injured. We have no idea what to do and no one to help
us. If you don't want to help—" she leaned on "want" just
a little harder than she needed to "—perhaps you'd be kind
enough to tell us who might?"

He noted the accent. The china doll was an American,
which didn't surprise Matthew; he placed her immediately.
She and the little girl had been the source of Kangaroo

Island gossip for the last month. Americans weren't unheard of; they visited along with the throngs of other tourists who swept on and off the island with the regularity of the tides. But few Americans had ever chosen to make their homes here. From what the locals could tell, this one and her daughter planned to stay.

Matthew had heard all sorts of conjecture; he had even heard how lovely the foreign stranger was. And he had to concur. She was small and delicate, with features sculpted by a master craftsman and pale gold hair that didn't quite skim her shoulders. Her eyes were a blue so light they were startling. No, the gossips hadn't exaggerated, but now, as then, he wasn't the slightest bit interested. "Koala? Are you certain?"

Alexis forced herself to be polite, even though the adrenaline rush of the morning had stripped away much of her natural courtesy. "I'm certain. He's lying under some bushes in our front yard, and he was alive when we left."

"He knows we're trying to get help," Jody added. "I told him."

Matthew's eyes flicked to the little girl. He didn't smile. "And he listened?"

"Of course." Jody tilted her head. "Why aren't you wearing a shirt?"

"Because it's five o'clock in the morning."

"I'm sorry," Alexis apologized, pulling Jody toward her to silence her. "We won't bother you any longer."

Jody gasped in protest. "But—"

Alexis tightened her grip on her daughter's shoulder. "Come on, Jody."

Matthew couldn't deny that they were bothering him; they were. He'd barely had time to shake off his nightmares, barely had time to escape behind the walls that were his only way of making it through each day. But neither could he deny that they had done the correct thing by seeking him out. Even if koalas hadn't been protected under Australian law, he would have been the right person to ask for help. He knew about suffering, and he'd be damned if he let any creature suffer needlessly.

"If you'll wait just one minute, I'll come with you," he said gruffly. "Just let me get some clothes on."

As if drawn by his words, Alexis's eyes dropped to his bare chest. The ranger was tan and fit, a man who spent his days outdoors under the sun. He was broad-shouldered, but narrow-hipped and long-legged. Somehow the strong, rangy lines of his body were more comforting than the austere contours of his face. He was a handsome man—or would be if he smiled, but there was nothing warm or reachable about him. Even though he'd said he was coming with them, it still wouldn't have surprised Alexis to have him shut the door in their faces and never open it again.

"We'll wait in our car," she said, raising her eyes to his face. Nothing there had changed. He was still regarding them with an expression she could only characterize as frozen.

She had a sudden flash of compassion. Wounded recognizing wounded. She had never learned to cover her own wounds so thoroughly, but then, women were taught in childhood to be wide-eyed and vulnerable. It was training she had never quite been able to overcome.

She wondered what had put the sorrow behind the ice in his dark blue eyes.

Matthew knew how rude it was to ask the woman and child to wait in their car. The morning air was chilly, and the little girl had just shivered to prove it. But he didn't want them in his house. He guarded his privacy as he guarded his expression. He reached for the doorknob. "On second thought, go ahead and drive on back. I know where to go. Just don't approach the koala again, please. They can be nasty tempered, and I wouldn't want you to get hurt."

"We'll be careful," Jody promised. "But I've got to check on him and tell him you're on the way."

For just a moment something passed over the ranger's face. Alexis saw it, and knew it was pain. She knew something more. She wanted to soothe it away. She wanted to find its source and give the comfort she so badly needed herself. And that frightened her almost as much as Jody's scream had.

"Just stay back when you do," Matthew cautioned Jody, his face blank once more.

Jody nodded.

Alexis heard the door shut behind them as she and Jody followed the path to their car. For just a moment she wanted to turn, to shout through the closed door that she had changed her mind, that she would find someone else to help. Instead she walked on.

She had awakened to a scream, and she was still over-wrought. That momentary desire to reach out to the ranger was nothing more than the product of a nervous system gone haywire and an imagination that would be better con-fined to the new book she had just begun writing.

She walked on, one arm slung casually around Jody's shoulders. By the time they reached the car, the pain in dark blue eyes no longer haunted her.

As much.

The Bartow farm was the closest property to Flinders Chase. But "close" was deceptive when it meant seven miles of corrugated gravel roads and dirt tracks that wound through thick stands of mallee scrub and eucalyptus and pine forest. The main road to the park accounted for four of the miles, the drive leading to the farm's homestead the other three. On the advice of her landlord, Peter Bartow, who lived in Victor Harbor on the South Australian coast and held the Kangaroo Island land as investment property, Alexis had bought a brand new four-wheel-drive wagon. The shocks had been worthless in a week.

From the first moment Alexis had stepped off the ferry to gaze at the island that was to be her new home, she had felt like a stranger. Since that had been the whole point of com-ing to Australia, she had refused to let herself be over-whelmed by loneliness and a longing for the familiar. She had tried to accept each facet of her new life with grace and patience. Grace and patience ended abruptly when it came to the Kangaroo Island roads, however. Only a little of the island had anything as civilized as asphalt. The rest was a maze of gravel lanes or, worse, deeply rutted dirt paths.

Getting anywhere was a major expedition. For a city woman used to having civilization at her fingertips, the roads were a symbol of Alexis's new and profound isolation.

Now, after miles of teeth-jarring jolts, she pulled to a stop in front of the fading-to-gray frame house that was her new home. Before she had turned the key to silence the engine, Jody was out of the car. Alexis watched her crash through the underbrush, and, with resignation for what they might see, she got out to follow.

The koala was still alive, its dark eyes a chastisement.

"The ranger'll be here in a few minutes," Jody told the animal. "He's going to take care of you."

Alexis kept a careful eye on the little girl as she carried on her soothing monologue, reaching out once to halt her when Jody got too close. "Listen, I hear a car," she said when Jody's stream of reassurances had almost petered out.

Jody peeked through the bushes. "A truck—ute," she corrected herself. "Sometimes I forget."

Very rarely, Alexis thought. Jody had taken to the Australian vocabulary with enthusiasm. But then, she had shown a remarkable facility for languages from the moment they had begun spending weeks in places with names like Bora Bora and Waimauri. The long and circuitous trip to Kangaroo Island had been a nightmare for Alexis but one marvelous adventure for Jody.

"It's the ranger," Jody announced.

"Mr. Haley."

"He came quick." Jody pushed aside the bushes as Matthew descended from his ute. "We're over here."

If the ranger was surprised to be summoned through a dense growth of scrub, he didn't show it. He had pulled on a khaki shirt sporting a park insignia on its left sleeve, and he carried a burlap sack and rope in one hand and a small black bag in the other. He was all Boy Scout preparedness and clean-cut good looks. He was also all business.

"Step back, please," he said with no additional greeting.

Alexis moved to one side, taking Jody with her. "He's still alive," Jody said, wriggling out of her mother's grasp to peer over the ranger's shoulder as he squatted to get a closer look at the koala.

Then he moved even closer. He began to speak reassuringly to the little animal.

Alexis was stunned by the warmth, the sympathy, in his voice. It was hard to believe this was the same man who had almost shut his door in their faces.

"That's right, mate, we'll take care of you. There's nothing for it, though. We're going to have to bundle you up in this bag until I can put you in a cage for the trip back to the park. No worries, though. You might be a bit crook now, but we'll have you climbing trees again in no time." Matthew reached out to touch the koala, frowning when it didn't try to escape.

Jody couldn't see the frown, but she explained the koala's lack of response anyway. "He knows you're trying to help," she told Matthew. "He'll let you."

Matthew could feel the little girl right behind him. She was almost leaning against his back. He wanted to snap at her and tell her to stand clear, but he couldn't make himself do it. She was so concerned, and no matter his own needs, he couldn't make himself add to her unhappiness. He sat back on his heels and opened the sack, reaching in for a pair of thick leather gloves. "I'm going to have to take him back to the Chase. We can care for him there and see what his problem is. He won't want me to move him, and koalas can be quite nasty when they're disturbed. You'd both better wait on the porch."

"But he knows me," Jody said. "He'll feel better if I'm here."

Alexis reached for the little girl's hand and tugged her toward an opening in the scrub. "Come on, honey. You'll need to do as Mr. Haley says."

"But he knows me!"

Alexis did the only thing possible under the circumstances. She picked Jody up and started toward the house. Matthew turned to watch her go, reluctantly admiring the way she had taken charge of the situation. She seemed almost too slight to bear the burden of the little girl's weight, but she managed without complaint, like a woman who had always managed alone. For the first time he wondered what circumstances had brought her here, and why she was making her home in this godforsaken spot on an isolated island in the Southern Hemisphere.

Then he turned back to the koala, all thoughts forgotten except how he was going to rescue the animal.

On the porch, Jody tried to wriggle out of her mother's arms. "But I didn't want to leave," she said for the fourteenth time.

"Sometimes you have to do things you don't want to." Alexis set her daughter down but wisely didn't take her hands off her. "You know that. Sometimes you have to do what other people tell you because you're not always right."

"I almost always am."

"You almost always *think* you are," Alexis corrected. "Now, can I trust you to stay here without disturbing Mr. Haley?"

Jody's expression was rebellion incarnate, but she nodded, and Alexis knew she'd stay. "I'm going inside to start breakfast. Call me when Mr. Haley is finished." She cupped her hand under Jody's chin. "Come on. Smile."

"Is that one of those things I *have* to do?"

" 'Tis."

The smile was reluctant and brief. Alexis bent to kiss the heart-shaped face so like her own, then went inside to set the table. It was only minutes until she heard Jody's call. When she emerged from the house, Jody was in the drive, watching the unsmiling ranger transfer the koala from the burlap sack to a wooden cage in the back of his truck.

"What's wrong with him? Do you know? Will he be all right?"

Alexis hurried off the porch to rescue the ranger from Jody's questions, but he was already answering them.

"I'm guessing he'll be fine. You don't need to worry."

"Can I come see him?"

Alexis reached Jody just as the little girl noticed a bandage on the koala's shoulder. "What's the bandage for?" she asked accusingly.

Matthew fastened the lock on the cage before he turned. His eyes sought Alexis's, and she knew he was trying to phrase his answer carefully. "He was bleeding," he said finally, turning his gaze to Jody.

"What from?"

"A bullet hole."

Alexis drew in a sharp breath, and she instinctively reached for the little girl. But Jody had already figured the worst. "Poachers?" she asked, her high childish voice at odds with the adult word. "Was it poachers?"

Matthew frowned, puzzled. "How did you know that?"

"Koalas are protected. Only a poacher would shoot one."

He looked to Alexis for explanation. "She reads everything," Alexis told him, shrugging. "Is she right?"

He nodded, and concern broke through his carefully neutral expression. "I'm afraid so. This isn't the first koala that's been shot at, and I doubt it will be the last. It takes a ruthless man to kill one. Until we find out who's behind it, you may want to reconsider living way out here by yourself."

"Why? It's koala skins he wants, isn't it?"

"Right. But you might as well be a koala if you get between one and the man who wants it. A poacher's bullet could be as deadly to a woman or child as to an animal. And next time our poaching friend might do more than injure his target."

Chapter 2

Alexis hadn't zigzagged her way around the globe to this remote island only to pack and move once more. Somewhere on the long journey between Michigan and Australia, she had made a decision. She was tired of running. She had spent more of her adult years running than standing still.

Sometimes she had run without moving an inch. Every time she had suffered Charles's abuse she had run to a safe place, a serene haven in her imagination where no one touched her, no one threatened her life.

Then, later, she would wake up and discover that running hadn't saved anything except her sanity. And sometimes she had questioned even that.

So somewhere, in some remote Pacific port—the place was no longer important to her—she had decided not to run anymore. She would go to Kangaroo Island, to the Bartow property where no one would know her and no one would threaten her again, and she would stay. She would give Jody the home she deserved, and she would write her next book in solitude and peace.

"No." Alexis was surprised how good the word felt as she said it. "I'm not leaving."

The concern was erased from Matthew's face, replaced once more by a chilling blankness. "I'm not certain you understand—"

"I understand that you're telling me I should leave because one animal has been shot at. I don't think that's enough reason to fear for our lives."

"You can take my word for it."

A cool breeze swept through the yard, and Alexis felt it raise chills on her exposed arms. In her month on the island she had discovered that days here seemed to have no relation to each other. One could be warm, the next a reminder of their proximity to the Antarctic. This promised to be one of the latter. The cold air braced her, strengthening her resolve. She ignored the ranger's answer.

"I've put out some things for breakfast. I'm sure we caught you before you had time to eat. Would you join us, please?"

The thought of eating with this woman and child gave Matthew no pleasure, but at the moment, responsibility weighed heavier than his own comfort. Alexis had already started toward the house. Angrily he realized he had no choice but to follow.

"Will the koala be all right in the cage?" Jody asked the two retreating adults.

Matthew knew the koala was all the excuse he needed to leave. He also knew the excuse wasn't good enough. Not until he had convinced Miss America to take her daughter and go back where she had come from. "There's not much we'll be able to do for him except watch the wound for infection and make sure he eats. Right now he just needs to rest, and he can do that in the cage."

"I'm going to stay here and talk to him."

"You need to eat your breakfast," Alexis called behind her.

"I don't want to eat now."

Alexis had learned long ago to save her strength for the arguments that really mattered. Jody would eat when she was hungry; stubborn as she was, she was incapable of starving herself for any issue. "I hope something will be left when you're ready, then. But if there's not, there's always lunch," she said philosophically.

There was a snort from the man behind her. Curiously, Alexis glanced over her shoulder. The lanky ranger was closing in on her, his mouth twisted in what almost passed for a smile. For one heart-stopping moment everything about him coalesced into a magnificently masculine whole. She had assessed him, body part by body part, facial feature by facial feature. She had even been drawn to the pain behind the cold mask he wore. But she had not seen the entire man, and she had not measured that man's effect.

The effect sent a slow warmth flushing through her body.

Facing forward again she sped toward the steps, appalled at her reaction. She waited for the jolt of fear that always followed attraction to a man. She waited in vain.

"She's an unusual child."

Alexis had the front door open before she answered. The ranger was right behind her, and she could feel him take the door's weight from her hands. "She's quite bright," she said, not looking at him.

Matthew imagined that Alexis Whitham was used to questions about her daughter. He also imagined that she had finally settled on the term "quite bright" as a suitably vague explanation of the child's intelligence. He suspected it was a polite understatement, but he didn't intend to stay around long enough to find out. "Mrs. Whitham," he began.

"Not Mrs.—Miss. But call me Alexis, please, Mr. Haley." Alexis walked down the narrow hallway leading to the sun-flooded kitchen that was her favorite part of the old house. She suspected the ranger was following her, although she hadn't looked at him since that one rusty twist of his mouth had warmed her blood.

Matthew didn't want to call her Alexis, but there was no way to avoid it without being rude. And rudeness wouldn't plead his case. "My name's Matthew," he said, and even to his own ears the words were a coldly issued formality. He might as well have told her bluntly that he'd prefer to be called Mr. Haley.

Alexis stopped at the round wooden table that stood in the center of the kitchen, breaking up the vast space where once a large family must have crowded at mealtimes. There had been moments in the last month, when she had stood alone washing the few dishes she and Jody had used for dinner, that she had heard echoes of that family's laughter. The farmhouse sitting on the edge of Hanson Bay wasn't haunted by ghosts but by the joys and passions of the people who had once loved and lived here. Sometimes at night, when Jody was in bed and Alexis was all alone, she felt the residues of that human warmth give her the strength to face the next day.

Now she could feel a different sort of warmth, the physical warmth of a man whose body was alive and throbbing with vitality but whose soul and heart were encased in ice. She understood men with hearts of ice; she had known one intimately, and she had barely survived it. Whatever Matthew's reasons for becoming the man he was, there was no place in her life for him.

Matthew came to stand behind her, speaking as he did. "I appreciate the invitation for breakfast, but I don't want to eat. I wanted to speak to you, and I'm glad the child isn't here to hear it."

Alexis faced him for the first time since entering the house. She felt the impact immediately. Her muscles tensed, and her chin lifted. "Then at least let me get you something to drink."

Matthew knew her answer was polite defiance. She was going to structure this conversation to suit herself. "Nothing, thanks. I've had my tea, and I do want to get the koala back to the park."

"You won't mind if I have something then, will you?" Alexis gestured to a chair. "Please sit down."

He sat unwillingly, stretching long legs to the side instead of beneath the table. There was nothing casual about the posture, however. His arms were folded across his chest like a man who was holding everything inside, especially anger.

Alexis wondered how long he would contain that anger before he vented it on her.

Once again she waited for the fear to come. It didn't.

Matthew began his persuasion. "Outside you said that one shot wouldn't make you leave."

Alexis busied herself with the coffee-maker. It was the only truly modern appliance in the kitchen. The stove and refrigerator were both ancient, although they still worked perfectly, manufactured, obviously, before the concept of planned obsolescence. There was no dishwasher, no trash compactor, no food processor or electric can opener. But there were thick slabs of Kangaroo Island gray slate under her feet and enough windows to feel as if the brilliant blue water of Hanson Bay was lapping at the table legs. And there were residues of laughter.

She spoke finally, wishing she didn't have to hear what he was going to say. "That's right. One injured koala is no reason to turn tail and run."

He changed tactics. "Do you know how the koalas were introduced to the island?"

"I haven't been here long enough to know much of anything."

Matthew felt an unwelcome tug of admiration. Her voice was sweetly feminine, but there was a calm note of determination in everything she said. Jeannie had possessed the same combination of sweetness and unswerving conviction. He knew intimately what he was up against.

"The koalas aren't native to the island. They were brought here in the twenties. There was a fear they'd be wiped out by hunters on the mainland, a fear that turned out to be nearly realized. Some far-seeing individuals brought them here to breed them in pens. Eventually they set them loose in the park to live in the manna gum trees. And that's where they've stayed until recently."

"They're spreading?" Alexis took a mug down from the cabinet, then turned to Matthew, holding it out in question. "Sure you won't change your mind? I grind the beans myself. Jamaican Blue Mountain."

The coffee smelled wonderful, so wonderful, in fact, that his resistance wavered. "One cup, then I'll need to go."

She nodded. No one could resist her coffee, not even this man who obviously wanted badly not to accept anything from her. She filled his cup, then poured one for herself and brought them both to the table on a tray with milk and sugar, choosing a seat across from him.

Matthew added milk, nodding curtly in thanks before he continued. "Koalas have a very specialized diet. They prefer the manna gum leaves, but they'll also eat pink gum and sometimes mallee or wattle. They drink little or nothing, absorbing the water they need from dew on the leaves."

"They must need a lot of trees."

"They do, which is why, even though they're now protected by law, they don't flourish in other parts of Australia. We've destroyed much of our bush land, and with it their habitat." Matthew swirled his cup, inhaling the rich aroma appreciatively before he took his first sip.

Alexis watched, surprised. For a man with so little emotion in his voice and his features, the frank, sensual appreciation of the coffee was a revelation. Her immediate surge of response was a revelation, too. An unwelcome one.

She ignored it, refusing to become flustered. "But there are enough trees to maintain the population here?"

"The park can plant new trees and protect old ones to keep them from being stripped completely until they regenerate. We've had no problem keeping the koalas in the park until a drought last year killed off some of the trees. Unfortunately it was a good year for koalas, and it seems that all the females bred. They began to disperse, a few at a time, to find new feeding grounds."

"And you couldn't stop them?"

"Koalas rarely leave their trees except at night. We would wake up in the morning, and there'd be fewer of them. An accurate count was impossible, but we knew we were losing them to nearby areas because we got reports. The decision was made not to retrieve or contain them. We had hoped. . . ." He thought of all the things they had hoped. That the koalas would be safe, that they would breed and roam free as nature had intended, that man, for once, would favor the needs of another species before his own.

"You had hoped no one would poach them," Alexis finished.

"Koala fur makes a stunning coat. There are people in this world who think it's even more stunning because the animals are protected."

"Bastards!"

Matthew's head snapped up. The word—a word he wouldn't have believed she knew how to say—had been spat out like the vilest poison. "Too right."

Eyes of the palest blue gleamed back at him, fury dotting them with silver ice. "Then you're sure it is poachers, not just farmers chasing them from their land? Not just hunters who've made mistakes?"

"A bullet's a bullet, no matter the reasoning that aimed the gun and pulled the trigger. But no, we know there are poachers. There have been reports of gunshots at night, and the screams of the bears as they fall." He hardened himself against the distress that crossed her face. "And in the morning there've been pools of blood...." He let his voice trail off, purposely letting the image of the slaughtered koalas do its own work.

"So you see," he said at last, when he guessed the silence had stretched as thin as her nerves, "the poachers are real, and they're hard-hearted men. And hard-hearted men are a threat to a woman and child alone. If you or your little girl—"

"Jody. Her name is Jody."

"If you or she gets in the way of what they want, even by accident, you could be hurt...or killed. We're doing what we can to stop them, but there's no way of telling when we'll catch them."

Alexis had finished half her coffee before she spoke again. "What makes you think they'll be back on this property? We've seen no koalas, certainly none near the house until this morning. And we've heard no gunshots."

"You border the park. It only makes sense that if the koalas are leaving the Chase, they're moving through your land. They're not easy to see if you're not looking for them. I imagine I could take you on a tour of this property and turn up half a dozen.'' He forgave himself for exaggerating. It was worth it if he could get her to leave.

''If there are that many, then the poachers *will* be back.''

''Precisely.'' Matthew finished the few swallows left in his cup. For just a moment he let the coffee, the sunny kitchen and the lovely woman across from him warm him. The sensation was a shock, and he shut it out quickly. It had been remarkably close to pain. He stood. ''Then you see why you should leave here, at least until the poachers are jailed?''

Alexis stood, too. Her eyes caught his and, surprisingly, held them. ''Oh, no, Matthew.'' She almost stumbled over the name, but she went on, as if she still had all the confidence that Charles had bled out of her, drop by drop, in the years of their marriage. ''I'm not leaving. If the poachers come back and no one is here, they can kill the koalas without any trouble. I'm going to be here to scare them away.''

His dark brows met in a fierce slash that told her what he thought of her foolishness. ''You're a woman alone. That makes no sense!''

''It makes all the sense in the world,'' she said quietly. ''I can't leave.''

''And why not?'' he demanded, forgetting that he had no business asking.

''It's simple.'' She smiled a smile that held all the world's sadness. ''Because I know what it's like to be hunted.''

She knew what it was like to be hunted. She knew what it was like to be so weary of running that you wanted to turn and give yourself up, give up fighting and pleading and screaming for help.

Alexis sat bolt upright in bed, her hand over her mouth to stifle the scream that had almost been torn from her. While she slept, Charles had found her. He had stalked her, gun in hand, the aristocratic lines of his face distorted by hatred. He had aimed the gun at her, then fired. And a koala had fallen at her feet. She had been racked with guilt, trembling with fear. And then the gun barrel had swung back to her. . . .

And she had awakened.

Moonlight touched objects in the room with familiar golden light. Nothing moved, nothing sounded except the high-pitched calls of a night bird roosting in the dense bushes at the clearing's edge.

"Charles?" she whispered. But there was no answer. Charles was a hemisphere away. And she was alone with Jody, beginning a new life.

She swung her legs over the side of the bed. The throw rug against the soles of her feet helped bring her closer to reality. She stood on trembling legs, holding one bed post to steady herself. When she was calmer, she made her way down the hall to Jody's bedroom. The little girl's door was ajar, and a night-light beamed its comforting glow into the room. Alexis could tell from the doorway that Jody was sleeping peacefully, sleeping soundly.

Sleeping as only a child can sleep.

Alexis sent a silent prayer of thanks that Jody could still sleep that way. After everything, she could still sleep as if the world were a safe place to be.

Turning, she started back through the house to her room. Halfway there she realized she wouldn't sleep again, no matter how many times she meditated or counted the breaths she took or told herself she was free from threat.

Instead she turned in at the first door past Jody's and switched on a small lamp. The walls were lined with bookshelves, and the windows by her desk looked out over the same view that graced the kitchen. There was just enough moonlight to touch the rock-strewn surf with platinum, and the sky was a magnificent abundance of stars laced with gossamer wisps of clouds.

"God's in His heaven, all's right with the world," she whispered, wanting desperately to believe it.

Hours later she was exhausted, but there were four new pages to add to the novel that she had begun a week before. She stood, stretching, then flicked off the computer she had mail-ordered to accommodate Australian current.

The novel was going to be good. She could feel it expanding inside her. Like her first, it traced a woman's personal growth. Unlike her first, it said little about her own struggles. Her first book had been therapy. Writing it had saved her life, although, ironically, it had also endangered it more. There was nothing of her life that anyone could pinpoint in this book. There was nothing to enrage the man who was always enraged anyway. Charles would know she had written the book, but there would be nothing there to make him search harder for her.

Once again she told herself that she was safe.

She turned off the light, but she was still unwilling to go back to bed, even though the hours left for sleeping were few. Instead she headed toward the kitchen for a glass of milk. She got it without turning on the light, then went to stand on the thick rug at the windows to see what was stirring.

Kangaroo Island was a place of night creatures. By day they existed somewhere in the thick stands of mallee and yacca scrub. But at night they prowled the island scavenging for food.

Some of the night creatures were quickly becoming Jody's friends. There were wallabies, the miniature kangaroos with soulful eyes and bony animal hands that clasped whatever scraps they were given like skid row bums with newly donated dollar bills. There were possums, Australian-style, who sat on their hind legs and begged, snatching food from human fingers with the adeptness of trained dogs. And there were other night creatures she and Jody never saw but knew were there from their scurrying feet under the front porch, the tip of a tail, the squeak or squeal or growl from an animal throat.

Kangaroo Island was a long way from Grosse Pointe, the exclusive suburb of Detroit where Alexis had lived with Charles. There the only night creatures had been policemen silently cruising the tree-shaded streets in constant vigilance, and garbage men who came quietly sometimes after midnight to whisk away the trash that wasn't allowed to defile the curbsides after dawn.

There, wallabies and possums and koalas had been creatures to be seen in a well-stocked zoo.

Alexis thought of koalas, and then she thought of Matthew Haley. It wasn't the first time that night. His face had intruded as she had worked on her novel. She had pictured the man who would inhabit the pages of her book, and his hair had darkened from sandy to medium brown, his eyes had turned a deeper blue, his eyebrows had become a slash of black over a long, perfect nose.

She wondered if, despite the training of her marriage to Charles, she was still susceptible to cold good looks, to men with eyes that looked right through her and lips that had never learned to smile. Yet this time she had also seen torment behind those eyes, and she had seen the lips twist into something that had been the saddest expression she'd ever witnessed.

And it had been the torment, the smile that had almost bloomed, that had intrigued her.

"Matthew Haley."

As if the name had called something from the shadows, she saw a movement behind the scrub that bordered the path leading down to the beach. She squinted, then pressed her face against the glass. It was cold against her cheeks, and she shivered. At first she saw nothing, and she wondered if her imagination had distorted reality. Then she saw movement once more. She stepped back, afraid suddenly that she might be seen. There were heavy old curtains lining the window's edge, and she stepped behind them so that the silhouette of her body wouldn't be visible from the ground below. She leaned against them, turning just far enough so that she could still view the bushes.

There was nothing for a minute; then, as she watched, a man's figure appeared out of the shadows. He was tall and broad-shouldered, but she could tell little else. He turned and looked toward the window. She squinted, frantically searching his hands for a gun, but he was too far away for detail.

Then, as she watched, he started toward the house, walking directly toward the stairs up to the kitchen door.

Heart pounding, Alexis flattened herself against the narrow wall between kitchen windows. She always locked the house, and yet, in her terror, she couldn't remember if she had locked it tonight. It only made sense that after the talk of poachers and memories of Charles she would have locked the house and checked it yet again.

Still she couldn't remember. She knew if she passed in front of the windows to check she might be seen. But she had no choice. Being seen was less important than being.... Her brain refused to name her fear. In one quick movement she fled to the door, grabbing the key in the keyhole to test the lock.

At the same moment there was a light rapping from the other side of the door. The key was already in position; the door was safely bolted. She stepped away from it and thought of all the glass windows in the house and how easily they could be shattered with a rifle butt or a swift kick. How easily the man standing on the kitchen stairs could gain access.

"Miss Whitham." A pause. "Alexis." The voice was quiet but stern. It was also unmistakably Australian.

Alexis felt such a surge of relief that her knees grew weak. Tears clouded her eyes as she turned the key and let in the man who moments before she had worked so hard to keep out.

Matthew stepped into the room, and then, with a muttered oath, grabbed her just as she slid to the floor.

Chapter 3

She was as light as the china doll she resembled. Matthew could have borne her weight without having to tense one muscle. But every part of him was tensed anyway. Through her dressing gown he could feel the softness of her breasts pressed against him, her hips cradled against his. He could smell the floral bouquet of her shampoo and hear the soft gasps that proclaimed her struggle for control.

When he could abide the sensations no more, he swept her over one arm, forcing her head down. "Keep your head low. It will stop you from fainting."

She leaned over his arm, but she protested as she did. "I'm not going to faint. I'll be fine in a moment."

"Miss Whitham, if I took my arm away, you'd crumple like a fifty-dollar suit. Now be quiet and breathe."

She took several deep breaths, because she knew he was right. With the fourth, she straightened. The room spun, then miraculously halted. Then, and only then, did she realize that she was still in Matthew Haley's arms.

And it felt like she had come home.

She pulled away immediately, anger and apology fighting for prominence. Before she could speak, he did. "Are you all right now?"

"I was all right before I saw you sneaking around in the shadows!"

He felt a twinge of regret at what he had to say next. But it didn't stop him. "And if I had been a poacher? Would fainting at my feet have stopped me from killing koalas?"

"I didn't think you were a poacher."

He saw her straighten her shoulders, but he also saw that she still trembled. He remembered how she had felt trembling against him, and his voice was sharper. "Then who did you think I was?"

Alexis knew she had said too much already. She hadn't come all the way across the world to blithely tell her life story. She had come to hide. "Suppose you tell me why you were out there, instead."

Matthew remembered the way she had avoided answering him earlier that day, too. He had asked her what she meant about being hunted. She had smiled her sad smile again and shaken her head. Then the little girl had come in, and his chance to persuade them to leave had passed.

But the look in her eyes had stayed with him through the rest of the day and into the night. He hadn't been able to forget the sadness, or something else he'd seen: resignation.

He wasn't going to tell her that the sadness, the resignation, had brought him here tonight. He told her the other half of the truth. "I came because I was hoping the poachers would come back to find the koala they'd shot. I've been waiting for them since dark."

She felt protected. And the feeling was so new, she wasn't certain what to do with it. "You've been out there since then?"

His nod was curt.

"Why didn't you let me know?"

"I didn't want an audience."

"You must be freezing and exhausted."

"Not necessarily in that order."

"Sit down and let me get you something to warm you up." She saw that he didn't move. "It's the very least I can do if you're going to stand guard for me all night, but if that's too much to accept...."

His eyes narrowed, but he moved toward the table and sat down in the chair he had used that morning.

"Soup or a hot toddy?"

Matthew was too tired to care. "Whatever's easiest."

Alexis flicked on the light over the stove, then busied herself mixing milk, cinnamon and vanilla with just a touch of honey. She stood with her back to Matthew, avoiding the small talk that neither of them wanted. When the mixture had heated, she poured Irish Whiskey into two mugs and added the milk. Only then did she go to the table.

Matthew's eyes were closed. In repose, his features didn't seem so austere. He seemed warmer, gentler, safer to know. This was more the man who had given up a night's sleep to watch her property for poachers and less the icy-hearted ranger.

"Matthew?" she called softly. "Are you awake?"

He hadn't been, but as he opened his eyes and chased sleep away, he wished that he hadn't given in to his exhaustion. He felt defenseless, as if the moments napping had robbed him of something vital. He held out his hand, and she gave him the mug. He cupped it in both hands for warmth. The first sip flowed through his chilled body like lava.

The last woman to take care of him this way had been his wife. And without thinking of the consequences, without thinking that he hadn't said her name out loud in three years, he spoke. "Jeannie used to make a toddy like this."

"Jeannie?"

"My wife."

Alexis's eyes flicked down to his hands. There was no wedding band there, but then, many men didn't like wearing visible signs of their marriage. Charles had been one of them. "And what does Jeannie think about you skulking in the shadows all night?"

He wasn't sure he could make himself say the words. Like her name, like Todd's name, they were words that had lodged in his throat every time he had tried to force them out. God help him. Three years had gone by, and he was still tongue-tied with grief.

Alexis saw the anguish melt across features that she had thought were austere. She drew a quick, silent breath. Suddenly she understood so much. "I'm sorry." She reached across the table and touched his arm. "You must have loved her very much."

He looked up, surprised. He had said nothing, but somehow she had known. He didn't want sympathy. He didn't want her understanding, or anyone else's. He just wanted to be left alone. And yet the words came anyway. For the first time in three years, they came.

"She's dead." He felt an explosion inside him, as if he had just killed her himself. "Dead," he repeated, "for three years."

Alexis had never known that a man could love so deeply. Through the years of Charles's abuse she had made herself believe that men were different from women, colder, rigid, filled only with anger and hatred that they vented on those weaker than themselves. Charles hadn't been the only man she had known who was like that, but he had been the worst. Matthew had seemed to be a man made from the same cloth. But now she knew better.

She pulled her hand from his arm and found that anger had replaced sympathy. Anger at a world where some people were given everything and others didn't even get to share their crumbs. "She was a lucky woman."

His mug slammed against the table, and he grabbed her wrist. "What do you know about it?"

"I know you loved her," she said, too caught up in her own feelings to be frightened at the violence in his touch. "I know that she was loved, and that she died knowing it. I know you've mourned her for three years."

"She died in a plane crash! My son was with her. They both died, and they knew for long, long seconds that they were going to." He dropped her wrist. "Lucky?"

"Not lucky that they died, though there've been times in my life when that was all I wished for." Alexis's anger at the world faded, and the void it left filled with tears. "I didn't mean to hurt you," she said softly. "But Jeannie died knowing you loved her. Sometime in those seconds, Matthew, she thought of that, and it's so much more than most of us will ever have to comfort us."

Three years, and he hadn't talked to anyone about Jeannie's death, hadn't even said her name. Now he sat across the table from a stranger who didn't know to step softly, didn't know that he kept his memories of his wife and son locked away inside him. He wanted to scream his protest.

At the same time he wanted to offer her the comfort it was obvious that no one else had.

There was a noise in the doorway. He turned and saw the child standing there, her hair tumbled around her shoulders, her eyes wide and frightened.

"Mommy?"

Alexis turned, then sprang from her chair. In a moment she was at Jody's side, lifting her against her chest. "It's all right," she soothed.

"I heard you fighting. With Daddy."

Alexis rocked her back and forth, trying to abolish what couldn't be abolished. "Daddy's not here, sweetheart. You heard me talking to Mr. Haley. That's all."

"Make him leave. You were fighting." Jody buried her head against her mother's shoulder.

"Not every conversation a man and a woman have is a fight, sweetheart."

Matthew stood. "I'd better go."

Alexis silently pleaded with him not to. "If you leave now, Jody will think we really were fighting," she said as calmly as she could.

He didn't know what was expected of him. He only knew that something was, and it had to do with the resignation he had seen earlier in Alexis's eyes. He was under no obligation to help her. She was a stranger, a woman from another country. He was a man who wanted to be left alone.

The child lifted her head to stare at him. He hadn't seen the resemblance to her mother before, but although the coloring was different, her features were remarkably the same. In her eyes, he saw traces of the same fears.

"Well, I wouldn't mind another toddy," he said, although it was the furthest thing from his mind. He motioned to the little girl. "Come sit at the table with me while your mother fixes it."

"A good idea," Alexis said, setting Jody down. "I'll get you some milk."

Jody clung to her for a moment, and Alexis brushed her hair back from her forehead. Then Jody approached the table. She sat across from Matthew, but she didn't meet his eyes.

Matthew remembered the child of the morning, proud, stubborn, brighter than she had a right to be. That child seemed to have disappeared. He felt the change like a reproach.

He didn't want to be involved. He didn't want to care about this child or her mother. But something had changed tonight, and what he wanted was no longer as important as it had once been.

"You *were* fighting," Jody said finally, rebelliously. "Don't you hurt my mother."

Matthew didn't try to reassure her. He didn't reach across the table to pat her hand or ruffle her hair. He just waited until she looked up at him. Then he spoke. "Aren't you going to ask me about your koala?"

"Is that why you're here?"

"In a way. I was checking to be sure no other animals were hurt. And I saw that your mother was up."

"Is my koala all right?"

"When I left this evening, he was sitting in the crook of a tree in our enclosure, and he was nibbling leaves. I'd say that was a very good sign."

"Then he'll be well soon?"

"Harry thinks he will be. And Harry knows how to take care of all the animals in the park."

"Harry?"

"Harry Arnold. He's a ranger, too."

"I'd never been to the park until yesterday."

Alexis set milk in front of the little girl. She took Matthew's cup to refill it, then returned and handed it to him before she seated herself. "We intended to go before," she added, embroidering on what Jody had said. "But we've been busy settling in."

"That takes a while. You've just been here a few weeks."

"Almost a month. Jody's in school already, though. And between school and the bus ride back and forth...."

"You haven't had much time." Matthew was uncomfortable with the casual conversation in a way that he hadn't been with the earlier eruption of feelings. That had been white-hot pain. This was slow torture. He had forgotten how to conduct small talk, and the realization shamed him.

"There were kangaroos right outside your door," Jody remembered out loud. "Lots of them. And ostriches."

"Emus," he corrected. "I'm afraid they're a spoiled lot. They're not that friendly in the wild. But protected as they are at the park, they've grown tame."

"I'd like to see them again."

"The park's open every day."

"When can we come, then?"

Matthew realized the little girl was waiting for an invitation. It was one thing to force himself to converse with her to reassure her. It was another thing to invite her to visit him at the park. He glanced at Alexis. She was leaning on folded hands, gazing at her mug. Her fine blond hair swung forward to veil her eyes, but he knew what he would see if they were visible.

"Why not tomorrow?" Matthew held up his watch, then shook his head. "Today, actually. But after the sun comes up a bit. You can see for yourself how your friend is doing."

"He'll need me to tell him everything's all right," Jody said gravely.

"I knew a little boy once who talked to animals," Matthew said.

"Did the animals talk back?"

"At times it seemed they did." Matthew shoved his chair back. The kitchen suddenly seemed too small, the hour too late, life too painful. "I'll be going now."

Alexis stood, too. She tried to catch his gaze, but he didn't look at her. "Thank you, Matthew. For everything."

He nodded, heading for the door. "Lock this after me," he reminded her.

"I'll be sure to." Alexis followed him, then watched as he strode down the steps and disappeared into the shadows once more.

Jody spoke from just behind her. "I thought that he was mad. Like Daddy."

Alexis locked the door, then faced her daughter. "And what do you think now?"

"I think he's crying inside. Like you."

Alexis groaned, then swept her daughter into her arms. "You know too much," she said, hugging her tightly. "You *see* too much."

"I only see what's there, Mommy," Jody said, fiercely returning the hug.

"The little girl will be glad to know the koala's fine." Matthew stood, hands on hips, gazing through the tall, wire-mesh enclosure, where the koala in question roosted comfortably on a tree branch, chewing eucalyptus leaves.

"Right-o. He's a dinkum survivor, that one. By all rights he should be a pelt in someone's winter coat." Harry Arnold closed the enclosure door behind him and stepped away. "I'll just be glad when he's out of here, I will. Trying to find enough young leaves low enough for me to reach is a test."

"He'll migrate again, as soon as we let him out."

Harry stopped, shook his head, then adjusted the nearly invisible hearing aid he was wearing. "I missed that."

"I said he'll migrate again, as soon as we let him out."

Harry nodded. "It's a chance we'll have to take. He wasn't meant to live in a cage, that's for certain."

"He wasn't meant to die at the end of a rifle, either."

Harry clapped Matthew on the back in silent agreement.

The morning sunshine had burned off the chill that had made Matthew's nighttime vigil so uncomfortable. Now the sun hung directly overhead, blocked only by the forest of tall gum trees behind the rangers' homestead where both Matthew and Harry had their houses. Matthew lifted his face to one ray of sun that pierced the thick foliage.

"The little girl and her mother might come today to see the koala."

Harry's hand went to his hearing aid, then dropped to his side before he could make an adjustment. "That so? You've been talking to them, have you?"

"I prowled the property last night to see if the poachers returned. The woman was up, and she saw me. I'm afraid I terrified her."

"You've become a terrifying man."

Normally, Matthew could block out Harry's comments. Harry was the one person he hadn't been able to retreat from, but he had learned to ignore anything personal Harry said. Now he found himself wondering if the older man was right.

He heard the slam of a door and turned to see Alexis and Jody getting out of their wagon. "Not terrifying enough to keep them away, apparently."

Harry turned at Matthew's words, and his eyes widened in appreciation. "Correct me if I'm wrong, but I don't remember you saying she was beautiful."

"That hardly seemed relevant."

"No? *I* can appreciate a beautiful woman."

"You can appreciate any woman."

"That was almost a joke, mate. Keep it up and you'll smile again, too."

Matthew glared, and Harry shook his head. "You haven't forgotten how," he told Matthew. "You've just forgotten why."

"Leave it, Harry. You presume too much."

"I presume you won't come unstuck when you hear the truth," Harry said, not at all offended. "I *presume* you're a right strong bloke."

"And you're a meddlesome busybody—"

"With an eye for a pretty face." The model of aging charm, Harry stepped forward to meet the two females. "G'day. I'm Harry Arnold, Matthew's superior. In every way."

Alexis saw twinkling hazel eyes, a full head of hair the color of sea foam, and a gnarled hand extended in welcome. Behind Harry she saw Matthew. He was scowling. She wished she hadn't come.

She held out her hand to Harry anyway. "Alexis Whitham, and this is my daughter, Jody."

"I believe there's someone here who knows you, Jody," Harry said, extending his hand to the child. "Would you like to go in the enclosure and visit?"

Jody nodded gravely. Harry put his arm around Jody's shoulders, chatting as he did, to guide her to the door. In a moment, the two of them had stepped inside.

"I'm glad you suggested this," Alexis said, speaking to Matthew for the first time since her arrival. "Now Jody will be sure the koala's all right."

Matthew didn't know how to answer her. He was uncomfortably aware of how beautiful she was, a fact he had been almost able to ignore until Harry had made a point of it. He had a sudden vision of the middle of the night when he had held her in his arms. He remembered the feel of her breasts against his chest, the fragility of her bones, the springtime fragrance of her hair. He remembered how strange, how wrong, it had felt to hold her.

She was wearing pink, a full skirt and blouse the same delicate shade as the blossom of the common heath that blanketed parts of the island. Her hair was pushed behind her ears to reveal tiny pearls, which were her only adornment, and she was smiling tentatively. He didn't know what to say.

Alexis reached out and touched his arm. The touch lingered, even though she withdrew her hand immediately. "I'm sorry about last night," she said softly. "I had no right to say the things I did. Nobody can understand another's pain."

"Do you always say exactly what you think?"

"Almost never. Particularly not to strangers."

"When I woke up this morning, the world was still spinning."

She smiled her gratitude. "It continues to do that, doesn't it? No matter what we fear."

He wanted to know what she feared. For the first time he found he really wanted to know. Why was she here? What had brought her from her native land to settle on a remote Australian island? Who had she believed was stalking her last night? But he could ask none of his questions. He knew she guarded her privacy as much as he did.

"Have you and the child eaten?" he asked instead.

Alexis heard "the child" and knew that Matthew was still refusing to give Jody a name. "We ate breakfast late. We both slept in."

"When she's done inspecting the koala, I'll put some things together for a picnic."

Alexis wasn't sure which of them was the more surprised at his offer. "You're sure it won't be too much trouble?"

"I'll keep it simple. But she'll enjoy eating in the picnic area. We've fenced the tables off from the roos so they won't nab food."

Alexis fell silent. From the cage she could hear Jody talking to the koala, explaining why he was there and how long he'd have to stay. Matthew was listening, too.

"She's certain he understands," he said when Jody had finished.

"She's certain about everything," Alexis said wryly. "And when she finds out she's been wrong, she's *certain* it wasn't her fault."

Harry emerged first, followed at last by Jody. "I told him I'd come back," Jody told her mother. "So we have to come or he'll think I've been lying to him."

"That could set back koala-human diplomacy a hundred years," Alexis said, ruffling Jody's hair.

"I *mean* it!"

"I know you do. And we'll come back to check on him again," Alexis promised.

"That's a bright little girl you've got," Harry informed her.

She hid a smile. There was always someone who had to point out Jody's abilities, as if they were afraid she had never noticed herself. "Thank you, but bright's not as important as kind. I didn't hear a thank-you, Jody."

Jody dutifully thanked the rangers, but her brown eyes were already darting back and forth, looking for new worlds to conquer. "Can I see the kangaroos now?"

"Why don't you take Jody to the picnic area," Matthew pointed through the trees, "and let her pet the roos? I'll be over in a few minutes with something to eat."

"I'll take her over," Harry offered. "Mrs. Whitham can help you get organized."

Alexis saw refusal flicker across Matthew's features.

"If you don't need my help—" she began.

"It'll be good for him," Harry said, interrupting. "Four hands are better than two, I always say."

"If you always say it, why haven't I heard it before?" Matthew asked. Harry touched his hearing aid, as if he couldn't understand what Matthew had said. Grunting, Matthew motioned for Alexis to follow him.

She was sorry the spontaneous offer of a picnic was being spoiled by new tension. Hurrying to match her shorter stride to Matthew's, she caught up with him. "Please wait," she said, breathing harder by the time she was at his side. "Tell me what you want me to do. I'll be happy to wait at the picnic grounds if you'd rather I didn't come inside."

He almost asked her to do just that. But he had a sudden vision of a man who had rarely allowed anyone into his house or life for three long years. The man was him.

"I could use the help." He slowed his pace, accommodating it to hers. "But I'll warn you, my kitchen's not as cheery as yours."

"Oh, I can make do, I think."

She was walking right beside him, and once again he was aware of the light floral scent he had noticed the night before. Hyacinths or wildflowers. He wasn't sure; he only knew it suited her, as did the pink she wore. She was a woman who wasn't afraid to be feminine, and he was a man who was trying not to appreciate it.

At his porch, he opened the door and held it for her. She slipped under his arm and stood in the hallway. "Old and cool and comfortable," she said.

"Old and cool and in need of a good tidying." He led the way down the hall.

Alexis followed, keeping her eyes straight ahead. Anything else seemed almost like a violation.

"I was planning for this to be simple," he told her when they reached the kitchen. "Cheese and fruit. Some biscuits."

"More than enough." Alexis took in the kitchen in one glance. Small and recently updated, it was almost antiseptic in its ungarnished simplicity. She wasn't sure what she had expected. Mementos of his marriage, perhaps. Faded, yellowing drawings done by a child's hand. Pieces of wedding china lovingly displayed. Instead his former life was conspicuous by its absence. This room belonged to a man alone. She was sure if she opened the cupboards she would find one cup, one saucer, one knife and fork.

"Why don't you wash the grapes?"

She started, and her eyes flashed to his. He was watching her, and he knew what she'd been thinking. Silently he dared her to comment.

"Are they in the refrigerator?" she asked.

He nodded, then turned away. Alexis opened the refrigerator door. The grapes were almost the only food inside. "Don't you sometimes long for a supermarket you can walk to?" She stopped and gave a quick laugh. "Or do Australians even have supermarkets?"

"You haven't been to our cities, then."

"Not to do more than change planes." Alexis knew they were getting uncomfortably close to discussing her past. She sought a way to change the subject, but Matthew continued it.

"I imagine you're used to more variety than you can get in Parndana."

Since Parndana—the place of little gums—was the clos-est town, a mere thirty-five miles away, Alexis knew Mat-thew would shop there, too. The trip was so rough, however, that she was sure that, like her, he didn't shop often.

"A great deal more variety. But I can always go in to Kingscote when I get feeling too cramped."

"You could fly into Adelaide."

She couldn't, although she wasn't going to tell him so. Adelaide, on the mainland, was one of Australia's bigger cities. And tourists, American tourists, stuck to cities. She was safer here. Even Kingscote, Kangaroo Island's largest town, with a population of 1200, was a risk. "I could," she lied. "It helps to remember that."

The grapes were washed and the cheese sliced in silence. Alexis was surprised at how efficiently she and Matthew worked together, although the room seemed too small for both of them. Matthew was a large man, and he seemed larger here, where he took up all his space and a portion of hers. It was difficult to ignore him, to disregard his lean strength, the economical way he used his body, the perfec-tion of his coordination. It was difficult not to notice that when he stood close to her, he warmed the cool tempera-ture of the kitchen.

Matthew finished his preparations, taking care not to brush Alexis, not to linger too long near her. He remem-bered nights when he had fixed meals with Jeannie here, nights when they had laughed and kissed and touched.

The memories made Alexis more of a stranger and, also, somehow more desirable.

Jeannie was dead. Perhaps he wasn't.

Matthew's knife clattered against the counter, and he snatched his bleeding finger to his mouth to silence the curse he wanted badly to utter.

"Oh, you've cut yourself." Alexis dropped the plastic bag she had been sealing to move to his side. She reached for his hand automatically, cradling it in her own. "Let me see."

He wanted to push her away and raised his other hand sharply, in fact, to do just that.

It was then that he saw the fear in her eyes. Alexis stepped back with a low cry, and her hands blocked her face in an age-old gesture of self-preservation.

She had been beaten. Someone had beaten her as if she were a stray dog! Matthew's own feelings were suddenly meaningless. His hands dropped to his sides. He felt powerless to help her, powerless to take back the gesture that had frightened her so. He wanted to grab her and hold her against him, whisper reassurances against her pale blond hair, drive away her fears with his own strength. But he couldn't, not without frightening her more. He gave her a moment to see that he had meant no harm; then, as he moved toward her, he lifted his injured hand slowly, carefully.

Alexis had recovered by then. Her shoulders were thrown back, her hands at her sides. But her eyes held residues of fear and humiliation. He lifted his hand in front of her and watched her struggle not to flinch.

"I'm used to taking care of myself," he said with a gentleness he hadn't used with another person since Jeannie's death. "I might have stopped you from coddling me, but I would never have hurt you."

Her cheeks flushed. "I didn't think you would. You just startled me."

He nodded, although he knew she was lying. "Have you ever tried to bandage your own fingers?" He attempted a smile and failed.

Alexis swallowed. She wanted to cry; she wanted to run away. "Not lately."

"It's damnably hard to do. Maybe it wouldn't be coddling if you could help me."

She heard the gentleness and saw the smile that wouldn't come. She swallowed again, and the lump of tears dissolved. "Maybe not."

"I'll get a plaster."

He turned slowly, then left the room.

Alexis watched him go and wondered why she had run all the way across the world to escape Charles, when Charles and the evil he had done were still living deep inside her.

Chapter 4

Monday morning dawned cool and fog-shrouded. By the time Alexis finished helping Jody get ready for school and prepared breakfast, rain had fallen, washing the fine film of dust from a week of dry days into the Sou' West River and Hanson Bay. Over cereal and toast, she and Jody watched white-capped breakers crashing against the bay's white sand beach, stirred by a rising wind.

"It takes me an hour and fifteen minutes to get to school," Jody said, reaching for another piece of toast. "Sometimes it takes longer. Today it will because of the rain."

"Do you mind the ride very much?"

"I pretend I'm a pioneer and the bus is a covered wagon." Jody spread honey on the toast, biting her lip in concentration as she made sure every exposed surface was coated. "I think a covered wagon would be more fun though. Not as bumpy."

"I know it's a long way, but some of the children travel twice as far as you do."

"I miss the Academy."

Alexis swallowed more than her toast. Regret. Bitterness. Jody had left a magnificently equipped private school for the gifted to come to a rural public school where gifted education was unheard of. "I'm sure you do." She rested her hand on Jody's. "But you'll learn things here you never would have learned there."

"They make me do baby math."

"They're trying to find what's best for you." Trying with the help of records that Alexis had forged to look as if they had moved from California instead of Michigan. "Do they ever ask you about San Francisco?" she asked, reaching across to wipe Jody's chin.

"Sometimes. I make up stuff."

"Not too much, I hope. Someone may actually have been there."

"I get tired of the game sometimes."

Alexis's hand lingered at Jody's cheek. "I know you do. But we're starting over. We needed new names, a new place to say we came from. It's a special secret."

"Are you going to tell Matthew?"

Alexis sat back. "No. I'm not going to tell anyone."

"Matthew wouldn't tell anybody."

Alexis knew Jody was right. The man was so isolated, so intentionally alone, that there would be no one for him *to* tell, anyway. "The fewer people who know," she explained, "the better the chance of keeping a secret safe. And that's what we have to do."

"Because you're afraid of Daddy."

Alexis had never told Jody that. When her desperate plan had finally fallen into place and Jody had been spirited out of the country, her explanation had been that it was a game, an important one, and that Jody mustn't tell anyone her real last name or where she was from. Together they had chosen Whitham and San Francisco, Whitham because it had been her grandmother's maiden name, and San Francisco because she and Jody had once been there on vacation. But never had Alexis linked their disappearance to Charles. Jody had just known it, because Jody never missed a thing.

"Your father was very angry at me," Alexis said carefully in answer. "I think he will be less angry if he just doesn't see us anymore."

"He was always angry."

"Not always, Jody. But a lot of the time, I'm afraid."

"He hit you."

Alexis looked down at her cereal. "Yes, he did." She thought of Matthew and the way she had reacted yesterday when he had lifted his hand. "Men don't usually hit women, Jody. Your father just couldn't stop himself." It was the most positive thing she could say. She couldn't add that Charles hadn't wanted to hit her, because that would be a lie.

"Do you think Matthew hits women?"

"No, I don't think so." Alexis thought of the gentleness she had seen in Matthew's eyes when he'd realized he had frightened her. She remembered the way he had lifted his hand, slowly, so slowly, and held it in front of her. She felt the same jab of humiliation she had felt then. "I'm sure Matthew doesn't hit anyone," she said, standing to clear the table. "And I don't want you worrying about it anymore, either. No one's going to hit anyone here. We're far away from all that."

"They didn't have kangaroos at home. Except at the zoo. I saw one at a zoo once, and it was losing its fur."

Alexis set down the dishes she had been collecting and dropped her arms around Jody's neck for a quick hug. She knew the little girl was trying in her own childish way to comfort her and tell her that she would try to be happy here. "No kangaroos and no koalas. There are things to learn here, Jody. We'll be fine."

Jody suffered her embrace, then twisted free. "I've gotta get my shoes on."

"Then I'll drive you to the bus stop."

"Can I wear my new yellow slicker?"

"May I? Yes, you may."

"Super!"

Alexis smiled at the way Jody intoned the word. There was no question that the little girl would adjust to their new life. She was already developing an Australian accent.

Half an hour later Alexis sat behind the steering wheel, waving goodbye to Jody to the swish-and-clack rhythm of her windshield wipers. Jody had said very little about the other children she had met on the bus, but this morning Alexis was gratified to see that another little girl moved over to make room for her, even though the bus was nearly empty. They both seemed to be giggling by the time the bus pulled away.

Jody would adjust because she had the resilience of youth. Alexis would adjust because she had no choice. She turned the wagon around in the drive, skidding slightly, and started to head back to the house. Halfway down the rain-slick track she stopped. The road was hard to navigate under the best weather conditions. Now, although she was in no danger of being hurt if she skidded, she was in some danger of getting stuck, even with four-wheel drive. The track traversed a region of ancient limestone dunes covered with dense mallee scrub. But beyond the track, in a straight line toward the house, was a thick forest of gum trees and acacias. The acacias were in bloom, their golden blossoms bright spots of sunshine amidst the gray rain.

On impulse Alexis turned off the engine and grabbed her slicker, a twin to Jody's, and matching southwester. Outside, the rain was still falling, but it was a fine rain and warm enough that she wasn't instantly chilled. The renewed earth smelled richly fertile, like a tropical rain forest. And even the common pink and gray galahs that called from the gum trees seemed wildly exotic.

Alexis was well into the forest before she realized she was walking back to the house because she wanted to. She laughed a little and wondered why she'd had to rationalize leaving the wagon on the road. She was responsible to no one. After a life of doing what was expected of her, nothing was expected. She didn't need to make excuses for taking a walk in the rain. She didn't need to answer to anyone.

She slowed her pace, enjoying the smells and feel of the spring rain. Bees buzzed around the acacias and the low-lying multicolored blossoms that carpeted the forest floor. One scarlet bottlebrush seemed to hum with life as the bees were drawn to its brilliant color. She hadn't been on the island long, but she knew the bees were its pride. They were the only pure Ligurian bees left in the world. Valued for their gentle nature and golden color, they were a resource for beekeepers everywhere.

She walked on, face turned to the sky. The rain was washing away her worries. She had lived her life in Detroit's suburbs. A day in the country had meant a drive to some quaint town for lunch and poking through antique stores. She had never milked a cow, planted a vegetable, or gotten up with the roosters. Nor had she wanted to. Now she was beginning to understand what she had been missing. Perhaps she wasn't here by her own choice, but being here might—as she had told Jody—teach her something.

She wondered what being here had taught Matthew. He was a man at home in the Australian bush. For all she knew he had never lived anywhere except the island. Yet there was nothing simple or unpolished about him. He was a strong man, and she suspected he had once been a gentle man.

He had been gentle with her yesterday.

Alexis hated herself for ducking, for covering her face with her hands when she'd been afraid he was going to strike her. She was not a coward. She had lived through an ordeal that any coward would have died rather than face. But that ordeal had changed her. She wondered what Matthew had thought. Twice he had seen her at her worst. And once she had dared to tell him that his grief was misplaced.

In spite of all those things, yesterday he had sat in the shade of a sugar gum forest and talked about the animals around them. He had been a different man then, talking about the job that he loved. He hadn't smiled, but his eyes had been warmer, his body more relaxed. And Jody had sat beside him, openly hanging on every word.

He had said goodbye soon after, but not before Jody had asked if they could visit him again. Alexis had sensed emotions that didn't show on his strictly controlled face. She sensed that part of him wanted to be rid of both the little girl who asked too many questions and the woman who cowered, and part of him wanted their company. She wondered now if those two parts still battled, or if he had thrust them out of his mind, going his solitary way once more.

It didn't really matter, because there was no room in her life for Matthew or any other man. No one else should be asked to live in her private hell. Perhaps if a year went by, and then another, she would know she was safe. Then, and only then, could she think about her future. Now she had to take one day at a time. And those days would have to be gotten through alone.

She crossed through a stand of smaller trees, trees stunted once by fire or storm. Overhead the sun was trying to break through, and the rain had slowed until it was no more than a heavy mist. She was gazing up through the trees, hand shading her eyes, when she saw the koala. It clung to the top of a gum tree as if it were a statue. She would never have noticed if she hadn't been looking directly above her. And even then she wasn't sure for a moment that the animal was real.

When the statue came to life, however, when it began to snort and wheeze like a wild boar and sway from side to side, she knew. She was entranced with the performance, almost as if the teddy bear that Jody had so loved as a baby had come to life above her. This koala was different from the one who had lain in her yard staring at her with wide, accusing eyes. This koala was alive and full of vitality, and he was putting on quite a show.

"Looking for a lady friend?" she called to him. "You might need to try the park."

The koala continued to sway, his occasional snorts the percussion section of a magpie symphony from the next tree. Alexis stood below admiring his gray-brown coat and white ruff. She had a sudden vision of the fur wrapped around the shoulders of a viciously bored socialite, and she shuddered.

She had been right to stay here. There was little she could do to prevent poachers from killing the koalas, but there was no doubt in her mind that her presence would make them wary. And if she patrolled the area each day, walked the land looking for signs of poaching, they would be warier still. Koala fur was not worth the risk of harming an innocent person, even to supremely selfish men. It was certainly not worth the possibility of getting caught in the act.

She lifted her head to tell the koala she planned to do what she could when a shot rang out. It slammed through the wood of a nearby tree, silencing the magpies and her own planned speech. Instead Alexis screamed, a clear, high scream that echoed through the grove until it seemed as if a chorus of women's voices was responsible.

"Jay—sus! Where'd she come from?"

The thickly Australian voice drifted down to Alexis from a low hill to her left. They were the only words she heard. By then she had plastered herself against the gum tree, and the pounding of her own heart drowned out everything else.

Had she really believed she could make a difference? Frantically she tried to decide what she should do next. Her bright yellow slicker and hat made her an easy target—a fact that could be good or bad depending on the poacher's intentions. Taking no chances, she unbuckled the slicker and dropped it to the ground, following it closely with her southwester. The rain had picked up again, and she was soaked immediately, but she didn't care. Above her the koala snorted once, then grew silent.

Alexis ran to the next tree, keeping it between her and the hill where the man's voice had come from. There were no more shots as she made her way from tree to tree. There were only the sounds of her footsteps and her heart pounding in her ears. The forest began to change subtly. The gum trees began to give way to mallee and scrub as she neared the house. She ran past the ruins of a barn and the overgrown thicket that had once been a pasture. Over a slight rise she saw the house, a weathered haven that promised safety if she could just reach it. She was almost there when she heard a roar. For one agonizing moment she believed it was another gunshot. Then she realized it was the backfiring of a car. She stopped at the base of the last gum tree before the clearing in front of the house and listened to the car speed away.

Then, in the far distance, carried over the sound of falling rain, she heard the snort-wheeze of the koala. And in the tree overhead, she heard the second movement of a magpie symphony.

Matthew knew better than to drive the island roads like a Grand Prix racetrack. But knowledge was no deterrent today. He gripped the steering wheel of his ute tightly in his hands, expertly speeding back and forth across the road to avoid the worst ruts. He gripped the steering wheel so hard it was in danger of snapping into pieces.

He wished the steering wheel had been the neck of the man who had dared to fire a gun in Alexis's direction.

It was a miracle that he had been there when she called. He had awakened before dawn, as always, but it wasn't Jeannie he had thought of first. He had awakened thinking of Alexis. In his dreams he had moved to touch her, and she had thrown her hands in front of her face for protection.

The dream had been as subtle as a cockatoo's feathers. He might as well have stayed awake all night brooding over the episode in his kitchen. He had frightened her yesterday, and frightened her good. But then, Harry had told him he was becoming a frightening man.

Now she was frightened again. Luckily the phone had rung just as he had come in from the hike meant to scare away visions of a woman with her hands in front of her face. He had come in to shower and change out of his wet clothes, and suddenly new, more frightening visions had taken over. Visions of Alexis shot and bleeding in a grove of gum trees. Visions of Alexis crying for help when there was no one for miles to help her.

He slammed the palm of his hand against the steering wheel in helpless anger. The ute jumped in response, and he had to fight to keep it on the road, but the fight chased away visions of Alexis dying because she was too stubborn to move away.

He slowed just before the turnoff to the Bartow farm, then stopped to investigate tire tracks. As he had feared, the rain had washed away any evidence that might have helped pinpoint the poacher's vehicle. There were signs that a ute or car of some sort had been there, but even as he stooped beside the faint tracks that were still visible, they dissolved into puddles.

"Damn the rain!" Matthew got back in his ute and started down the track. As he drove he cursed the first Bartows who had tried to eke a living from this infertile piece of ground. Why had they chosen a spot so remote that camelback would have been the preferred method of getting there? And why had Alexis come to live here now?

Halfway to the house he came to her wagon parked squarely in the middle of the road. He revved his engine, then widened the track to get around it by flattening bushes with his wheels. He went on, expertly taking the twists and turns of the remaining track without a pause for ruts or potholes.

Alexis was waiting on the porch, gazing toward the grove of gum trees as if staring alone could prevent certain death for the koala. She had been inside for only a moment, and that had been to call Matthew. She hadn't changed; she hadn't showered. She had come back outside and listened for the sound of a gunshot.

Now she steeled herself not to run to him. Who was he but a stranger, a man she'd already involved in her life too many times?

"What are you doing out here?" he demanded, leaping down from his seat.

"Waiting for you. Waiting for another gunshot."

He stared at her as if she'd gone crazy. "You're dripping wet, woman. And you must be freezing!"

Alexis looked down and saw that he was right. She was wearing a cotton shirt and pants, and the cloth was thin enough that it clung to each place it touched. She pulled the blouse away from her chest, only to feel it settle against her once more as soon as she'd dropped her hand. She shivered, cold, frightened, angry. "He shot at that poor koala, and I was right there! If I hadn't been, he'd be dead!"

"And if his aim had been worse," he paused for effect, "or better, *you'd* be dead!"

"He wasn't after me." Alexis watched Matthew climb the stairs. She knew he was angry, and she could understand why. "He could have shot me if he'd wanted to. But he didn't know I was there until I screamed. I heard him ask where I'd come from."

He stopped a few feet from her. Her eyes were wide, and he could see her tremble. But she stood straight, her shoulders thrown back, her chin up. It was her courage that finally wrenched a groan from him. "Come here," he said, stepping toward her.

She wasn't sure who moved first, whether Matthew came to meet her or she went to him. She only knew that in a moment she was in his arms, held tightly against the rough oilcloth of his raincoat. She clasped her arms loosely around his waist and collapsed against him.

"You little fool, you could have been killed."

"I didn't ask him to come, Matthew. And I didn't know he was there."

One hand lifted to stroke her hair. It hovered over the fine gold mass for long seconds before he tentatively touched her. Her hair felt like the choicest silk, cool and damp against his fingertips, but soft and slippery, too. It was different from Jeannie's hair. Jeannie's had been thick and curly, springing back as he touched it. Alexis's was more like a child's.

But she didn't feel like a child against him.

"You're wishing you'd never heard of me."

His hand paused at the nape of her neck, and he kept her head pressed close to his chest. "Mind reading?"

"I don't normally cause this much trouble for people I don't know."

"I think we've graduated to the 'people I know' stage."

"I'm so sorry I've involved you again. But I didn't know who else to call. Who should I call?"

He wanted to tell her to call anyone but him. He wanted to push her away, tell her to get out of his life.

He wanted to kiss her.

Matthew felt a shudder run through his body, and he didn't know whose it was.

He shut his eyes, but he didn't release her. "The island police know about the poachers. There's little they can do. We're expected to keep them informed and take care of it ourselves until we have any real information."

Alexis stood in the shelter of Matthew's arms and wondered when she had last been held this way. She wasn't sure she ever had been. He was a man driven by grief, by anger, and yet he could hold her so that she felt safe and whole again.

Her arms tightened around his waist. "Thank you," she said softly. "I know this isn't where you want to be."

She was right, and she was wrong. He was caught somewhere between torment and hope. And the place was called guilt. He was holding another woman in his arms, a woman who wasn't the wife he had loved beyond all else in the world. And the woman felt as if she belonged there.

As if by unspoken agreement, they parted at the same moment. Alexis lifted her face to Matthew's and saw the struggle in his eyes. She knew hers looked much the same.

"You'd better change," he said gruffly. "Or you'll catch pneumonia and the poachers won't have a target next time. I'm going to look around, but I'll be back. We're going to talk."

"I'm not leaving here. I haven't changed my mind."

"We'll talk when I get back."

He was in his ute, pulling back down the drive, when she turned and went into the house.

Half an hour later she was showered, dressed in dry clothes and starting on her second cup of coffee when Matthew returned. He came to the kitchen door and entered without knocking. The small intimacy surprised and pleased her.

He sat at the table as she rose to pour him a cup, adding milk as if she had been sharing coffee with him all her life. He didn't speak until she was seated across from him.

"I found the bullet. And the koala. He didn't seem to realize his days were numbered here."

"Can you take him back to the park?"

"He's in a sack in the ute right now. Not happy to be there, either."

"I guess Jody should be here to reassure him."

"When can you be packed and out of here?"

"I told you, I'm not going."

"Then think of the child if you won't think of yourself."

"The *child* will be all right. I'm going to keep her near the house. And I'm going to post signs all over the property."

Matthew sat back, his face clearly showing his disgust. "Oh, that will do it, certainly. Why didn't we think of that before? A few signs and the poachers will run home with their tails between their legs."

Alexis wanted to be angry. Instead she laughed. The sound surprised them both. "I didn't know you had a sense of humor, Matthew. It's a lovely surprise."

He looked at her as if she had gone mad. "There's nothing funny about this situation."

"If I don't laugh, I'm going to cry. Have a preference?"

"My preference is for you to get out of here."

"I've run so far that if I run any more I'll be right back where I started."

Matthew knew she had just given him the perfect opportunity to ask what she meant. But he couldn't. He could see she was unhappy that she'd said so much already.

He swirled his cup, staring at the whirlpool. "What kind of signs?"

"Danger to Poachers. You Are Being Watched."

"It had better not be true."

Alexis added sugar to her coffee, just for something to do. She couldn't look at Matthew as she said her next words. "I am going to be watching, Matthew. I'm not going to let them come in here and slaughter those beautiful animals. I saved that one today just because I happened to be there. I can save more. If the poachers know I regularly patrol the property, then I think they'll stay away."

"And if they don't?"

"I'll be armed."

His cup clattered against the table. "That's insane!"

"I have a gun, and I know how to use it."

"Where did you get a gun? You're not even an Australian citizen."

"Peter Bartow gave it to me."

"He was a fool to arm a woman!"

She thought about his words. Peter Bartow wasn't a fool. He was cautious, concerned, even courageous. He was one of the few people in Australia who knew her story. And his response had been to purchase a gun in his own name and give it to her.

"Would he be a fool if he'd armed a man?" she asked.

"He'd be a fool to arm anyone. The world doesn't need more guns."

"I agree completely. Unfortunately not everyone does. Including the poachers."

"And what about your daughter? What if she gets hold of it? What if you shoot the wrong person?"

"There's a better chance I won't even manage to shoot the *right* person. As for Jody, she knows I have the gun and that it's off-limits. I keep it in a locked drawer, and I keep the key in my pocket."

"You've thought of everything, haven't you?"

"You must know I respect your opinion." Alexis leaned forward. "I've dragged you here over and over, begged for your help, nearly fainted with fright in your arms. If I could do what you ask, I would. But I can't. I can't run away. Work with me, Matthew. Let me help do what I can."

He didn't want her help. Sooner or later the poachers would slip up. Someone would see them; someone would report them. It was only a matter of time, because on an island as small as this one, secrets were hard to keep.

He didn't want her help, yet he couldn't turn her down, because no matter what he said, she was going to help anyway.

He didn't want *her*. He didn't want to stand holding her in his arms again, comparing the texture of her hair to Jeannie's. He didn't want to wish he could forget everything and kiss away her past and his own. He rose and took his coffee cup to the sink; then he turned, lounging against the counter, arms folded.

"What else are you asking me for?"

She seemed puzzled. "Nothing. I don't know what you mean."

"Are you asking for comfort? For someone to hold your hand if this gets a bit rough? I don't have that to give."

She wondered how he could pretend he hadn't already comforted her. "I'll remember that."

"And you'll keep the child near the house?"

"The child's name is Jody."

He didn't want to think of the child. He didn't want to think that she was the age Todd had been when he'd died. He didn't want to think that she talked to animals and knew they heard her.

He straightened. "Watch for signs that someone's been on the property. And keep an ear out for gunshots. If you feel you have to patrol, do it when the sun is high in the sky, not at dusk or dawn, when you might not be seen. Whistle or sing as you go, and if you see trouble, scream. It worked for you today. If you've a bit of luck, it might work again. I'll be over every day or so to comb the property myself, but you're to call me if you see or hear anything out of the ordinary. And you're not to interfere with the poachers. No gunshots of your own, no going after them. If you see anyone at all, try to get a look at their faces, but don't let them know."

"You give orders like a pro." Alexis lifted her coffee cup to him in a mock toast. "But the advice is good, and I'll take it."

He was halfway to the door before she spoke again. "Matthew?"

He stopped, but didn't turn.

"Thank you for coming. And thank you for holding me."

His sigh was almost a snarl. In a moment he was gone.

Chapter 5

It's boring here! And if you won't let me explore, it's even more boring!"

Alexis looked up from her computer and met Jody's rebellious gaze. "We agreed that you wouldn't come in here until ten o'clock."

"I didn't know that ten o'clock would take so long to get here!"

Alexis's eyes flicked regretfully back to the computer screen. Then, with a sigh, she pressed the required keys to shut it down for the day. "I've told you why you can't go wandering around, sweetheart. You're old enough to understand."

"There haven't been any more gunshots. You told me that last night."

There hadn't been any gunshots in a week. Alexis had put her plan into action immediately after talking to Matthew. She had ordered a dozen large signs from an old gentleman near Parndana who was glad for the work. Then she had posted them on all sides of the Bartow property. One stood conspicuously in the grove where the koala had been shot at.

Additionally she had begun to patrol the farm twice a day, never at the same times, but never at dawn or dusk. She sang as she walked, usually old Beatles songs, and she kept her eyes open for any twig, leaf, or clod of dirt that looked out of place.

In a week's time, nothing had been. Apparently Matthew had found everything in order, too, because, although she sometimes heard the distinctive purr of his truck and knew he was checking the grounds, she hadn't seen him once.

Alexis stood and stretched. She had been at the computer since early morning. Normally she avoided working on weekends when Jody was home, but today she'd felt inspired. She had awakened understanding something new about the heroine of her book, and she hadn't wanted to wait until Monday to get it down on paper.

"There haven't been any more gunshots, Jody Marie Cahill, but we're not safe until Matthew tells us the poachers have been caught. You know that."

Jody's eyes widened in delight. "You made a boo-boo. You made a boo-boo," she singsonged.

Alexis clapped her hand over her mouth as if she hadn't realized full well what she was doing.

"You called me by my real name. You have to pay a forfeit!"

Alexis was pleased to see that Jody's mind was off her own boredom. "So I do." She crossed the desk and draped her arm around the little girl's shoulder to lead her from the study. "What'll it be? Your favorite dinner tonight?"

"No. I want you to take me someplace today."

"That's a pretty big forfeit."

"I want to see the seals. You keep saying you'll take me, and you never do."

Alexis felt a twinge of guilt. With everything else that had been going on, she hadn't made much of an attempt to introduce Jody to the island that was her new home. They had been so busy settling in; then there had been the poachers...and Matthew.

"I think that's an excellent idea." She squeezed Jody in a one-armed hug. "Let's make it a picnic."

"And ask Matthew."

Alexis stopped, frowning. "Matthew's probably working today. I don't think—"

"He was outside a little while ago, walking around. I saw him through the window, and he waved."

"He's probably gone by now."

"He's in the kitchen. He likes your banana muffins. I let him have two."

Alexis looked down at the shabby but infinitely comfortable chenille robe she'd thrown on over her gown. She had written her first book wrapped in its voluminous folds, and it had become her good luck charm. But good luck or not, it was a poisonous bright red that drained every drop of color from her pale skin.

"I'd better change."

A masculine voice answered. "Don't bother. I'm leaving anyway."

Alexis looked up to see Matthew in the doorway. His eyes were lit with humor. Of course, he could afford humor, because he looked wonderful in a crisp white shirt and freshly ironed khaki shorts.

Alexis told herself that apologizing for what she chose to wear in the privacy of her own home would be ridiculous. "Good morning," she said with a polite smile. "I understand you've eaten all my muffins."

"I was under great duress."

Her smile warmed even though she told herself to be careful. "Been having your daily prowl?"

"There was nothing to see. Just the way I like it."

"Thank you anyway."

He nodded.

"Can Matthew go with us to see the seals? Please?"

"May Matthew go," Alexis corrected automatically.

"Of course he may," Jody answered, her dark eyes dancing. "Say you'll go, Matthew. I've never seen seals before."

"They're sea lions, actually." Matthew searched for a reason to say no to the child's plea. He had been trying to get away ever since she had seen him through the window.

"I'm sure he's too busy, sweetheart." Alexis didn't know why she couldn't stop herself from adding the next sentence. Perhaps because for a week she'd silently listened to a replay of his voice asking if she expected comfort from him. He had hurt her, and now she couldn't stop herself from hurting him a little in return. "I'm sure Matthew has better things to do than enjoy himself."

Jody looked confused, but Matthew looked stunned. Immediately, Alexis wished she could call back her words. She'd meant them to sting, not wound.

He shook his head. Alexis's quip would have meant little to him if he hadn't heard it before. Jeannie had said it, too. Whenever he had gotten too involved in his job, too intense, too serious, she had reminded him that way. And the gentle sarcasm had become a signal that he had to loosen up or risk hurting the two people he loved.

"Matthew, I'm sorry." Alexis stepped toward him. "That was uncalled for. I know how busy you are. We understand if you can't come."

"I don't understand," Jody said, obviously puzzled by the tension between the two adults. "It's Sunday. Do you work on Sunday?"

He shook his head again. "Not this month I don't."

"Then come with us!"

Matthew wasn't sure why he no longer wanted to refuse. He just knew that suddenly he couldn't. "If I won't be in the way."

Alexis was too surprised to answer immediately, but Jody answered for her. "You can tell us about the seal—sea lions. You can tell me what to say to them!" She skipped down the hall toward her bedroom. "Mommy, I'm going to wear the shirt Julianna sent me last week!"

They listened to the slam of Jody's door. Then they both started to talk at once.

"You don't have to—"

"Are you sure you want—"

They stopped and stared at each other. Alexis pointed at him. "You first."

"Would you rather I didn't come?"

"No." She searched his eyes. "But do you want to? You made it pretty clear that you don't want to be friends."

He was beginning to understand that friendship had little to do with their relationship. Something more basic, more elemental, shimmered between them. "I didn't say that. I said I had no comfort to offer you."

"Perhaps I can't hear the difference."

"I was trying to tell you there was nothing left inside me to give anyone."

"You only wish that were true." She raised her hand to stop his reply. "As for today, I'd love you to come, because I'm not sure how to get there."

"Then I'll come."

"Then I'll change."

She smiled, hoping to coax the same from him, but his expression remained serious. "Must you?" he asked. "You're easier to ignore in that robe than anything I've seen you in yet."

Her smile faded. He felt the pull between them, too. And he was letting her know he planned to fight it. She knew she should be glad, because he was a complication she didn't need. She didn't feel glad, though. She felt resigned. Hiding her feelings, she looked down, shoving her hands in her pockets and spreading them wide. "Maybe I can find something more suitable that's just as unattractive."

He reached out to finger the tattered chenille. Strands came off in his fingers. "I'm afraid this is one of a kind. Don't try to top it." His hand lifted to softly graze the side of her cheek. Then it dropped to his side. "Shall I get some food together while you dress?"

She found it hard to speak. She looked up and nodded instead.

His gaze locked with hers. Then he smiled.

Alexis had no doubt that the smile had been worth waiting for.

* * *

The smile *had* been worth waiting for. The *day* had been worth waiting for. Although the preceding week had been chilly, with fierce winds sweeping in from the south, this day was warm, a fine summer day in the midst of spring. Alexis wore shorts and a blouse of the palest pink, and Jody wore her favorite overalls of Day-Glo orange over an orange and black aloha shirt.

At Alexis's suggestion, Matthew drove her wagon, although Jody begged to take the ute so she could sit in the open back. Alexis knew that after one mile of jolts Jody would end up in the cab on her lap or squeezed next to Matthew, and the last thing Alexis wanted to do was crowd him. So instead they took the wagon. Jody pouted for the first mile, then forgot to be unhappy when Matthew began to point out landmarks.

The South Coast Road was, if possible, more corrugated than the road to Parndana. Their progress was slow, but nobody cared. Jody entertained them from the back seat, reciting plans for her future. Jody's plans changed daily. In the past year she had firmly decided to be a writer, a stand-up comedian, a nuclear physicist and the president of the United States. Now that she was living in Australia, she wasn't sure about the latter any longer, but the others were distinct possibilities still, with about a thousand alternatives thrown in for good measure.

"Maybe I'll be a veterinarian," she said, with a sudden flash of creativity. "And I could write books about my patients."

"I'm afraid that's been done," Alexis told her.

"Maybe I could be a physicist and write funny stories about atoms and things."

"That's certainly original."

"Did you know my mommy writes books?" Jody asked Matthew.

Alexis looked straight ahead, wondering what else Jody would inadvertently reveal. She had schooled the little girl to silence about their past, and they had practiced telling things about themselves that wouldn't give away any important information. But Jody was only nine, and secrets were hard to keep.

"No, I didn't." Matthew glanced at Alexis and saw the way she was studiously ignoring the conversation. He chose to ignore her signals. "What do you write?"

"A little of this and a little of that."

He translated correctly: she didn't want to tell him.

"She writes novels," Jody answered for her mother. "Big ones. I'm not allowed to read them."

Matthew glanced at Alexis again and saw that she was blushing. His imagination caught fire. He wondered what sort of scenes Alexis wrote that couldn't be read by a nine-year-old girl. She was the epitome of graceful femininity and gentility. On the outside she was reserved—except when she was angry or frightened. Perhaps she wasn't reserved when she was aroused, either.

He wondered if her cool blond beauty hid a passion that only appeared in her novels, or if that passion could be uncovered by a man.

He wondered why he cared.

"Have you been published?" he asked, watching the color rise in her cheeks.

"Once." She didn't add that she had only written one book, or that the book had been a best-seller. She didn't add that she was known throughout the publishing world as D.A. Meredith, or that the book had almost cost her her life.

"And you're working on something else now?"

"The island's a beautiful place to work. If I wasn't writing, I'd be taking photographs. Everywhere I look there's something to see." She pointed out the window. "What's that giant bird?"

Silently he congratulated her on a neat change of subject. "A wedgetail eagle."

"I saw some gorgeous birds the other day when I was patrolling. There was a small flock of them. They were large. Black with yellow tails."

"Our yellow-tailed black cockatoos."

She tried to think of something else to ask him about, but he was a step ahead of her. "Is your new novel set on the island?"

"I've just begun it. I don't know much yet."

"It's about a little girl growing up," Jody said. "And she has brown hair like me."

"Will your daughter be allowed to read this one?" he asked Alexis.

"That remains to be seen." Alexis turned her head to gaze out the window and cool her heated cheeks. As best-selling women's fiction went, the love scenes in her first novel had been only mildly spicy, more off-stage than on. But the thought of Matthew knowing about them was doing something strange to her insides. The book had uncovered secret wells of sensuality that she hadn't known she possessed. Certainly Charles had never uncovered any of her secrets, but then, Charles had never really tried. He had been too busy satisfying his own twisted desires.

They turned off on a road that made the one they'd been traveling look like a superhighway. Matthew apologized. "Did you realize it would be such a long trip?"

"Any trip is long when your top speed is thirty miles an hour."

The trip *was* long, but Alexis found she didn't mind. She liked sitting next to Matthew, watching him drive. She liked the hard line of his jaw, the uncompromising set of his mouth, the dark slash of his brows over his far-seeing blue eyes. He was a man in control, and although she liked being in charge of her own life, she found that letting him assume control of something as simple as the driving was relaxing.

She didn't know him well, but she already knew some things about him. Matthew was a man who did what he had to and did it well. He was a man who could be counted on, a man whose strengths were numerous. Even his most glaring fault was a strength that had ranged out of bounds. He had loved too well, wrapped too much of his life and himself around his wife and son. If a man needed an imperfection, his was one of the best.

As a young woman Alexis had dreamed of having a man like Matthew in her life. Now, for the rest of the time it took to get to Seal Bay, she imagined how different her life would have been if she had waited for one.

Matthew parked the wagon in a parking lot above the heath-covered dunes leading down to the water. There was a picnic area farther up the beach, with tables and barbecues, but Jody couldn't wait that long to see the sea lions. She raced to the walkway leading down the beach, then stopped, dismayed.

"They're dead! All of them! The poachers killed them."

Matthew's grunt was surprisingly close to a laugh. "No one's killed them. They're sleeping. Look." He went to her side and pointed. "See those specks in the water out there? They're sea lions, playing in the waves."

Jody shaded her eyes and squinted into the sun. "The ones on the beach look dead to me."

"You'll see they're breathing when we go down."

"You're sure it's safe?" Alexis asked, although she could see from their vantage point that other people were walking in and out between the sea lions, seemingly unafraid.

"Perfectly safe if we don't get too close." He made sure he had Jody's attention for the next sentence. "Remember, though, don't bother them, especially the cows with pups, because they'll defend themselves, and their teeth are razor-sharp."

"There are so many," Alexis said. "I didn't know we'd see dozens."

"There are several hundred who live in the bay. They represent about ten percent of the Australian sea lions left in the world. Once there were hundreds of thousands."

"Do you have problems with poachers here?"

"This beach is patrolled, so there's been no trouble. But we also have colonies of the New Zealand fur seal that breed on other parts of the south coast, and we've had reports of problems with them in the past."

"I don't understand why man feels such a need to hurt anything weaker than he is."

"Not all men feel that way."

Alexis risked a glance and found that Matthew was look-ing at her as if he could read her mind. She wanted to deny that she had meant anything more than a simple reference to the poachers, but she doubted he would believe her.

Jody was already halfway down the steps when Alexis and Matthew started after her. The beach was sheltered by cliffs and white sand dunes, gloriously ablaze with patches of blooming wildflowers. The beach itself was flat and strewn with large rocks that, from a distance, were difficult to dis-tinguish from the sea lions. The bay was a glistening blue broken by projecting rocks that created surf for the sea lions to glide on and clear pools to dive in.

Jody waited at the foot of the steps, obviously awed. "Some of them are as big as I am," she said when Matthew and Alexis had joined her.

"Some of them are almost twice as long and weigh three times more than *I* do," Matthew told her. "Which is one excellent reason not to get too close."

But close was a relative thing. The sleeping sea lions, who did indeed look dead because they slept so soundly, were very approachable. They slept in groups, warm bodies piled in heaps, as if each had been too tired to find his own space. Matthew led Alexis and Jody right up to them, and Jody finally agreed that they were alive as she watched them drawing deep, even breaths. She stayed with Alexis and Matthew at first, cautious because of Matthew's warning. But as the sea lions ignored her, preferring to sleep or find their way to the water for a swim, she grew bolder, running on ahead to investigate on her own.

Alexis stopped to gaze out at the water. She could feel Matthew behind her, and from the corner of her eye, she could see Jody, twenty yards down the beach, carefully checking out the next sleeping cluster.

She never felt so far from home as she did when she gazed out on one of the many seas that separated her from all she had known before. The distance seemed endless then, the changes too infinite to comprehend.

Matthew seemed to know what she was thinking. "Do you miss your home?"

The smile he couldn't see was sad. "Little things, mostly. Getting the *New York Times* delivered to my door. Baseball games. Chocolate-chip cookies."

"Manhattan in the rain? The snow-capped Rockies?"

He had surprised her. "No to both. I wasn't there often enough to miss either of them. How would you know about Manhattan in the rain?"

"I lived there until I was twelve."

She looked over her shoulder. "You're an American?"

He shook his head. "My father had a teaching position at Columbia, and we lived in New York until he decided to come home. I've been back often, though. I did a year of my university training at Columbia for old times' sake."

She tried to absorb the fact that Matthew had a connection to the States. She wondered how much he kept up with American news, American publications. "When were you last there?" she asked, trying to sound casual.

"Five years ago." He didn't want to think about that trip. It had been a second honeymoon surprise for Jeannie. They had gone, leaving Todd with Jeannie's parents, and the two weeks had been two of the best in their marriage.

Alexis relaxed a little. Her book hadn't even been written five years ago. Five years ago she had still been living in the depths of hell. "I wondered if you'd always lived on the island. You seem to fit perfectly here."

The sun moved behind a cloud, and the wind coming off the water blasted them in chilling gusts. Alexis folded her arms at her waist, rubbing the exposed skin with her fingertips. For a moment she envied the sea lions their fur.

"Cold?"

"The sun will be back out in a moment."

Matthew knew she was right. And he knew something else. Just for this moment he wanted to warm her. The sea had stirred his loneliness, too. It was a loneliness that had become so much a part of him that he could hardly remember its name. It was a loneliness he would live with forever, yet for this moment he wanted to thrust it away.

Tentatively he rested his hands on her shoulders. His touch was so light that for a moment she wasn't sure if she was imagining it. "Lean back," he said, his voice low.

"I'm all right."

"Lean back," he repeated.

She knew how good it would feel to have his arms around her. She had dreamed of this kind of warmth, this simple sharing of body heat and pleasure. Surely at some time in her life someone had offered her as much, although she couldn't remember when.

She swayed a little, and Matthew was encouraged. His hands slid down her arms, slowly, tentatively; then, as he felt her begin to relax against him, his arms closed around her waist.

She was small, and Jeannie had been almost his height, yet Alexis felt good in his arms. If not right, if not the same, then undeniably good, anyway. Her hair fanned out against his chest, and he lowered his face to it, inhaling its fragrance. He could feel the slight fullness of her hips and buttocks just brushing his legs, and he had to stop himself from pulling her fully against him.

He had been without a woman for three long years, and his body knew what his heart refused to discover. He needed a woman. He needed Alexis. Not to take Jeannie's place, because that was impossible. Not to take any real place in his life, because that was traitorous. But he needed her in the most primal of ways. He needed her moving under him, the heat of her body surrounding him; he needed the moment of oblivion that only sexual release can bring.

Before Jeannie had tamed him, he'd never lacked for women. He had been discriminating, choosing the ones he could leave with a hug and a fond farewell. In the intervening years he'd forgotten much of what he'd learned from those young, careless days. But he did remember one thing. Sex didn't always have to be the mind-shattering union of souls that it had been in his marriage. Sex could be comforting, if both people were looking for the same thing.

And he and Alexis shared that much.

She was a woman alone with a child in a strange country. She needed comfort. He was a man alone in the world. He needed comfort, too.

She relaxed against him still more. He could feel her breasts against the back of his arms. She was slight and fragile, but her breasts were large enough to brush against him as he held her. He imagined them exposed to his gaze, to his touch, to the pressure of his lips. They would be porcelain-white, like her skin, and rose-tipped. They would taste like the wildflower scent she wore, and she would sigh and murmur as he took them in his mouth.

His arms tightened around her further, and she sighed. For a moment he was so caught in his imaginings that he almost believed she was naked in his arms.

Alexis felt lethargy stealing through her. She was standing on a beach strewn with the dark bodies of sea lions, yet she felt transported. She was acutely aware of each place Matthew touched, acutely aware of his clean, masculine scent and the warmth of his bare arms. She wanted to run her hands down those arms, feel their hair-roughened texture, know the rock-hard strength of each separate muscle. She wanted to turn as he held her and press herself against his chest to feel her breasts flatten, then swell against him.

She wanted to know his taste, the hot probing of his tongue in her mouth, the rush of sensation that comes when two people join.

She wanted to know all those things, because she had never known that kind of ecstasy before.

But she knew just how devastating it would be to have them with Matthew.

She felt his arms tighten around her, and she knew they were both held prisoner by something that would soon be far beyond their abilities to control. She shut her eyes, and despair dulled her senses. Hadn't each of them been punished enough?

"Mommy!"

For a moment Alexis couldn't locate her daughter. She turned her head, but there was no bright spot of orange nearby.

"Mommy!" With a sudden stab of panic, Alexis realized that Jody's cry was echoing from a spot halfway down the beach.

Matthew felt the sudden jerk as Alexis's body returned to tense awareness. She spun out of his arms, already running in the direction of her daughter's voice.

He was beside her in an instant, passing her in two. He knew she saw the danger at the same moment he did, because he heard the sharp catch in her breathing as he saw a massive bull sea lion bearing down on the little girl.

He had told the child to be careful of cows with their pups. He hadn't told her that the bulls resented anyone coming between them and their harem in the spring. Somehow, inadvertently, she had gotten too close at a time when the bull was most sensitive. As Matthew ran he saw the bull lumbering toward her, cutting off her escape and forcing her toward the water's edge. Rocks along the shoreline prevented her from retreating.

Matthew had left Alexis far behind him in the sand, but the sea lion was closing in on the child and the rocks as he ran. He saw that he wasn't going to reach her in time. "Get up on the rocks!" he shouted.

The little girl was crying, edging along the rock shelf that grazed her legs. If she heard him, she didn't understand.

Matthew didn't take time to think that he had never used her name, that if he used it now she would be real to him forever after. He just shouted with all the breath left inside him.

"Jody, get up on those rocks. Turn around and do it now!"

Her name, or the authority in his voice, made the difference. Jody turned and scrambled on to the rocks, climbing higher as Matthew ran toward her. He snatched a long piece of driftwood from the shore's edge just as he neared the bull. Brandishing it like a spear, he ran straight for the animal.

The bull, who was no longer separated from his harem by the pesky child, looked at Matthew as if to say that violence was uncalled for, then turned and lumbered back to his cows.

The moment the bull was no longer a threat, Jody launched herself into Matthew's arms from the rock above. Matthew caught her and spun her around. But he didn't put her down when he had finished. He held her tight, her head pressed to his shoulder.

"I didn't do anything," Jody said in a scared voice. "I didn't. I wasn't close—well, maybe just a little close. But they were sleeping. And I didn't see the big one because he was behind the rocks."

"Jody!" Alexis caught up to them and held out her arms. Matthew gave the child an extra squeeze.

"You went too far!" Alexis said, reaching for Jody to hold her in a death grip. "You weren't supposed to go so far alone."

"I didn't mean to. I didn't know. I—"

"Matthew told you to be careful!"

Matthew touched Alexis's shoulder, his fingers lingering as he spoke. "She's learned her lesson. Haven't you, Jody?"

Jody looked at him as if something had changed, although it was clear she wasn't sure what. "You saved me."

"You saved yourself. You did exactly what you needed to do."

The man and the child looked at each other with new understanding. Jody smiled at him. Then she reached out, as if she were asking to be held once more. "Thank you."

Matthew saw the extended arms and the plea that was no less poignant because her face was so like her mother's. He had the sudden knowledge that if he reached out for her, nothing would ever be the same again.

His eyes flicked to Alexis's, and he knew that whether he reached out for Jody or not, nothing would be the same again anyway.

"Come here." He took the little girl in his arms, relieving Alexis of the burden of her weight. "Are you too old for a horsey ride?"

Jody giggled. Matthew set her down, then stooped so that she could climb up on his back.

Alexis stood quietly beside them and watched.

Chapter 6

Just put her on the bed. I'll make her comfortable." Alexis led Matthew into Jody's bedroom and over to the small narrow cot that was her bed. They had left the States with little more than the clothes on their backs, and building a household from the floor up took time. Luckily the farmhouse, though furnished with old, worn pieces, was well enough equipped that they weren't uncomfortable. There had even been a real find or two in the spacious attic, including the kitchen table, which Alexis planned to refinish someday.

Someday they would have more of their own things around them. When it was safe to make a shipment, one would be made. Meanwhile, they pretended to be gypsies, and they collected new things as they saw them. The long trip here had been wonderful for that.

Matthew set the sleeping child on her bed, then stepped back to let Alexis sit. She began to untie Jody's sneakers. Jody slept on, oblivious to the world around her.

"Was it such a tiring day?" he asked curiously.

They had stayed at Seal Bay until the sun threatened to leave before they did. Then they had driven home, stop-

ping near the turnoff to another picturesque bay for sand-
wiches and ice cream. Jody had fallen asleep immediately
after, lulled perhaps by the continual swaying of the wagon
as Matthew expertly avoided the worst spots in the road.

"Wonderful days make kids tired." Alexis looked up to
smile at him. After Jody's encounter with the sea lion, the
afternoon had been noticeably free of tension. They had
eaten and explored and laughed together. Jody had con-
versed with the sea lions—from a safe distance—and later
Matthew had guided them along cliff tops, where wind and
salt-scoured heath hid a multitude of small animals who
scurried furtively as they approached.

"Do you need help?"

Alexis shook her head. "I'm just going to slip off her
overalls and cover her up. Her shirt's warm enough if she
loses some of her blankets tonight."

"Would you like me to make a fire for you before I go?
It's going to turn cold."

She was so unaccustomed to anyone's help that for a
moment she thought of refusing. Then she smiled again.
"I'd like that. Yes."

The potbelly stove in the living room was already giving
off heat by the time Alexis joined Matthew. He was squat-
ting beside it, adding wood when she entered the room, and
she stopped in the doorway to admire the expert way he
coaxed the stove to perform.

"My fires take hours to warm the house," she confessed.
"I should be practicing, not depending on you."

"You don't have much wood left."

"I'll be sure to order more before the fall."

"Then you'll be here that long?"

"I told you, I plan to stay."

He stood, brushing his palms against his shorts. "You've
never said for how long. It doesn't look as if you plan to
settle in for any length of time."

She gestured to the nearly-empty room. "Because the
house is so bare? It takes time to settle in. Months. Years
before a house really becomes a home."

"You brought almost nothing with you."

"It was a long trip."

He had reached the point where curiosity had overtaken caution. Caution was useless now, anyway. He had thrown it to the wind that afternoon when he'd held her in his arms.

"Why are you here, Alexis? Why did you come to the island?"

She pretended she hadn't heard. "I'm thirsty. Are you? Why don't I make you something to keep you warm on the trip home?" She left the room without waiting for his answer.

Matthew felt a stab of impatience. He wanted an answer, but he hadn't been strictly honest with himself. It wasn't just curiosity that had prompted his question. It was concern.

He shut the stove door hard enough that he could hear the wood scattering inside. He gazed around the room as if it could tell him Alexis's secret. But the only thing it told him was that she traveled light. There were two pieces of furniture. Both, he imagined, had been here already. There was a small scatter rug in front of the chair, and potted plants on the floor beside the sofa that sat in front of the window. The room was otherwise empty, except for an open crate of books beside the plants, serving halfheartedly as a bookcase.

Without even a twinge of guilt he strode to the crate, bending over it to search for the city from which it had been shipped. But there was no address other than the post office at Parndana. The books themselves were a conglomeration of titles ranging from philosophy to light reading. Most of the books were old; some looked well-loved, as if they had been read time and time again. Only a few of them looked new. He bent further, to examine their titles, and was surprised to see that the three new books were identical. Not one of them looked as if it had ever been opened.

"*Before I Sleep*," he murmured. "D.A. Meredith."

The name tickled some elusive memory, buried under layers of more vital information. He knew he could stand there all day and still not isolate it, but he knew something else. It was no accident that Alexis had three seemingly untouched copies of the same book. She traveled light. Even her daughter's room was devoid of most of the small touches that would have made it seem like home. So the books had to be important.

"D.A. Meredith." He wanted to lift one from the crate and thumb through it, but he knew Alexis would come looking for him if he took any longer. Eventually he would remember the significance of the name, and if he didn't, there were libraries on the island and a bookstore in Kingscote. Someone would help him remember, and someone would have the book.

In the kitchen Alexis put the finishing touches on Irish coffee, adding thick cream she had gotten the day before in Parndana. Silently she rehearsed the story she would tell Matthew.

He joined her silently. Before she could sit at the table, he stopped her, cupping his hand under her elbow. "Would you like to sit on the porch? It's a bit cold, but you could change into something warmer."

"What about you?"

"I'll be fine in this."

She liked the idea of sitting in the dark with him. The porch was wide and old, with benches spanning its length. She sat there often, listening to the rustlings of the night creatures and the surf pounding the shore of Hanson Bay.

"I'll just be a minute." She left him to carry their cups outside.

Matthew settled on a bench, leaning back against the wall, and waited for her. When she came out she was dressed in a jacket and comfortable baggy slacks that emphasized her tiny waist. She held out her hands. "I've got something here that might fit you. Do you call this a jumper like they do in New Zealand?"

"I grew up in New York calling it a sweater." He reached for the sweater, and their hands brushed.

Alexis pulled hers back as if she had given offense. "Try it on."

The sweater was hand-knit and as soft as the sheep it had come from. It was a snug fit, but its warmth was welcome.

"I got the sweater in New Zealand. It was made by an old Maori woman from wool she spun herself. She told me it would bring me luck."

"And has it?"

"That depends on how you look at it, I guess." Alexis had decided to volunteer enough of her story to keep Matthew from asking questions she couldn't answer. It was an old trick, one she had grown adept at over the years. She wished she'd never had to learn it. "A little while ago you asked me why I came here."

He was surprised she'd gotten so quickly to the point. "And you ignored me."

"It's not an easy question to answer. I'm not proud of why I'm here. I'm running away."

He turned so that he could see her face. There was just enough moonlight for him to distinguish her features, but not to read her expression. "From what?"

"A life I didn't want." She cupped her mug in her hands, but even its added heat couldn't keep her from shivering.

"You're cold."

"Not really. I just don't like talking about the past."

"You don't have to."

"Let me tell you. Then I won't have to tell you again."

He moved a little closer, hoping to warm her.

"I've been divorced for four years. The divorce wasn't...pleasant. Jody's father, Charles, is a difficult man. He's used to getting what he wants, and he didn't want the divorce. So..." She sipped her coffee, trying to phrase the next part in her head before she spoke. "It finally became clear to me that I wasn't going to have a life of my own unless I got away from him. I took Jody and left the country, hoping that if we were gone, he could begin to make a new life for himself, too. Jody and I traveled for a while, looking for a place to settle down. I found out about Kangaroo Island from my attorney. Peter Bartow is his cousin. So here we are."

He suspected she had developed condensation into an art form. "Jody doesn't miss her father?"

"They were never close." Alexis wanted to laugh at her own irony. It was certainly true. She had done everything she could to keep Charles from getting close to Jody, because it had been clear from the start that he wouldn't tolerate her normal imperfections any more than he tolerated his wife's. Alexis had shielded and sheltered her daughter, and Charles had continued to vent his hostilities where he'd vented them since the first day of his marriage.

"Does your former husband know where you are?"

"I don't think so." She forced herself to lie, knowing she needed to put the discussion to rest. "I doubt he cares anymore. Out of sight, out of mind."

Her explanation was as full of holes as the island's famous granite boulders at Cape du Couedic. It said nothing about the fear in her eyes, about her own admission that she'd been hunted, about hands protecting her face. It said nothing about a house empty of personal belongings and a decision to live in an area so isolated that only a jungle guide could have found her.

She might be telling less than the truth simply because she owed him no explanation, but Matthew doubted that was the reason. If the moon were brighter, he was certain he would see desperation in her eyes.

"What are you afraid of, then?" he asked softly. "Who did you think you'd see the night I came to your kitchen door?"

She exhaled sharply, as if she'd been praying he wouldn't ask. "No one," she said, too quickly. "It was late, and I was tired. Maybe I was afraid of ghosts. I don't know. My imagination knows no bounds. That's why I'm a writer."

He sat back. He knew she wasn't going to answer any more questions about her fears. "Was your book successful?"

She was counting her lies now, totaling them against her fear of exposure. "Moderately. Enough to pay the bills."

"What was it called?"

She laughed, hoping to throw him off track. "I'm not going to answer that one. You wouldn't believe the people who think they understand everything about me after reading my book.''

''But they don't?''

''No one understands anyone. How can they?''

He didn't need moonlight to *hear* desperation. It was the fine-honed edge to a voice usually musical and gentle. He set down his mug and moved closer to her. His arm crept slowly around her waist.

''No one can understand if they're not given the chance.''

''This is getting dangerously close to comfort.''

''Is that what this is?'' Matthew rested his other hand on her shoulder and turned her slightly so she was facing him. ''Perhaps I was wrong, then. Perhaps I have some comfort to offer you. And perhaps you have some to offer me.''

''The only man I ever offered my comfort to found it sadly lacking.''

''But we already know he's a fool.'' His fingers threaded into her hair, and his thumb caressed her jawline.

Alexis studied his face. There were shadows there that weren't created by the moonlight. ''Charles is not a fool. I only wish he were.''

He waited for her to say more, but she just continued studying his face. ''What do you see?'' he asked at last. ''A man like the others you've known?''

''I see a man who's suffered but never made anyone else suffer because of him. I see a man who's still suffering and doesn't believe it will ever end.'' She reached up to touch his lips to silence him. ''And I see a man who wants solace, but nothing more.''

He waited until her hand was in her lap again. ''Do you see a man who wants to kiss you?''

''I see a man who wants more than a kiss. He wants to lose himself in a woman. But then he wants to go back to his suffering.''

''It's not a choice, Alexis. I can't change the events of my life.''

''I know. Neither can I.'' She leaned closer, lifting her face to his. ''But I can kiss you.''

He hesitated only momentarily. Then his hand cupped the nape of her neck, and he held her still as he took her mouth. It was sweet and soft, and it molded to his as if he had always been kissing her.

She sighed and draped her arms loosely around his neck, moving closer. His other hand lifted to her hair, and he let it slip through his fingers again and again.

With feather-light strokes Alexis discovered the width of his shoulders, the warm skin of his neck, the slight wave in his hair. She opened her mouth to his exploration and felt the slow rhythm of his tongue in a place deep inside her.

The kiss became two, then three. And there was nothing comforting about the kisses or the concern on two faces when they finally broke apart. Alexis brushed Matthew's bottom lip with her thumb, then moved away from him to stare out into the night.

"A kiss seemed like a small thing to ask," she said.

"Yes."

"There's no place in your life for me, and I have no place for you. I have to make my way alone."

Matthew leaned against the wall and closed his eyes. His heart still slammed against his rib cage, a helpless victim of two people who wanted and couldn't have, who had tasted and learned that hunger couldn't be appeased by so little.

"Alone is all there is."

Alexis stared out into the night. "It would be easier if I believed you," she said at last. "But how can I, when I know you only wish it were true?"

Matthew spent the hour before dawn trying to put together everything he had remembered about D.A. Meredith. He had awakened with one fact a shining beacon on his search. *Before I Sleep* had been a smash best-seller, flying out of bookstores as if it had wings of its own. The thing that made it most unusual, however, was that D.A. Meredith was a pseudonym, and the author had refused to step forward to take credit where it was due. There had been conjecture in the press, but the universal consensus was that events in the novel were based on the lives of real people.

D.A. Meredith was said to be afraid to admit to writing the book, because if she did, fingers would be pointed and lawsuits initiated.

By remaining anonymous, no one could be sure who she had known and not known.

There had been more, but Matthew had quickly lost interest. The whole furor had seemed like nothing more than a publicity gimmick. He found such pleasure in reading that he didn't want to feel manipulated by publishers and booksellers. Too, his taste ran more to nonfiction, and what fiction he read was usually set in Australia.

Now he wished he hadn't been so indifferent. He knew there was more to the story, but memory had served him as well as it could. He either had to get hold of the book himself or talk to someone who had.

The someone who had was Harry Arnold.

Harry had been a Flinders Chase ranger for twenty-nine years. He always said that if he hadn't liked to read, they would have had to cart him to the nuthouse years before, because all the clean air, quiet nights and clear views of the Southern Cross were enough to drive any man insane. Harry read everything that came his way. It was all the same to him: mysteries, romances, cookbooks. The librarians in Kingscote and Penneshaw were his best friends—next to Matthew.

Now that Harry's hearing had begun to fail, reading was even more important to him. His wife had died twelve years before, and although he sent the hearts of every single island woman over fifty into overdrive, he had no thoughts of remarriage. He romanced them all, spreading his attentions with no thought of favoritism. But what Harry loved best was a good book.

He was in the middle of one when Matthew found him eating breakfast. "G'day," Matthew said, tapping Harry on the shoulder.

"I knew you were there." Harry finished his paragraph before he looked up. "I'm wearing me box."

Harry's "box" was tiny, almost invisible. To hear Harry tell it, it weighed sixty pounds and was slowly extending his ear lobe by an inch a week. The "box," however, kept Harry from having to take early retirement. And since everyone knew that the Chase wouldn't be the same place without Harry Arnold, everyone encouraged him to wear it.

"Mind if I have some tea?"

"You know where I keep the kettle."

Matthew hadn't used Harry's kettle for three years, but he found it anyway, filling it with fresh water and setting it on the burner before he returned to the table. "What are you reading?"

"You're a regular fountain of questions this morning." Harry turned the page and looked up, smiling to be sure his teasing wasn't misunderstood. "Have a good day yesterday?"

Matthew wouldn't have used "good" to describe it, but he decided it was safer to nod than to explain. "You?"

"I started this book." He held it up for Matthew to read the title.

"You're planning to take up scuba diving?"

"In me dreams." Harry marked his place with an old envelope, then set the book aside. "Now, what are you doing here, Matthew? Not that I'm sad to see you, you understand."

"Have you read a book called *Before I Sleep*?"

"It's on me bookshelf. I got it from the library last year, then bought me own copy."

"Then you liked it?"

Harry appeared to be considering the question. "I can't say I liked it," he said finally. "No, I can't say that. But it stuck with me."

"Why?" The kettle began to whistle, but Matthew ignored it.

"It's a bloody good book. Good story, good characters, and it made me think."

"But you didn't like it?"

"I *like* detective novels. I *like* books about the American west and the outback. I can read one, then go about me business. I took a while to do that after *Before I Sleep*."

"What's it about?"

"Why are you so interested? And would you please get the bloody kettle, or I'll lose what little hearing I've got left."

Matthew got the kettle, making a pot of tea to bring back to the table for them both. He sprawled across from Harry as he waited for it to brew. "Yesterday I noticed Alexis had several copies of the book. I was just curious why."

"You could have asked her. You are talking to her, aren't you?"

"There are things she doesn't talk about."

Harry nodded sagely. "She's one of the walking wounded, too, is she?"

"What's the book about, Harry?"

"It's been a while since I read it, but it's an American book. The main character is a woman trapped in a bad marriage. Her husband bashes her, but nobody believes it because the rest of the world sees a different side of him. There are other characters, too, a right good love story and lots of corporate shenanigans, even a bit about organized crime that makes *The Godfather* look like a child's primer. But the main thing I remember is the abused wife and her struggle."

Matthew made a tent of his fingers. For a moment he didn't want to go on with his questioning. The problem with questions was that sometimes you got answers.

"She dies at the end," Harry said when Matthew didn't speak. "She dies because nobody will help her."

Matthew jerked forward, reaching for the teapot. "What do you know about the author?"

"At first there was a big set-to about who wrote it. Seems the publisher made up a biography, but when reporters tried to find D.A. Meredith to interview her, they couldn't. Then there was speculation that she didn't exist. Some thought the book had been written by a collection of people, one of those 'you take chapter one, I'll take chapter two' schemes. But anyone who's read the book seriously knows only one person could have written it."

"Did they find the author?"

"They did, finally. Apparently the publishers had hid the trail to her so cleverly that it took most of a year, but some enterprising bloke finally located her. She was the former wife of one of the big shots in the automobile industry. She refused to admit she'd written the book, but the evidence was clear. When she couldn't deny it any longer she admitted writing the book but refused to admit that it had any basis in reality. There were those who thought she'd written it because her divorce settlement was so small." Harry held out his cup and watched Matthew fill it.

"You make a good cuppa," he complimented.

"Anything else about the author?" Matthew asked as casually as he could.

"Somebody got hold of the preliminary papers in her divorce suit. The main papers were sealed, but the preliminary papers were enough to link the woman's ex-husband to some thinly veiled incidents in the book. The publicity was fierce. If I recall, there was even a move to boycott autos from that company. It became a real women's issue. And all the while, D.A. Meredith kept right on refusing to say if the book had any basis in fact."

Matthew sat silently so long that his tea was cool before he raised it to his lips. "What finally happened to the author?"

Harry shrugged. "The excitement died down. People found something new. The author secluded herself somewhere to write another book. Her former husband lost his job but got snapped up by another automaker. Life went on."

"Secluded herself?"

"She just disappeared one day, and no one could find her. There were murmurs of foul play, but her publishers assured the world that she was fine, just riding out the publicity in seclusion."

"Do you remember her real name, Harry? Not her pseudonym?"

Harry wrinkled his brow. "Can't say I do. But I think it was Dana something. That's what the D was for. Dana Cahill. That was it. Her husband was Charles Cahill. Cahill's a big name in America. Ever heard of him?"

Chapter 7

Matthew took three nights to finish *Before I Sleep*. During the days in between, he brooded as he worked. He no longer had any doubts that Alexis had written the book. Everything fit. He could have satisfied any questions by driving to Kingscote to look through back issues of the news magazines for a picture of D.A. Meredith, but since he was already certain, he didn't bother.

Alexis had written the book. More important, as he read each chapter, delving deeper into the twisted psyche of the heroine's husband, he knew she had lived it.

She had lived with Charles Cahill, a man much like Terrence Garrick of *Before I Sleep*, and she was running from him now.

Running because she didn't want her own final chapter to mirror the novel's.

On the third night, when the last page had been read, he hurled the book at his bedroom wall. He'd had questions, and now he had answers. He wished, fervently, that the answers had been different.

The clock in his hallway chimed once, then was silent. He'd been up late for three nights, but there was no question whether he'd get to sleep that night. He wouldn't. His mind was churning with thoughts of Cynthia Garrick of *Before I Sleep*, and of Alexis Whitham.

He had an urgent need to check her safety. He had been patrolling her property more frequently since beginning the book, but he hadn't seen her. He had seen the light in her study, seen that her automobile was parked at slightly different angles each day, seen that Jody had left a plate of scraps for the wallabies she was training to come up on the porch. He knew Alexis and Jody were all right—so far. He wasn't sure they would remain so.

He rose from bed and pulled on his trousers and an old rugby shirt. In his haste to leave he slipped on loafers without any socks as he searched for the keys to his ute. At the door he almost tripped over the book. It was lying open, its white pages reflecting the light from his bedside lamp. He had the sudden vision of a childhood religious crusade he had once been forced to attend with his grandparents. The preacher, a powerful man with a lion's mane and eyes that shot fire, had stood at the front of the woolshed-turned-church and held the Bible aloft. It had fallen open, and its pages, too, had reflected the light.

"Judgment," the man had screamed. "Judgment!"

Matthew kicked the book to one side and ran out the door.

Alexis pulled Ron Bartow's letter from its envelope. She had memorized the contents, but she wanted to read it again anyway, hoping it would help her sleep.

She was still too keyed up to turn off the light and close her eyes. "Let it be true," she whispered into the silent bedroom. "Please God, let it be true!"

If it *were* true, then she could begin to hope again. If it were true, she could begin to live again.

" 'Charles is seeing a woman, Sandra Oliver, of the Ann Arbor Olivers. There are rumors of an engagement announcement in the not too distant future. There are also rumors that he may be in line for a job at the very top of the corporation.' " She read the words out loud like an ancient chant to ward off evil. "'And if everything our investigator tells us is true, it looks like he's stopped searching for you, Dana. He can't chance anything now. He has too much to lose.'"

Too much to lose! She was the one who had lost everything. Yet the words still thrilled her, even as the use of her real name, which now seemed to belong to a stranger, brought her past back too vividly.

She thought about the turn of events in Charles's life. She felt deepest regret for Sandra Oliver, but Sandra had been warned. *Before I Sleep* had warned the world. Now Alexis had her own life to struggle with.

She thought of what a dear, faithful friend Ron had been through the nightmare of the last years. From the beginning he had believed her stories of Charles's abuse when no one else had, or had wanted to.

Ron had been rising through the ranks of one of Detroit's most prestigious law firms when Alexis had been introduced to him at a cocktail party. She had liked him right away, liked the warmth in his eyes, the quiet way he listened, the loving way he treated his wife.

And she had liked the fact that his firm was prestigious, because she believed that only someone well-established and respected could help her get what she most desired: a divorce from Charles.

Looking back years later, she and Ron had pondered how they could have been so naive. The firm had terminated Ron without warning when he'd agreed to represent Alexis in her divorce attempt. The following night he had been stabbed and left for dead in his suburban garage. His wallet with less than four dollars had been taken, but his expensive gold pocket watch and a diamond-studded wedding ring had been passed over.

Alexis had withdrawn her suit, not only because of the harm done to Ron, but because that same night Charles showed her evidence that he'd had fabricated. The evidence suggested that she had both cheated on her husband and abused her infant daughter. He would use the evidence, he informed her, to get custody of Jody.

There had been no one to go to for advice. Ron had almost died because he had befriended her. She had made no other close friends, humiliated that they might discover the truth about the abuse she suffered. Her family more than approved of her marriage; they had engineered it. Charles Cahill was the perfect match for dear Dana. His feet were firmly on the ground, while her head was somewhere in the clouds. His bloodlines were impeccable, his education properly Ivy League, and his family's wealth rivaled their own.

Any stories Alexis tried to tell her family were considered flights of fantasy. She had always been considered the odd duck, the child who was more at home in her imagination than the real world. When Alexis had tried to confront her mother with the truth, her mother's response had been that she was to stop complaining and start giving dear Charles what he needed.

If her mother had listened, she would have known that Alexis had been giving Charles what he needed since the first day of her marriage: a target for a soul so warped that he believed any of his impulses deserved to be acted upon.

Ron had recovered, slowly, painfully. As he had recovered, he had lain in bed developing strategies to help Alexis. He started his own law firm, accepting cases sent his way by attorney friends who knew that he'd been victimized. He built the firm steadily until it was successful enough to shield him. Then he contacted Alexis through friends to tell her that he would help if she wanted to try again.

Jody was four by then, a chubby cherub who had seen little of her father and little of his wrath. But Alexis had watched Charles on the few occasions that he had been in Jody's company. She had seen signs that terrified her. The vein throbbing in his neck if Jody dared to interrupt him, the icy gleam in his eyes if she dared to reach out to him. On the day of her fourth birthday party, Alexis had found bruises on Jody's arms after Charles had carried her to her room for spilling cake crumbs. Alexis had known then that she had to try again. Somehow she had to try.

Ron's plan of action was uncomplicated and effective. He hired detectives and paid handsomely for the testimony of servants who refused to testify for any other reason. His most inventive strategy was to take statements from the so-called witnesses that Charles had threatened to use against Alexis the first time around. He got two of the witnesses to admit that their statements were made under duress and that the information in them wasn't true. In every way he bested Charles at his own game.

The day Ron was ready to spring the trap, Alexis left the Cahill estate to take Jody for a walk. She never returned. By Ron's arrangement, she was secreted in a hotel in the city with a twenty-four-hour-a-day bodyguard, psychological twin to the one who was escorting Ron himself. Negotiations took one week. In the end Charles gave Alexis what she wanted: a divorce and total custody of Jody. In return she gave him her word that she would never reveal the circumstances of the divorce to anyone. There was little reason for Charles to doubt that she would honor her promise. Alexis knew that all the Ron Bartows in the world couldn't stop Charles's wrath if she didn't.

The divorce and all the evidence that had secured it cost Alexis most of the entire small fortune she had inherited from her Grandmother Whitham. But her escape had been worth any price. She asked for no money for herself or Jody in the divorce settlement. She left her marriage with only the possessions and cash she had brought to it. She decided to stay in the Detroit area because Ron and the information he had secured offered her protection there. Anywhere else she would be friendless and completely alone if Charles set out to get revenge. She settled in a small house in Oak Park, miles from exclusive Grosse Pointe, where she had lived with Charles, and began to pull together the shattered fragments of her life.

The nightmares of Charles's abuse still haunted her, however. She tried talking to a counselor, but found herself unable to verbalize the terrors she had endured. She tried making new friends, taking a part-time job during Jody's hours at preschool, redecorating the little house. Despite everything, she knew she was fast sinking into a deep depression.

Ron had come to the rescue once more. He had suggested that Alexis begin a journal. If she couldn't talk about what had happened, then she could write about it. She was the only one who ever had to know what was in those pages. She was free to reveal everything.

The idea tugged at her until one day she took out her college typewriter and began. She discovered right away that putting down what had happened to her was as impossible as talking about it. But she also discovered that if she wrote her story as if it had happened to someone else, the words poured out. She changed names and facts. She became Cynthia Garrick; Charles became Terrence. The automobile industry became the shipping industry; Michigan became New York. She embroidered on some of Ron's information. During Ron's investigation Charles had been seen with a well-known Detroit crime boss. Ron had also turned up rumors of a corporate upheaval masterminded by Charles himself. She remembered bits and pieces of Charles's conversations, unexplained phone calls, the gossip of others. She wrote the story as if Terrence Garrick had Mafia connections; she used her imagination and intuition to weave together a picture of a man so evil that he seemed driven by the devil. And to balance the horror, the pathos, she invented a lover for Cynthia, a man who was the antithesis of Terrence, a man who was everything kind and courageous.

The novel took her a year to write. Once begun, it motivated every waking hour. *Before I Sleep* brought her back to life, and she found that life was truly where she wanted to be.

The novel would have remained no more than her personal therapy if she hadn't mentioned it to a friend. Nancy Carter had been a roommate during Alexis's years at Sarah Lawrence. The friendship had waned, as all her friendships had, during the years of her marriage. But it had been renewed one day when Alexis took Jody to New York for a short holiday after the book was completed. On a whim she had called Nancy, and they had met for lunch while Jody stayed at the hotel with a baby-sitter.

Nancy had recently been made an editor at a prestigious publishing house, Abercrombie Press, and the two women talked about her job until they sipped their after-lunch coffee. "You should write a novel," Nancy had told Alexis then. "You were always better with words than anyone I knew. You'd be a pleasure to edit."

Alexis had smiled and asked Nancy if she could keep a secret. Then she had told her about the manuscript locked in a Detroit safe-deposit box. "Someday, maybe I'll write something you can print," she said, her mind already busy searching for a new idea, one that could be published.

But Nancy hadn't been willing to let her get away so easily. "Let me read the one you've written," she'd said. "Maybe I can save you any mistakes on your next one. I'll be honest with you. We're friends."

Back in Detroit, Alexis thought about Nancy's offer. The book could never be published, but it was, after all, not really her life story. She wasn't breaking the promise that had secured her divorce. Nancy was the soul of discretion. She understood why the book could never be printed. And somehow the idea of just one other person reading it, one other person understanding what she had gone through, was too much of a lure to refuse.

Alexis copied the manuscript and sent it to New York. Then she forced herself to forget about it, knowing just how busy an editor's life is. She was on Nancy's personal slush pile, and she knew it would be months before the manuscript was returned.

Nancy called in five days. She was sending tickets to New York by courier for Alexis and Jody. She already had a nanny lined up for the three days Alexis would be there, and lunch with her senior editor for the first day Alexis arrived. She begged for permission to show him the book and promised that he would respect Alexis's wish for silence, if she still wanted it after they'd had a chance to talk.

Alexis had lived for years in terror and humiliation. Only writing the book had helped lift her from the morass her life had become. Now the respect and admiration in Nancy's voice were another lure she couldn't refuse.

She and Jody made the trip. The events that followed were like a snowball picking up momentum until it became an avalanche. Abercrombie Press offered her an unheard of advance on the hardcover rights to her book. Paperback rights and possible movie or miniseries options were almost guaranteed to bring it up above the million-dollar mark. More important, they promised that her real name would never be disclosed. No one would be able to trace the book to her. She would be safe and financially secure for life.

Alexis had discussed the proposal thoroughly with Ron before she'd said yes. In the end he'd been encouraging. The book was different enough from reality that even those who suspected that Terrence Garrick was Charles Cahill would never be sure. And if Charles came after her, threatening her life, Abercrombie Press would leak her identity. That was certainly a threat that would stop him. His hands would be tied, for if he made a move toward Alexis, the world would know he was really Terrence Garrick.

The plan had been foolproof, but unfortunately, the reporter who had relentlessly tracked her down had been nobody's fool. No one could have predicted the public's obsession with learning the true identity of D.A. Meredith. The mere fact that her identity was hidden sparked the imagination of women everywhere. And when she was finally exposed and what was known of her personal story compared to incidents in the book, the public had what they wanted most.

The name of the man on whom the character of Terrence Garrick had been based.

The nightmare had begun again after that. Alexis had refused to verify that *Before I Sleep* was based on her life story, but her refusals didn't matter to Charles. And her refusals didn't matter to the women who read the book, either. Every woman who had ever been threatened by a man saw herself in Cynthia Garrick and D.A. Meredith. Every woman who had ever been threatened by a man saw him in Terrence Garrick and Charles Cahill.

Charles's prestige slipped as the book grew in popularity. Mail poured in against him. A boycott against his employer netted more bad publicity than loss of profit, but Charles's work began to suffer. He was a man unused to losing, or to criticism. Flashes of the instability that no one except Alexis had ever seen began to show at work, until finally he was forced to resign. Although officially he left to pursue the possibility of starting his own company, the upper echelon of Motor City knew that Charles Cahill was a man in disgrace.

With nothing to lose and nothing else to distract him, Charles opened war on Alexis.

The war was invisible, the emotional equivalent of nerve gas. There was nothing Alexis could prove. She had moved to a modern condominium complex with top-quality security, but she arrived home one day to find her plants turning brown in their pots and Jody's cocker spaniel in convulsions. The veterinarian had been baffled, because no test he administered could pinpoint a cause. And even after the dog died and tissue samples were tested, no conclusions were reached.

She moved again, to another, safer condominium. This time her car was tampered with. She was driving Jody home from school one afternoon and suddenly the steering wheel locked. She was hit from behind when she attempted to stop, and her car smashed a guard rail, just missing a plunge into a deep creek.

Neither the police nor the mechanic who took the car apart and put it back together at Ron's insistence could find the cause of the problem.

By then Charles had found an important new position with another auto manufacturer. Despite rumors and boycotts, Charles Cahill was too brilliant, too talented, to stay unemployed for long.

The new job made no difference in his campaign of terror, however. The incidents grew, expanding in complexity and cunning. Never once did Charles incriminate himself. Alexis prayed he would slip up, leave just one piece of evidence so that she could charge him with harassment, but he was too clever for that. The same superior mind that had combined space-age technology and Yankee ingenuity to design some of the most innovative automobiles in the industry could also design new and foolproof ways to terrorize his ex-wife.

Then one night Alexis awoke to find Charles standing beside her bed. "If I die," she had whispered, frantic to make him leave, "Ron Bartow will make public every piece of evidence we found against you. The world will know you *are* Terrence Garrick and that you murdered me."

"When I murder you," he had said calmly, "the world won't care, because you and your life will be old news, and I will be in power again. And when I murder you, no one will know it's murder."

She had lain there in terror, waiting for him to beat her, to force himself on her. But he had smiled, the same confident smile that had attracted her to him in the first place, and left the room. With trembling fingers she had punched out the number for security, then Ron's home phone.

Security had listened to her story and searched the condo for clues. All the windows were locked; the back door was secure. Alexis had to admit that the chain and deadbolt had been in place before she had let them in. Both guards had thrown up their hands in defeat and left.

Alexis and Ron had talked through the rest of the night. Their conclusion had been mutual. Alexis and Jody had to disappear. It had taken months to make the arrangements, months when Jody and Alexis lived under the scrutiny of a bodyguard, months when incidents still occurred and the time for action seemed to be getting shorter.

In the end their plans had come together in a matter of days. First Jody disappeared, flying to Hawaii with a friend of Ron's as chaperon. Then Alexis disappeared, traveling to Hawaii by way of Canada. From there they had spent the next nine months traveling to different ports of call, sometimes disguising themselves, always keeping on the move.

The trip had been grueling, but there had been occasional moments of comradeship and pleasure. Jody had landed in Hawaii during a surprise hurricane. The man who had escorted her, Gray Sheridan, had taken her to the house of a friend, Paige Duvall, to wait out the siege. Jody had made close friends during those three days, and those friends, Gray, Paige, Gray's wife Julianna, and an Australian opal miner named Dillon Ward, had since proved to be friends of Alexis's, too.

Before coming to Kangaroo Island she and Jody had spent a week in Waimauri, New Zealand, with Paige and her new husband Adam Tomoana, and Jody had claimed Adam's son Jeremy as the little brother she had never had. Dillon and his wife Kelsey had joined them there toward the end of their visit. Alexis had been glad for the chance to thank them for keeping her daughter safe during Hurricane Eve.

Best of all, she had known when she left Waimauri that she had friends in the Pacific that she could count on. Even Julianna and Gray, who made their home near Honolulu, kept in touch with her through Ron, each time reminding her that they were less than a day away if she needed them.

Alexis hoped she never would. She hoped she would no longer need Ron's unselfish support, either. She hugged his letter to her breast and tried to imagine a life free of threat. She wanted only the things that others took for granted. The freedom to live without looking over her shoulder. The freedom to love without endangering her loved ones.

"'It looks like he's stopped searching for you, Dana. He can't chance anything now. He has too much to lose,'" she quoted in a whisper. She just hoped that Ron was right.

A light tapping startled her from her thoughts. Her eyes flicked to the bedside clock. It was one-thirty in the morning, but she had company.

She should have been afraid, but she wasn't. Perhaps it was the news in Ron's letter. Or more probably the fact that neither poachers nor a man intent on murder knocked first. She suspected immediately that it was Matthew at her kitchen door. He had probably been checking the property and seen that her light was on.

Displaying the proper amount of caution, she switched off her light, then crept through the dark hallway to peer into the kitchen. A man was silhouetted through the glass at her back door, and she recognized the erect posture and broad shoulders as Matthew's. She had the door open in seconds for him to enter. "Is something wrong? Are the poachers back?"

He had almost forgotten the poachers existed. He just wrapped his arms around her and stood in the dark, holding her.

Alexis felt his tension and the strength of his grip. He was holding her as if she had needed rescuing. "Matthew, what's wrong?" she asked, her voice muffled against his chest.

He wasn't sure how to tell her that he knew who she was, or that he had breached her privacy to find out. Worse yet, if he had discovered her identity, others could, too. She was certain to feel less safe.

Still he couldn't keep the truth from her. She had to know that he knew, but also that her secret was safe with him. She had to know that now, more than ever, he would work to protect her.

Alexis tried to pull away, and although Matthew resisted for a moment, he finally freed her. "What's wrong?" she repeated, looking for clues on his face. But there were no clues. The room was too dark and the man too skillful at hiding them.

"We need to talk."

"At one-thirty?"

"Your light was on."

She sighed. "Insomniacs, both of us."

"I haven't slept much for three nights. I've been reading."

"Reading?"

"Let's sit down."

"Let's go into the living room, then." Alexis led the way, turning on a lamp by the door before she sat on the sofa. Without hesitation Matthew sat beside her.

"Reading?" she asked again, a peculiar feeling forming in her belly.

"*Before I Sleep.*"

She sat back, turning her face away from him. "That's your problem, then. Reading before you sleep keeps you awake. Maybe you should try watching movies on your video recorder."

He decided to minimize the game playing. He reached into the crate beside him and pulled out a copy of the book. Silently he handed it to her. She took it without reading the cover. "Yes, I've read it, too," she said, struggling to sound calm. "It's a frightening book, and definitely not one to read at night."

"Stop pretending, Alexis. I know you wrote it."

"Get out." Alexis stood and pointed to the doorway with a trembling hand. "Get out right now!"

Matthew had expected almost any reaction except this one, but he didn't have to think of a response. He just reached up and pulled her back to the sofa in one swift movement. "I haven't told anyone," he assured her. "And I never will. Never!"

"And that's supposed to make me feel better?" Alexis tried to break free, but he held her steady.

"How much of the book is true, Alexis?"

She stopped struggling, but she didn't answer.

Matthew loosened his grip, rubbing his thumbs along the inside of her wrists. "I'm not a violent man," he said softly. "But when Jeannie and Todd died, I wanted to kill the pilot who'd been flying their plane. I couldn't, of course, because he'd died with them. But sometimes I'd wake up at night after it happened, and I'd wish he'd lived somehow, so that I could have the pleasure of killing him myself."

She shuddered, and her eyes filled with tears. But for whose sorrow, she didn't know.

"And when I finished your book tonight," he went on, "I knew what it was like to want to kill again."

"There's a piece of Charles in each of us, isn't there?"

He heard the tears in her voice and saw them on her cheeks. "No, there's not." He folded her hands and brought them to his chest. "Our anger is the other side of all that's good in us. The Charleses of the world maim and kill because they have nothing inside them except anger."

"You've only read my book. You don't know him."

Gently he lifted her hands and brought them to his lips. "Tell me, then."

"No!"

"I survived reading the book. You survived writing it."

"I don't talk about it!"

"Shall I ask you what's true, then? Scene by scene?"

"Why are you doing this?" Alexis wrenched her hands free, but she didn't move away, because she knew Matthew would just bring her back if she did.

"Because I have to know what we're up against before I can help you."

"I haven't asked for help."

"You have a record of not asking for help. How long did you live with Cahill before you asked?"

She was stunned that he would so quickly get to the root of her greatest humiliation. She stood, ready to fight him if he tried to stop her. But he didn't. He just sat quietly, watching her. The fight drained out of her before it had time to strengthen. She walked to the window, folding her arms against the chill wind that blew through the cracks in the sash.

When she spoke, her voice had no inflection, as if she were telling someone else's story. "My parents are important people, wealthy people. But they never let my brothers or me take that for granted. I was raised to be responsible. I suppose in a way it backfired, because I grew up *feeling* responsible for everything that went wrong around me. If my parents got angry with me—and they often did—I knew they were right. I deserved it because somehow I'd failed."

Matthew knew what she would say next, but he also knew she had to say it. He sat quietly and waited.

"I was raised never to complain. If I was punished, I was supposed to accept it quietly and be thankful my parents cared enough to punish me. And because I was different from my brothers, I was punished frequently."

"Different?"

"Absentminded. Inattentive. Poor at math and science and athletics, the pursuits that were important to them. I was a dreamer."

"For which the world is now grateful."

She didn't smile at his encouragement. "When Charles showed an interest in me, I think I saw a way to prove to my parents and brothers that I wasn't hopeless. Here was a powerful man, a man they respected absolutely, and he wanted their daughter. My stock rose in their eyes immediately."

"You married him because they wanted you to?"

"I can't blame my decision on anyone. I only know that when Charles asked me to be his wife, I felt like someone special. I realize now that Charles's aloofness, his arrogance, reminded me of my father. In some adolescent way, I wanted the love and approval from him that I'd never gotten at home. A substitute, I guess. I thought if I could make Charles love me, I would know I was worth anyone's love."

"You must have been very young."

"Immature." She shivered again, rubbing her arms for warmth she badly needed. "I didn't realize that Charles wanted me to satisfy his own unmet needs. I was young and virginal enough to appeal to his darkest fantasies. His behavior on our wedding night was unspeakable. When it was over, I knew I had made the greatest mistake of my life."

"You stayed with him anyway?"

She shook her head. "I went home, but I was too ashamed to tell my parents about the man I'd married. So I told them we had fought, and that I had grounds for an annulment. They were appalled. The next thing I knew, Charles was there, and then I was leaving with him. I suppose it was easy for him to convince my parents that I was just overwrought from the wedding and the tensions of starting a new life. Charles has a silver tongue. Perhaps I even believed him."

"You didn't!"

She was silent, filtering through all the memories, the feelings. "No," she said at last, "I didn't. But I did believe

that things would be better. Charles swore he loved me, that
he'd just been insane with passion, and that if he'd hurt me,
he was sorry.

"That was the pattern of our life together at first. Charles
would be brutal, brutal enough that sometimes I feared for
my life. Almost anything could trigger it, his shirts not being
ironed properly, my nightgown on the floor beside the bed,
artichokes for dinner when he'd wanted asparagus. The
brutality was always private. He never hurt me in front of
anyone. He never left marks. And he always seemed surprised if I was upset. He'd apologize, as if he were apologizing to a child."

"Yet you stayed with him?"

"He could be indulgent, too. Sometimes he could make
me feel like I was pleasing him, that I had finally learned to
be a good wife. And I was frightened and insecure enough
to believe that maybe he was right, maybe it had been my
fault before. Then the violence would begin again, only
worse. We had a swimming pool." She stopped, swallow-
ing because her throat had finally gone dry.

Matthew had read the book. He knew what was coming.
"You don't have to go on."

She did anyway. "We had a swimming pool. Charles
made me swim with him every night. He liked to play in the
pool. Rough-housing, he called it."

"Alexis, don't!"

"On good nights, we would swim laps together. But if it
was a bad night, Charles would wrestle with me in the water, ducking me. One night he held me under, held me under until—"

Matthew grabbed her shoulders. "Stop!"

"You can't bear to hear it, can you? No one has ever been
able to bear it. But it's true. I almost died in that pool. And
when I refused to swim with him again, he set fire to the
poolhouse when I was there napping one afternoon. I got
out in time, but only just. I knew Charles had set the fire,
although I didn't have proof. I was the only one at home,
even the housekeeper was gone. And when the fire chief said
the fire was arson, he looked at me as if I'd started it. I

learned later that Charles had 'smoothed it over.' He told the chief that I'd been unwell and inclined to be fanciful. Some money had changed hands, supposedly to ensure that *I* wouldn't be investigated. My family looked at me more strangely than ever after that.''

"Alexis . . .''

"What, Matthew? There's really nothing to say, is there? I found out the week after the fire that I was pregnant. I'd gone away without telling anyone where so I could think how best to end the marriage. When I found out I was pregnant, I told the doctor I couldn't have the baby. He was a country doctor in a country town. He made arrangements for me to have an abortion, but when the time came, I couldn't.'' Her voice broke.

Matthew knew nothing better to do than to hold her. His arms circled her chest, locking there, and his body molded to hers. He wished he could absorb her pain.

"Jody's my whole world. I know it wasn't fair to bring her into a horrible marriage. I know it wasn't fair to bring another helpless victim into Charles's life. But I realized I couldn't do anything but.''

"It was courageous to have his child.''

She sighed. "I know this sounds strange, but Charles comes from good people. His parents aren't twisted. He has a sister who's everything you would ever want a friend to be. I don't know why he's the way he is. He was the only boy on both sides of his family, and I know he was given everything he ever wanted because he was loved so much. Maybe that was it, or maybe there's something deeply wrong inside him. Perhaps he was born without a soul. I don't know. I've tried to understand. But as I was preparing to end the pregnancy, I knew, somehow, that I couldn't punish my unborn child for Charles's insanity. I knew that baby was innocent of the taint of its father. The baby would be good, like all the myriad generations of Cahills before it. And she is. She's everything her father could never be.''

"Of course she is. She's an extraordinary little girl.''

"So I went home, and I told Charles I was pregnant. I intended to leave him, but he seemed like a changed man after that. He was solicitous of my every need, generous, protective. I wasn't fool enough to believe he had repented completely, but I did believe that maybe he was trying. I started questioning all the things that had happened. Maybe I really had deserved his anger, if not his punishment. Maybe he really had just been playing in the pool, unaware of his own strength. Maybe the fire in the poolhouse wasn't arson, or if it was, maybe someone else had started it.''

Matthew just held her tighter.

Alexis took what courage she could from the warmth of his body. ''When Jody was born and Charles found out he had a daughter, he was livid with rage. He'd wanted a son. He told me I'd failed him again, just as I always had. I wanted to believe he was just disappointed. I went home from the hospital hoping he'd see reason. But, of course, he didn't. Things went from bad to worse, and the abuse began again in earnest. I tried to secure a divorce, and he almost killed my lawyer. Charles had enough connections to get almost anything he wanted. Jody was four before I was able to get away from him. By then he'd almost killed me again, and I thought he might start on Jody next. The divorce was nasty, as it had to be. I hoped afterward I could begin a new life, and for a time it seemed like I might be able to. Then *Before I Sleep* was published.''

She turned, and Matthew saw tears in her eyes. ''And here I am. I've come all the way across the world to hide myself, and the only person on Kangaroo Island who knows anything about me has already discovered my identity. There is no place to hide, is there?''

Chapter 8

Don't, Alexis." Matthew stroked his hands up her back and neck until he cupped her head, forcing her to look up at him. "You're safe here. No one else will find out who you are."

"You found out, didn't you?" She tried to pull away, but the effort was halfhearted. She needed his arms around her.

"I was looking for answers, and I saw three copies of the same book sitting in the crate."

"I've been so careful, and I still made a mistake. What other mistakes have I made?"

"I don't know, but I do know that running could be the biggest mistake of all."

"There's no place left to go."

"Is that bastard still looking for you?"

She wanted to say no. She wanted to tell him that Charles had lost interest in her. But somehow Ron's letter didn't seem as important now. Her momentary optimism had been foolish. How many other times had she believed that things would be better? How many other times had she believed that Charles had changed? What was wrong with her that she couldn't face reality?

"Is he?" Matthew repeated.

"I want to believe that he's stopped."

"But you can't."

"I don't know what to believe. I wanted to believe that no one would find out who I was, too." For just a moment she let her eyes and her voice betray her need to know that everything would be all right someday, that someday she and Jody could live a normal life.

Matthew couldn't look into Alexis's eyes anymore. He had come to protect her, not to get pulled into the depths of her soul. He wrenched his gaze from hers. "If you have any doubts, you'll have to continue to be very careful. I'll help every way I can."

Alexis saw the way Matthew's eyes lifted to her hair. That, more than his words, indicated his feelings—or lack of them. He was a good, considerate man who had come to help a neighbor who was in trouble—nothing more. She had no right to entangle him in her private sorrows. He had more than enough of his own.

She shook her head, freeing it from his grip. "You've done too much already. I don't want you involved in my life any more than you have been."

Matthew had pulled inside himself for protection, and now he found there was nothing to protect himself from. Instead of gratitude he felt shame. He covered it with gruffness. "I'm not talking about involvement, Alexis— Dana, whatever you call yourself. I'm talking about your safety and your daughter's."

"My name is Alexis Whitham. I left Dana Cahill behind a long time ago." Alexis retreated until she could feel the windowsill against the small of her back. There was no feeling in her voice as she spoke. "And I discovered a long time ago that the only person I can count on to keep me safe is myself. I appreciate your concern, and I'll welcome your nightly patrols around the property, but what you've discovered doesn't really change anything."

Matthew felt Alexis's retreat chill him like the Antarctic wind belting Hanson Bay. For years he had felt only his own sorrow, his own isolation. Now, for the first time, he realized he was not alone and never had been. The world had continued to revolve after Jeannie and Todd died. People had laughed and suffered and reached to offer reassurance while he struggled to shut them out. Alexis's suffering had been far worse than his. At least he had known love. She never had.

With the moonlight bathing her ivory skin, she seemed untouchable—a marble statue that had come briefly to life but now, once again, was cold and still. Cold and still because of the coldness, the stillness inside him. Suddenly he was ashamed. Isolating himself had become a way of life, and now he had hurt someone else—someone who was coming to mean more to him than he wanted to admit. In that moment he wanted only to revive her. And to revive himself.

He stepped forward, knowing as he did that he was moving from one phase of his life to another. He took another step and slowly lifted his hand. She didn't flinch. "It changes things," he said softly. "I'm not sure how, and I'm not sure why. But it changes things."

"The very last thing I need is pity."

"And admiration for your courage? Do you need that?" His hand settled against her cheek and slid into her hair. Her eyelids fluttered shut.

"No."

"What do you need?"

"To be left alone." She shook her head, but his hand stayed in her hair. "Matthew, I'm asking you to go. We're two lost souls. We have nothing to give each other except sorrow. And there's no more room inside me for that."

"You've said there was room for comfort."

"Comfort is a drop in the bucket."

He knew she was right; he knew he should go. Instead his thumb stroked her cheek, then traced the edge of her lashes. They were suspiciously moist. He didn't know what he wanted to give her: pity, admiration, comfort, or something that surpassed all three. He only knew that he couldn't leave her. He moved closer, and his other hand settled in her hair, turning her face to his.

She didn't open her eyes. He suspected she was waiting for him to hurt her. He knew he was still so confused that he might.

His lips touched hers. He expected her to pull away, but she didn't. Instead she sighed, warming his lips with her breath. He could feel tension in the muscles of her neck, and he began to stroke it away as he deepened the kiss. He coaxed her to respond with his lips and with the slow massaging of his fingers, but she stood motionless.

"Alexis," he murmured. "Open for me. Open *to* me. I'm not going to hurt you." He said the words and prayed they were true.

She began a protest, but Matthew pulled her closer, silencing her objections. Alexis knew she should struggle. If she did, he would release her. But she didn't want to struggle. She didn't know what she wanted, but it was not to fight with Matthew, not to push him away. And despite what she had told him, it was not to be left alone.

Tentatively she touched his back, then slid her hands lightly to his shoulders. Her lips parted, and suddenly she couldn't get enough of him. Each texture, each taste, was both familiar and new. Each curve, each angle, was both a homecoming and a revelation.

His tongue danced with hers as his hips sought to cradle her. She could feel the broad expanse of his chest pressing against her breasts and her nipples hardening in response. A rush of heat suffused her body, and she moaned softly, adjusting so that she could feel more of him against her. He was aroused, more than ready to dispense with this preliminary to lovemaking, and the thought that she had been the one to arouse him enhanced her pleasure until it was almost unbearable.

He shifted his weight, pulling her away from the sill so that he could fit his hands to her hips. Through the thin cotton of her gown, she could feel his long fingers kneading her soft flesh, guiding her against him until it seemed as if they would merge that way and in that moment.

Three years of silence and sorrow had given birth to a need so strong that for a moment Matthew clutched Alexis,

shaken by the demands of his body. In only seconds he had
gone from kissing her to needing to possess her. Desire this
potent was foreign and frightening. And still he wanted to
forget the past had ever existed; he wanted to extinguish all
thoughts of the future. He wanted only the present, this
woman and himself with nothing between them except the
all-consuming need for completion.

He groaned, and his hands rose to her shoulders, dip-
ping into the scooped neckline of her dressing gown. Her
skin was warm and satin-sleek, and he could feel her rapidly escalating pulse beating against his fingertips. His
mouth left hers to roam across her cheek, stopping at her ear
lobe to taste and tantalize, then moving to her throat. She
moved against him, throwing her head back to give him access. He heard her soft moan of satisfaction and felt the way
her hips swayed against his. Her response inflamed him
further, and he delved deeper, caution disappearing on a
wave of passion.

Alexis felt the cool night air against her skin as Matthew
began to unbutton her gown. She had wondered for years if
she would ever be able to respond to a man after the hor-
rors of her life with Charles. She had no time or inclination
to wonder now. She could only feel. Feel the memories of
that other life fade and disappear, feel Matthew's hard
strength wiping away all traces of the man who had abused
her, feel the exhilaration of her sensuality reborn.

But no matter her delight, she was hesitant to touch him
back. On her wedding night she had learned not to initiate
and not to respond. Now response was out of her control,
as if someone new were inhabiting her body and the woman
she had been was gone forever. Still she was afraid to caress
him, fearing that somehow she might anger him and release the same raging beast that had dwelled inside Charles.
Her hands ached to stroke his skin; her lips throbbed with
the desire to kiss him, to explore the rasp of his cheeks, the
smooth skin of his neck. Instead she stood in his arms and
felt the fine trembling in his hands as he bared her chest.

"Alexis." He made the word into a prayer, although what
he prayed for, he didn't know. He moved just far enough

away from her to see the pearly gleam of her breasts dressed only in moonbeams. He cupped one and felt his own callused fingers rasp against her velvety softness.

She was a lovely woman, but even her beauty hadn't prepared Matthew for the luminescence of moonlight reflecting off rounded breasts, breasts that had been made to be molded by a man's hands and lips. She was the goddess, each man's dream of what a woman will be. Softness and warmth and the ancient promise of fertility.

Then, as he gazed at her, he had the terrible vision of her softness, her warmth, tormented by the man she had married.

Alexis watched Matthew's face, not wanting to care if he approved of her, but caring anyway. For a moment she saw something akin to awe, and then, in horror, she saw the dawning of anger. She jerked away, as if he had slapped her. Desire disappeared, washed away by shame. Her hands fell to her sides in defeat, and then swiftly rose to push him away so that she could draw her gown together. She rested the back of her head against the window. "Go home, Matthew."

He wanted to tell her that until that moment her life with Charles had been fiction. He had read her book and heard her story, and he had felt the distant fury of a man watching a war on the television news. Now he had held her, kissed her, felt her life pulse against his hand. And as he had gloried in her absolute perfection, he had envisioned Charles Cahill brutalizing her.

He couldn't tell her, though, because there were no words to capture that vision and his own rage. And there were no words to capture his own confusion. He had wanted her with a single-minded desire that had been so strong he had willingly surrendered to it. As he had kissed her, caressed her, he had known instinctively that with only a little encouragement, Alexis would have surrendered, too. He had needed her. She had needed him.

Then, in one blinding moment of truth, he had realized that both of them needed so much more.

"Go home," she repeated, weary to the depths of her soul. She had risked more of herself with Matthew than with any man except Charles. And she had seen anger. He had not hurt her, but the anger had been there. Disappointment, disillusionment, anger. She knew them all well. They were the only emotions she inspired in the men to whom she tried to give herself.

He lifted his hand to her cheek again. Alexis didn't mistake the caress for abuse, but for a moment, for the smallest fraction of a second, she looked at him and saw Charles. She saw Charles and all the rejection and pain, the humiliation and terror, of six interminable years of marriage. She lifted her hand, too, and struck him.

Matthew's head spun with the force of her blow. He heard Alexis's sharp gasp before he faced her again. When he did he saw the horror on her face and the tears welling in her eyes. He swallowed his fury, swallowed his demands for an explanation. As calmly as he could, he reached for her hand. She had made a fist of it to cover her mouth, and he pulled it gently toward him, bringing it to rest against his reddened cheek. He held it there, as if her touch could somehow soothe away his pain.

Alexis knew that in the moment it had taken to slap Matthew, her sanity had been questionable. "I'll leave," she said, tears choking her voice. "I'll take Jody and go."

"No, you won't." Matthew shut his eyes, suddenly more tired than he could ever remember. "You won't leave, and we won't stop seeing each other. I'll look at you, and I'll still see Jeannie, and the bastard who abused you, but it won't stop me from coming here. You'll look at me and you'll see—"

"A man who touches me and finds me wanting!"

For a moment he couldn't believe he had heard her right. "Wanting?"

She tried to jerk her hand away, but he held it tight. "I saw the anger in your eyes, Matthew. I know what it meant. You needed a woman tonight, and you almost convinced yourself you needed me. But I wasn't good enough, was I? I wasn't the woman you needed."

He had seen no scars as he'd gazed at her moonlit skin. He had felt no scars as he had held the sweet ripeness of her breasts in his hands. But the scars were there, deep and disturbing. He turned his face into her hand and kissed her palm. For a moment he thought he might cry.

When he could speak, he spoke into her hand, as if he were giving her a gift to hold and examine when he was gone. "I thought you were the most beautiful sight imaginable," he said. "I thought it wasn't possible to want a woman as much as I wanted you. And then I thought about Charles Cahill, and I wanted to kill him for the things he had done to you. Perhaps that makes me no better than him, but there is one difference." He lifted his head and held her eyes with his. "I take no pleasure in destroying a miracle."

Alexis struggled to believe that he hadn't found her lacking, that he hadn't changed his mind because she was less of a woman than he needed. She struggled to believe that he had cared enough about her to hate the pain she had suffered.

Matthew could see the struggle in her eyes. "It was only because you are so much a woman that Charles set out to destroy you," he said softly. "And it's only because you're so much a woman that I'm leaving now." He brought her hand to his mouth without taking his eyes from hers and kissed her palm once more, folding her fingers over the kiss.

Then he was gone. For a long time afterward she stood at the window and held her hand over her heart.

There were no more middle of the night encounters, although one morning a week later Alexis awoke to find a bouquet of island wildflowers on the porch. She put them in water, and each time she looked at them she thought of the man who had picked them.

Life settled into the uneventful routine that she had often longed for. Jody's teacher developed strategies designed to challenge the little girl, and Jody began to enjoy school more. Another little girl in her class invited her to a birthday party sleepover, and Jody spent the week prior to the big night packing and unpacking her overnight bag. Alexis's own life was unmarred by anything more ominous than an occasional spring thunderstorm. Every day she added pages to her novel and took long walks through the property.

But Matthew and the last words he had spoken to her were never far from her mind.

On the morning of Jody's sleepover she helped the little girl do a final check of her overnight bag before she zipped it once and for all.

"And you won't forget to pick me up tomorrow? At four?"

"When have I ever forgotten to pick you up?" Alexis gave her daughter an impromptu hug. "Besides, I might even be glad to see you by then."

"You're always glad to see me!" Jody stowed her books under one arm and the overnight bag under the other. "I'm ready."

"Now you're sure you gave your teacher the note yesterday so that you can ride Annie's bus home with her after school?"

"I told you already. I gave it to her yesterday morning. Besides, all the girls in the class are going to ride that bus."

"Annie's mother is a saint."

"Can I have a sleepover someday?"

"*May* I?"

"You're too old!" Jody giggled. "But can...may I someday? I never had one at home. You never let me."

Alexis thought of all the ways that their lives had been constrained by fear. Jody had never had a sleepover because Alexis had never been sure it was safe. She had tried to make it up to the little girl by entertaining her friends in public places, but Jody had missed out on one of the pleasures of childhood. Even now, Alexis wasn't certain a sleepover was a good idea. Not yet.

"We'll see," she hedged. "Right now we've got to get you out to the bus so you can go to this one."

The house seemed emptier than usual when Alexis came back from dropping Jody at the bus stop. Without the promise of the little girl's return that afternoon, the day seemed forty hours long, and the evening promised to be longer. She forced herself to write, even though she had nothing she wanted to say, but by three o'clock, she knew her efforts were hopeless. She had squeezed out two agonizing pages that would probably have to be rewritten. Flicking off the computer, she went to see what she could make herself for an early dinner, since she hadn't bothered with lunch.

She settled for a ham sandwich and a glass of milk, taking them out to the front porch, where she could see the distant surf lapping at the white sand beach. It wasn't as lonely outside. There were silver gulls circling Hanson Bay, and a lone osprey who repeatedly poised and dove into the water with the regular rhythm of the waves.

Then there was the koala sitting snugly in the branches of the eucalyptus tree that was closest to the house.

For a moment Alexis wasn't sure that the koala was real. From the porch it looked almost as if the little animal were a shadow created by leaves and slanting sunrays. She frowned and set her dishes down, then walked to the steps for a better look. The tree was twenty yards from the house, a lone survivor of what must once have been a grove. Directly beyond it the scenery changed to the sea coast heath and mallee scrub that were most common on this part of the Bartow property. The tree was an unlikely roost for a koala. But it was a roost nonetheless.

"Well, where on earth did you come from?" Alexis wouldn't have been so surprised if she'd seen another koala in the grove closer to the road that ran to Flinders Chase. The injured koala that Jody had found under the scrub bordering the porch had fallen from a higher perch somewhere and, in his shock and pain, sought protection in the bushes. But Alexis had never expected to see another one this close to the house.

The koala swayed, proving once and for all that he wasn't a shadow. Alexis wondered what he would do and where he would go if she approached him. She decided to find out. She was standing directly under the tree when he finally moved. He lumbered down to a lower branch as if to get a better look at her.

"Now who's on display here?" she asked, delighted by his antics.

The koala snorted, as if in answer.

"Jody should be here. She'd probably know what you were saying." Alexis shaded her eyes, peering up at her new friend. It was only then that she saw the scar on the koala's shoulder. It was barely visible, but the fur had been shaved around it, and even though it was growing back, the patch stood out. The new friend was an old friend. This was the koala Matthew had rescued the day they had met. "You've come back," she said. "That took faith, didn't it?"

The koala just stared.

Alexis wished she could tell the little animal to go back to Flinders Chase. He wasn't safe here, but apparently he was willing to take the chance just to establish himself in new territory. She wondered if she should call Matthew. In the two weeks since she had seen him, she had searched for excuses to talk to him. The koala was certainly an excuse, but not one she wanted to use. She knew Matthew would take him back to the park, and just as surely she knew that she didn't want him to. She understood the koala's need for freedom. She understood it only too well.

Surely there would be no danger from poachers this close to the house, and Jody would be delighted tomorrow to find her friend was back.

Alexis said goodbye, then went back to the porch to finish her sandwich.

Afternoon and evening melted one into the other. She took the long, leisurely hike along the beach that she had promised herself since coming to the island, stopping to examine each piece of driftwood, each adaptable plant that clung tenaciously to the bits of soil in rock crevices, each sea creature trapped in the tidal pools until the tides turned once more. Until she had come to the island, she hadn't understood the lure of nature. Now the island was teaching her. She understood why Matthew spent his life preserving a small piece of wilderness, and for the first time she realized that the island was no longer just a place to escape Charles, but a living piece of natural history, a link in a chain that had begun millennia ago.

She was falling in love with Kangaroo Island. And she was dangerously close to falling in love with the man who was its embodiment.

She didn't want to love either the island or the man. She couldn't afford the ties that loving brought. Her life had to be lived one day at a time, one moment at a time. It was the only way she had survived so far, and it might be the only way she would continue to.

If she were going to risk love, it should be for an uncomplicated place and an uncomplicated man. Neither Kangaroo Island nor Matthew fit that description. Especially Matthew.

Somehow, though, reminding herself of Matthew's complexities only strengthened his attraction. He was a man whose love for his wife and child had been strong and pure. What woman didn't want to be loved that way? What woman didn't want to give a man like that a child?

She had given him every reason to despise her, yet he hadn't abandoned her, even after she had struck him. He didn't want involvement—he was still too racked with grief—but he had set his own grief aside to reach out to her when she had needed him. And he had looked at her with awe when he had undressed her.

She had written *Before I Sleep* to purge herself of Charles's abuse. But she had never purged herself of its aftermath. After her divorce she had avoided men, sure that she would only find more of what she had escaped—if not terror and pain, then the humiliation of knowing that she wasn't good enough. She could look at herself in a mirror and see two Alexises. The first was the girl who had married Charles—young, innocent, shyly confident that she had something to offer. The second was the woman she had become—no longer innocent and no longer confident. That Alexis saw only the faults that had pushed Charles into rage after rage.

But Matthew hadn't seen those faults. He had looked at her with awe, and he had desired her. Just as miraculously, she had desired him.

She was dangerously close to falling in love, but right along with the terror that thought inspired came jubilation. After everything, there were still warmth and hope and possibly love inside her. Knowing that, she knew that someday perhaps all her wounds would heal.

It was almost dark when she began to make her way back to the house. She hadn't meant to stay out so long, but there had seemed to be no reason to go home earlier. Now, as the sun disappeared behind a bank of low-lying clouds, she wished she had hurried. There was a world of difference between walking through the bush in the sunlight and in the dark. She hadn't realized how quickly darkness could come when there were no streetlamps to smooth the transition. She hadn't even thought to leave a porch light burning, and not one light shone through any of the windows.

She forced herself not to move too quickly. The sky was darkest purple, and the deepening twilight played tricks on her eyes, so that she stumbled over a root and nearly fell. By the time she got close to the house, the darkness was almost impenetrable.

She had lived too long with fear to question her instincts. Five hundred yards from the house something made her stop and shrink back against the mallee that led up the hill from the beach. She stood absolutely still, becoming one with the contorted scrub behind her, and listened intently. She wasn't sure if she had heard something, or seen something, or just felt something different in the air around her. But as she stood there, all her senses alive and finely tuned, she became more and more certain that her caution wasn't misplaced.

A minute passed, and then two, as her concern and certainty grew. The wind had picked up as night fell, and it whined and moaned around her, portending a storm. Carrying over the whine was the faintest whisper of a human voice.

Alexis listened closely, trying hard to calculate the distance between herself and the source of the whisper, but the wind defeated her. She couldn't even tell the direction the voice came from, because the wind blew in gusts, changing directions to whip through the mallee, then down from the hill where the house stood. The voice grew no louder, but changed in quality until Alexis realized she was hearing two separate voices. The men—and she was fairly sure the voices belonged to men—weren't coming any closer, but neither were they going away. They were standing somewhere within hailing distance, and until she knew who they were—and *where* they were—she was trapped.

Another minute passed, then two. She crept out from her hiding place, staying low, to assume another vantage point behind a large chunk of granite. She could see the house more clearly now, and the path leading up to it. There were no moonlit figures, no ominous, threatening shapes. The path was clear. She gauged the time it would take to scramble up it, cross the porch and unlock the door. Inside she would be safe while she called the police—or Matthew.

But she needed too much time. She would be vulnerable too long, and although it was possible that she would be out of sight anyway, she wasn't ready to take the chance.

She strained her eyes, making a slow, calculated turn as she searched for some sign that would betray the men's whereabouts. Just as she was about to drop back into the safety of the mallee scrub, she saw a pinpoint of light. It came from a ridge beyond the house, and as she watched, it was joined by another.

The men were poachers. She had never been more certain of anything. The ridge was the beginning of the eucalyptus grove. The men were searching for koalas, feeling perfectly safe because there were no lights on in the house. Even her car was parked out of sight in the old barn, because the last week's thunderstorms had been so severe she had been afraid of damage.

At that moment she remembered the koala in the tree near the house. The men weren't close yet, but how long would it take them to venture closer? They believed they were undetected. They could take their time. Koalas didn't run away, and they didn't hide. They waited patiently for their death, and Matthew had told her once that they cried like little children when they were shot.

She was filled with such anger that all fear was forgotten. She could not hide in the scrub and listen to the cries of a dying koala. She had cowered before Charles for six terrible years. She would cower before no man again.

She was scrambling up the path before she had even made a conscious decision to do so. She was on the porch and inside the house in the next minute. In the darkness she stumbled to the telephone and dialed Matthew's number, trying desperately to come up with a plan as she waited for him to answer.

Her options were cut short when she heard a gunshot followed by the shouts of the men. The receiver fell from her fingers, and she cried out in anguish. There was nothing Matthew could do, not in time to stop the poachers. They had found their prey, perhaps already slaughtered it. If they were to be stopped from more destruction, she would have to be the one to do it.

She ran through the house, turning on every light as she came to it. In her room she unlocked the bedside drawer that held the pistol Peter Bartow had given her. She took it out and loaded it, then headed for the back porch. At the door she almost lost her courage. She was only one woman, and there were at least two men intent on hunting the koalas. They were dangerous men, lawless men, and she was risking too much.

But she knew what it was like to be hunted.

She opened the door and went to the railing. "I've called the police," she shouted. The words seemed to hang in the air. There was no answer, but another gunshot rang out.

"Murderers!" Alexis pointed the pistol to the sky and pulled the trigger. Her ears throbbed as the roar echoed the one before it. "The next shot goes right into the trees and maybe into one of you!"

She was temporarily blinded by a strong beam of light directed toward the porch. She stepped into the shadows, behind a pillar and clutched the gun to her chest with shaking hands. The gun frightened her almost as much as the men.

The light was extinguished. She heard the men's voices, but they were so low she couldn't distinguish any words. She listened intently, her fear magnifying every gust of wind, every falling leaf.

Finally she heard a noise. It was the revving of an engine on a nearby road—probably one of the many overgrown dirt tracks that had once crisscrossed the farm. The revving became a distant purr. And then there was silence.

Chapter 9

Matthew was in the shower when the telephone rang. He was tempted not to answer it. The day had been a difficult one. All the campgrounds were closed for renovation, and along with all his other duties, he was supervising the extensive repairs. If the campgrounds were to reopen in time for summer there was a lot to be done. He had worked without a break, and he was exhausted. The shower was the closest thing to a moment of peace that he'd had since breakfast.

On the third ring he realized that the caller might be Alexis. He turned off the water and jerked a towel off a hook, drying himself as he hurried into the kitchen. He answered the phone and stood waiting, but there was no voice on the other end, just a sequence of unidentifiable noises.

He frowned, repeating his "hello" louder. Again there was no answer, although it was clear the connection hadn't been broken, because there was no dial tone. He waited another moment, then just as he was about to place the receiver back in its cradle he heard a shout. He pressed the receiver back to his ear. "Hello!"

There was no response, but he heard another noise, fainter than the shout. It sounded like distant fireworks. Then, clearly, he heard a voice screaming "Murderers!" and the loud crack of a gunshot.

He didn't need to hear any more.

Alexis stumbled up the ridge that led to the eucalyptus grove where the poachers had been. She was afraid of what she would find, but more afraid not to search. Five minutes had passed since she'd heard the poachers leave. She knew she was alone on the property once more. Alone except, perhaps, for a dying koala. She had already made certain that the koala in the tree near the house was all right. He had been agitated—noisy and restless, as if he sensed what had transpired—but he had been untouched. She doubted he would have remained so if she hadn't shot blindly into the night.

Her flashlight barely penetrated the darkness. There was a thin sliver of moon overhead, but storm clouds obscured it more often than not. Each step was treacherous enough, but with the wind skipping leaves and debris across her path, she had to inch along for fear of falling.

With a sense of foreboding she reached the grove. What moonlight there was shone in pinpoint patches. She had to depend completely on her flashlight. She spotted an empty beer bottle and footprints in the boggy ground at the base of a large tree. Methodically she searched for more signs, deadlier signs, that the poachers had been there.

She had expected the final piece of evidence. In the deepest part of the grove, in an area of rotting stumps and thick undergrowth, she found an ominously fresh stain on the forest floor. The stain was blood. With a sick feeling in the pit of her stomach she identified it, then turned off her flashlight. She sank to her knees and began to tremble, fighting back tears. She had done her best, risked her own safety, but she hadn't done enough. The poachers had killed a koala.

She had felt a brief sense of triumph when the poachers had driven away, but now she knew just how ineffectual she had been. What was one woman against men intent on slaughter? She was worse than useless. She was like a child trying to hold back a thunderstorm with a prayer. She had no power; she had no strength. She had only the worthless conviction that she had to make a stand.

She began to cry. Fighting tears was useless. Women cried, and they died a little inside each time they faced their weaknesses.

Once released, her tears were a torrent. She cried for all her failures, for the terrifying years she had spent with Charles, for the loveless years with parents who had tried to mold her into something she wasn't, for the last minutes when the depth of her failures had been revealed. And she cried for the koala, who, like her, had been the innocent victim of men who could not be stopped from violence.

She knelt beside the blood of the sacrificed animal, and all her hope drained away.

"Alexis?"

She felt hands on her shoulders. In her misery she didn't even question how Matthew had found her, how he had even known to look.

"They killed a koala," she said, wailing as all women who mourn the dead have wailed. "They killed one right here. I heard them, and I was too late to stop it. I let them kill it."

"You didn't let them. You had no choice."

"I was too late. I stopped to call you. I should have gotten the gun first. I should have shouted."

"*You* could have been killed!" Matthew knelt behind her and tried to take her into his arms, but she continued to rock back and forth in agony.

"I didn't do enough. I'll never be able to do enough."

"You've done more than anyone should be asked to. You've made this a crusade." Matthew wrapped his arms firmly around her chest and pulled her back to rest against him. "Shh.... Be silent." He forced her to stop rocking, holding her as she fought him. He sensed her growing hysteria as he tried desperately to calm her. "Shh.... Alexis, be still. It's over. There's nothing you can do about what's happened here. You've got to get hold of yourself."

"And when is the rest of the world going to get hold of itself, Matthew?" She wrenched away from him, but he brought her back against his chest. She turned in his arms and searched his face, grappling to find an answer. "When is the rest of this damned world going to get hold of itself? When are the *men* in this world going to get hold of themselves? You kill, you maim, you laugh at suffering! And it doesn't matter who suffers, does it? Anything smaller than you, weaker than you, is fair game."

He let her shout at him, knowing that neither of them had a choice. But when she fought to get away again, he held her tight.

"Don't hold me!"

"You need to be held."

"I don't need anything from you or any man!"

She needed more than he could give her. She needed more than *anyone* could give her. For a moment he faltered, wondering if he wanted to give, or if giving was an excuse for taking. Then he knew it didn't matter, because both were really the same. She needed so much, but he needed just as much—maybe even more. They could only go on together. They could only risk failure on the slim chance they would succeed.

"You need me," he said, holding her still to bury his face in her hair. "You need me, and I need you. I need you, I want you. Don't fight me, Alexis. I didn't do this thing, and I'm not like the men who did."

His tone more than his words began to penetrate. She was shaking with fury, with anguish, but even riding the crest of her emotions, she knew that Matthew wasn't to blame for the problems of the world. He struggled to make the world a better place. And because he cared so much, he had lived with despair.

She calmed, gradually. He whispered into her hair, and his hands made slow circles on her back. Her breath caught once, twice, until she was breathing evenly. Tears dried on her cheeks, and her trembling began to ease.

His arms encircled her tighter. His lips sought her forehead, her eyelids. He tasted salt and the beginnings of desire. "Come back to the house," he whispered before he took her mouth.

She leaned against him, letting him kiss her. The wonder of being held, of being cared for, began to steal over her. She had been so cold inside that she'd thought she would never know warmth again. Now it crept through her, slowly, in ripples that began in the places where he touched her. She sighed, letting go of her anguish inch by inch.

"Alexis, dear one." He traced her jawline with his lips until his face was buried in her hair once more. "Come back to the house with me."

She pushed away from him and stood, anxious now to leave the place where the koala had died. He stood, too, and took her hand, leading her back through the forest.

The rain began before they reached the house. One moment the wind grew still and the moon appeared through the dense thunderheads. The next, the wind was roaring in from Hanson Bay carrying rain so cold that whatever warmth they had found together was immediately extinguished. Alexis slipped, almost crashing to her knees in her hurry to escape it. Before she could recover, Matthew had lifted her in his arms for the last steps up to the porch.

Inside, he didn't put her down. She was shivering again, from shock and cold. He didn't want to leave her. Without a word he carried her into her bedroom. Outside her window, lightning split the sky, followed immediately by a burst of thunder. She shuddered against him.

At her bedside, he laid her gently on top of the covers. The red robe lay carelessly tossed over the footboard, and he reached for it, using it like a towel to begin drying her hair.

"I'll be all right," she said, embarrassed to be treated like a child.

"Yes, you will be." He sat beside her, rubbing her hair. He followed the path of the robe with his fingers, smoothing the fine blond strands back from her face as he dried them.

"But you're wet, too."

"Shh. . . . I don't care."

She looked up at him, and he saw traces of fear in her eyes. He smiled gently, encouragement lighting his face. He cupped her head, forcing her to turn away so that he could dry the rest of her hair. She lay still, but he could see her breathing accelerate. He moved away only long enough to turn off the overhead light, then returned.

He smoothed the robe along her cheeks and down her neck. Then he began to unbutton her blouse.

"Matthew. . . ."

"Shh. . . ."

She remembered his anger when he'd looked at her before. Her hands went to his to stop him, but he ignored them. "I've thought about the way you looked," he said quietly. "I've thought about little else. Let me see you again."

She turned her face away, wanting to believe his words, afraid at what she might see in his eyes.

He unfastened the last button, smoothing open her blouse. She wore no bra, and, finding that, his hands trembled. "So beautiful," he said reverently. "So perfect." He touched her with the robe, passing it tenderly across her chest and over her breasts. He didn't want the cloth between them, but he wanted even less to startle her with his hands.

She remembered the abuse Charles had hurled at her the first time he had seen her undressed. She swallowed painfully. "Please, don't say anything else."

"No?" He lifted her, sliding the blouse over her shoulders and arms until she was free of it. "I'm not allowed to tell you how you make me feel? That I never believed I would feel this way again?"

Her head turned, and her eyes sought his. There was no anger there. Awe, and perhaps a touch of sadness, but no anger.

"Do you feel pity?" she asked softly.

"For you because you've lived in hell? Not pity. Sadness, concern, anger that it had to happen. But you don't deserve pity. You walked out of hell alive. Now you're in my arms." He swung his legs on to the bed and stretched out beside her. He dropped the robe on the floor and began to caress her with his hands.

Alexis wondered if she had ever known tenderness before. Matthew's hands weren't casual or punishing. They stroked to give her pleasure, to give *him* pleasure. They moved over her with the delicacy of a butterfly's wings and with the strength of a gentle man. Where his hands stroked, his mouth followed, tasting, testing. She was ready for more long before he gave it to her. She held back her response, afraid she might spoil the miracle that was happening, but when she could hold back no longer, she sighed brokenly, inching closer to him.

His mouth dipped lower to cover one breast. As if she had asked. As if he had known what she needed. This time she couldn't suppress a moan, and his fingers tightened on her shoulders as she did, as if he had felt the sound inside himself.

He covered her other breast, washing her nipple with his tongue, suckling until she was bent beneath him, reaching for more. His hands slid under her and down to her hips, stopping at her waist to explore its narrow contours before he arched her hips to his. His mouth took hers, beginning a slow rhythm with his tongue while his hips began a slow rhythm against hers. She was all breathless wonder and warm acquiescence, but she didn't touch him, not even to clasp him against her.

"Put your arms around me," he whispered against her mouth. "I want you to hold me."

Her breath caught. "Do you?"

"I want you to touch me. Anywhere. Everywhere. Don't hold anything back. I want whatever you have to give me."

He had given her freedom, but she found that she couldn't take it. Not yet. Charles held her hands as surely as if he were in the room. She tried to comply, but she was limp with distress.

Somehow Matthew seemed to understand. "My shirt is wet," he said. "And I don't want to stop touching you."

She undressed herself every day. She helped Jody dress and undress. But the distance to his top button seemed an endless mile. He felt the tremors in her hands and wanted to strangle the man who had put them there. "Yes," he encouraged her. "Your hands against my skin are wonderful."

The next button was easier, and the next. But the last was hardest of all. Matthew buried his face against her shoulder. "I want to feel all of you against me," he said more harshly than he'd meant to. "Don't make me wait."

She reacted by stiffening, and he cursed his own impatience. It seemed a part of him, a slowly growing beast that was demanding satisfaction before she was anywhere near ready to give it. He cursed three years of abstinence and the allure of the woman in his arms.

"Alexis, if I wanted you less, this would be easier."

The last button slipped out of its hole. She slid her hands over his chest and against his shoulders, pushing the shirt away. He knew better than to clasp her tightly. He knew enough to go slowly, to let her learn the feel of him inch by inch. He knew better, but his control was fast slipping. He groaned and positioned himself so that he could feel her breasts press against him. His mouth sought hers once more, to apologize, to coax.

She was overwhelmed by sensation. He was so much larger than she, so much stronger. For a moment she panicked, struggling against him. He moved away a little, and his mouth slid to her cheeks, to her nose, to her forehead. "I'm sorry," he whispered.

"I'm sorry," she said fiercely. "This can't be what you need!"

"You're what I need, and I'll take you any way you give yourself."

Her indrawn breath was a sob. Involuntarily her arms went around him, not to push him away, but to hold him close. He groaned and let her, giving in to the luxury of her body pressed to his.

She began to lose herself in his warmth. She began to feel his strength as a gift, not a threat. She began to move with the age-old rhythm of desire until he slid off the shorts and panties that still clung soddenly to her and she was naked against him.

The buckle of his belt dug into the soft flesh of her abdomen. She slid the tongue from its hole and pulled the belt out of the loops of his jeans. "Yes," he said against her mouth. His hands moved over her body, faster, surer, learning what pleased her, teaching her what pleased her. He waited for her to finish undressing him, and the wait was torture. He knew what she suffered, and he knew he couldn't cure her. She had to act willingly or not at all.

She was flooded with longing. He knew her intimately now, knew that she was afraid, knew that she wanted to be set free from fear. And still he held her, made slow, perfect love to her. He was everything she had once dreamed a lover could be and every dream she had since abandoned.

And all she had to do to bring back dreams was to finish undressing him. Her hands wouldn't move. Once, in the nightmare of her marriage, Charles had tied her hands and left them tied all night. He tied them just as effectively now, although only she knew they were bound. She fought her fear, named it and tried to cast it away, but she couldn't. She could only, finally, beg for help.

"I can't undress you," she whispered, close to tears. "Matthew, please help me."

If he was chilled by her refusal, he was warmed by her plea. He covered her hands with his, moving them to his hips, then around to his zipper. He held her hands in his as he slid it down, and his hands continued to cover hers as he slipped them inside his jeans to inch them over his hips.

Now she felt as if she had been set free. Her hands glided beneath his briefs, inching them off, too. In moments he was naked beside her. Her hands, unbound now, began to explore him, tentatively at first, but with more assurance as his breath grew harsher and his hands moved more quickly over her. She shuddered as he spread her legs and began a slow kneading rhythm that seemed to focus all the blood and sensation in her body in one glorious place.

Matthew knew she might not be ready, might never be ready for his lovemaking, but he knew, too, that waiting forever, waiting even seconds longer, was impossible. Perhaps neither of them was ready, but both of them had to know.

He moved on top of her, framing her face with his hands. "Say my name," he said, kissing her deeply after he had said the words to reassure her.

"Matthew," she said, her lips still pressed to his. "Say mine."

"Alexis." He parted her legs, waiting for her to show him she wanted him. She spread her legs, winding them around him. He had needed a small sign; she had issued an unmistakable invitation. With thought suspended by that small, significant act, he thrust once, entering her with such a thrill of pleasure that he was dizzied by its intensity.

She cried out in surprise and wonder. She had expected a gentle entry, a coaxing. Instead he had lost control, and suddenly she knew the depth of his desire and the magic of her attraction for him.

He heard her cry and felt a terrible remorse, withdrawing. His head dropped to her shoulder, and he was too shaken to speak. Worse yet, he still wanted her so badly that he wondered if he would survive.

She knew. Somehow she knew what he had thought. She tried to tell him, but there were no words to explain. Instead she fitted herself against him once more and rose to meet him.

He shuddered as she began a regular rhythm. She was warm and liquid, pulling him down farther inside her until he was part of her. She cried out again, and this time he understood. He wove his arms around her until she was clasped as tightly as he could hold her, and as he moved against her, he murmured her name until it was a litany of thanksgiving.

Alexis knew that tears were sliding down her cheeks, tears far different from the ones she had cried earlier. She cried now because dreams could be found, because men could be gentle and strong, and because for the first time in her life she knew what it was like to be touched by love.

Then the tears stopped, and the dreams were at last discovered, safe and whole. And love . . . love began in earnest.

"What about Jody?"

Alexis stirred in Matthew's arms. She had been asleep, a deep, peaceful sleep like none she could remember. "Umm. . . ."

"I didn't even think about Jody." Matthew turned her to him. He was whispering. "Is she going to walk in on us any minute?"

"She's away overnight. At a sleepover."

"Then we're alone."

"Except for the koala in the tree out front. It's the one you rescued the first day." Alexis yawned and opened her eyes. The room was dark, but her eyes adjusted quickly. Beside her Matthew seemed huge and impossibly, gloriously male. She wondered how there was enough room in the bed for both of them.

"So he came back."

"Blind faith. When the shooting started, I was afraid they'd find him next. It seemed as if that would be the ultimate injustice."

"And so you got your gun and went shooting, too."

She heard the censure in his voice. "I'd do it again. Next time I might shoot right at them."

"You could have been killed."

"You said that earlier."

Matthew pulled her head to his shoulder. It surprised him how well she fit against him. But everything surprised him: the shattering pleasure he had found in her arms; his pride that she had trusted him; his mounting desire to have her again. Perhaps most of all he was surprised that he wasn't racked with guilt that he now held another woman. But what had happened didn't touch what he'd had with Jeannie. It was different and would always remain so.

"I've lived so much of my life in fear," she said minutes later, knowing Matthew hadn't gone back to sleep. "I won't live that way anymore."

"There's a thin line between courage and recklessness. Promise me you won't go after the poachers again."

Her voice was husky and tempting. "You sleep with a woman, Matthew, and then you begin asking for promises?"

"Only if I think I have a small prayer of getting them."

"We just haven't reached that stage yet," she said, turning over so that her leg caressed his and her breasts brushed his arm. "That's a big promise."

His lips turned up in a slow smile—a smile by degrees. "What is it you Yanks say? Something about feeling your oats?"

"Now what would make you say something like that?" She glided one hand across his chest, taking her time so that every texture, every muscle, knew her fingertips before she'd finished.

He just caught the hint of shyness behind the sexiest smile he had ever seen. He took her hand and moved it lower. "You've just begun," he said. "Let's not waste an excellent start."

"Still looking for promises?"

He threaded both hands into her hair and began to pull her closer. "Right now, enchantress, I think I'm looking for something more immediately satisfying."

Neither of them mentioned it, because both of them were afraid to. But when Alexis lay beside Matthew once more, wrung dry and aching from spent pleasure, she knew he would stay the night. His breathing slowed, and he turned a little to gather her closer.

She wondered what he was feeling. He had made it clear from the day they'd met that he wanted no one in his life. Now he was sleeping peacefully beside her, sharing her blankets, sharing her warmth.

And giving warmth. She'd never known that warmth could be exchanged, could spread and grow until it was a raging conflagration inside both of them. She had never known that she was capable of such fire. Her own flames had been banked, not extinguished as she had thought. And out of the ashes of her past Matthew had fanned her passion into flames once more.

She wondered if she had done the same for him. He had wanted her; he had found joy in their lovemaking, joy, she thought, in their tenderness. But she wondered what it meant to him. He didn't talk about his feelings. He had said next to nothing about his past, nothing about his wife and son. He had let her know that he was thinking only of her when they had made love, but now she wondered who he thought of as he slept.

There had been no promises exchanged, only warmth slowly building to fire. She could make no promises. Not yet. Not until she knew she and Jody were safe at last.

But when that day came, would there be promises to make, or would the ashes of both their pasts smother the flames that had ignited tonight?

She didn't know. She only knew that for the first time in many years, she could hope.

Chapter 10

Do you love Matthew?" Jody lay belly-down on her mother's bed, finishing a crossword puzzle.

"Is the answer 12 Across or 44 Down?"

Jody rolled her eyes. "Do you?"

Alexis stood in a full slip, gazing into her closet. She and Jody were meeting Matthew at the park in half an hour to go on a picnic. Alexis had only seen him once in the week since they had spent the night together, and she was looking forward to having a whole afternoon with him. Fleetingly she wished there could be even more, but Jody had to be considered. For now she and Matthew would have to be content with stolen mornings, mornings like the one several days before when, after Jody's school bus was far down the road, he'd appeared with fresh muffins and stayed for more than morning tea.

"I'm wondering why you've asked," Alexis said, reaching for a blue chambray gathered skirt and matching blouse. She wasn't sure the outfit was entirely appropriate for a picnic, but she liked the way it flowed around her legs in the breeze, and she suspected Matthew would, too.

"I'd like it if you'd love somebody," Jody said with a child's candor. "Annie's mom and dad held hands under the table at the sleepover. I saw them." Alexis turned and saw that Jody was frowning. "Did you and my father ever hold hands?"

As Jody grew, she asked more and more questions about Charles. It was only natural, but Alexis's aversion to answering them was just as natural. She didn't want to turn Jody against the man who had helped conceive her, but neither did she want to paint a warm, glowing picture that not only wouldn't jibe with Jody's own memories but might someday send her in search of him.

"I was very young when I married your father," she said at last. "Neither of us was really in love. That sometimes happens, sweetheart. People marry for the wrong reasons, even if they don't know it at the time. Your father and I were very wrong for each other, but we did one right thing. We had you." She smiled, hoping to lift the frown from Jody's face.

"I'd like a new father." Jody bent her head back to her puzzle book.

Alexis didn't know what to say. She began to rummage in her jewelry box for a necklace to wear.

"*Do* you love Matthew?"

Alexis imagined she'd hear the question again and again until she finally answered it. "I don't know."

"You have trouble telling, don't you?"

"It's not as easy as they make it look on television."

"I'll be able to tell."

"When I fall in love, or when you do?"

"When I do. I'm going to marry a man like Matthew, or maybe like Gray or Dillon." She put her pencil eraser in her mouth and chewed on it as she thought about her choices. "Or Adam—except I think I might get tired of all those sheep after a while."

Alexis laughed and sent up a silent prayer of gratitude. After a tough start, Jody was learning about men from some of the best in the world. "A man like any one of them would do nicely."

Just as Alexis thought the subject had been put to rest, Jody added one last thought. "A man who doesn't hit me," she said, closing her puzzle book. "Not a man like my father."

Cape du Couedic lay at the extreme southwest tip of Kangaroo Island and Flinders Chase. Until 1940, the cape had never seen a motor vehicle, but it *had* seen several tragic shipwrecks. A rustic stone lighthouse loomed well back from the cliffside as testimony to the South Australian government's vigilance in keeping the coastal waters safe.

Matthew parked Alexis's wagon near the lighthouse and came around to help her out. The nine mile drive to the cape had been along a narrow, winding road that, although perfectly safe, had been rutted and rough. To prove that this new road was a vast improvement over the one the lighthouse keepers had once traversed, Matthew had told hilarious stories about the trials of those days as reported to Harry by rangers before him.

"It's beautiful here." Alexis took Matthew's hand and let him help her out of the seat. She found almost any excuse for touching him a good one. He didn't drop her hand when she was standing beside him. He tucked it under his arm and extended a hand to Jody.

"And this is where the lighthouse keepers live?" Jody bounded out of her seat, pulling Matthew and Alexis toward a group of houses that was set back from the lighthouse itself.

"Not anymore, I'm afraid. The lighthouse is automatic now."

"Oh. . . ." Jody stopped, obviously disappointed. "I wanted to know what it was like to live here."

"Very lonely. No telephone. No television. Not even a mail delivery. Every two weeks or so the keepers sent their children along the road back to Rocky River to fetch the mail."

"They walked?" Jody was truly astonished.

"Walked or rode an old horse. There's one story about a new keeper, a fellow who had never ridden in his life.

Someone had to go fetch the mail, and since he was the newest, they sent him. They told him to just sit on the horse's back and the horse would know the way.''

"Did he make it?" Jody hung on every word, just as she'd hung on every word Matthew had said that day.

"Afraid not. It was a hot day, and he fell asleep on the horse's back. The horse was hot, too, so when he came to a fork in the road, he just turned around and went back home. When he arrived, the keepers woke the poor bloke up and sent him on his way again. They say it was almost midnight when he finally got back with the mail.''

"And I'll bet they had to pry him off the horse." Alexis tucked her arm more solidly under Matthew's. He clasped her hand and smiled down at her. Their eyes held, and communicated the feelings they had never really put into words.

"I'd like to ride a horse like that," Jody said enthusiastically. "It would be fun to get the mail."

"Is this the same girl who has to be shoved out of the car to run into the post office for me?"

"That's different." But to be sure there was no argument about why, Jody broke free and skipped toward the lighthouse without them.

"You're a good mother," Matthew observed.

Alexis rubbed her cheek against his shoulder in gratitude. She had always effectively been a single parent, and it had rarely been easy. "I try." She waited, hoping that Matthew would say something, anything, about his own days as a parent. But he didn't. He never mentioned his marriage or his son, as if his memories were still too painful.

"She hasn't had a smooth childhood, but it doesn't show. You've gotten her through it."

"Life will never be smooth for her. She's too intense. She sees too much. I'm just trying to teach her how to take everything one step at a time and how not to expect perfection."

"Is that how you manage?"

"That and dreaming."

He wanted to ask her where her dreams took her now, but he knew he wasn't ready for an answer. Since the night they had first made love, his own dreams had been confusing and agonizing. His nightmares of Jeannie and Todd's deaths had been replaced by nightmares where Alexis and Jody were in danger. There was one that had especially haunted him. Jody and Alexis were sitting in a grove of gum trees. He was running to warn them they were in danger when, from the distance, he could see the bodies of koalas begin to fall from the trees. He ran, but couldn't get closer. As he watched in horror, a man stepped from behind a tree and pointed a rifle at them. It was the evangelist from his childhood memories, and as the man pulled the trigger he screamed "Judgment!"

Matthew couldn't tell Alexis about his dreams. He wasn't even sure he could bear to dream them. He only knew that after the worst night, he'd had to see her. He had gone to her house that next morning to be sure she was all right, and when he'd seen that she was, he had thrown away his nightmares and made love to her.

"I'm glad we're seeing more of the park with you." Alexis wondered what Matthew was feeling. He held her close, but he didn't speak of his emotions. She wanted no promises, but she wasn't above needing reassurance.

"The Chase is a special place. I want to show you all of it. It's so vast, so different from one end to another, that you can never grow tired of it."

Alexis knew Matthew had just tried to provide the reassurance she had craved. He was talking about the future. "You have a wonderful job. In a way, you have more destiny in your hands than almost anyone I've known."

He was surprised she would think so. Jeannie had never really liked his job. She had been a Sydney girl, and the city was where she felt most at home. She had come to Kangaroo Island with him willingly, and she had never complained. But he had known her well enough to understand that she often longed for more than the island could give her. She had turned her considerable energy into making a home for her husband and son, but it had never really been enough. To compensate, she had made frequent visits back to Sydney, and it was at the start of one of them that she and Todd had been killed.

He squeezed Alexis's hand as he led her toward Jody, who looked as if she were trying to think of a way to unlock the lighthouse door and climb the stairs. They explored the base of the lighthouse and then the path leading to the cliffs overlooking the ocean. Alexis found each step interesting. The ground was smooth gray granite, yet wildflowers, succulents and grasses of every form and hue decorated crevices and pockets in the rock. The ocean itself was a brilliant blue, and at the edge of the cliffside they descended slippery steps to view the Admiral's Arch, a gaping cavern where the sea surged and receded with each crashing breaker.

Their clothes were damp, but not their spirits, when they drove to nearby Weirs Cove to see the limestone ruins of the storehouses where the lighthouse keepers had kept supplies. Nearby was the remains of a gully that had been gouged from the cliffside and rigged with a "flying fox" to haul supplies from a small jetty built at the base of the cliff. A series of crude, crumbling steps led far down the precipice to the teeming surf below. Neither the steps nor the gully itself had been used since the lighthouse keepers had joined the ranks of the unemployed. But they still stood, a monument to a different time.

"Imagine living here," Alexis mused out loud. "Imagine standing here four times a year and waiting, just waiting for the ship to come."

Matthew laughed. "Sometimes it would come and the weather would be so rough it couldn't berth for weeks."

"Then imagine standing here, knowing that your food stores, the clothes you'd ordered, the few luxuries you'd saved for, were all out there, almost at your fingertips, and you couldn't do a thing about it."

"I feel a story coming on."

"Mine? Or yours?"

He smiled, something he did more frequently now, but each time Alexis still felt it deep inside her. "Back in the twenties, one of the keepers had a wife with a bad leg," he began. "She landed down there at the jetty, but she couldn't climb the steps."

Alexis looked down and shuddered. "Smart woman."

"So they settled her in a basket on the flying fox and began to haul it up."

"And?"

"The motor broke down. I guess they all wished they'd stuck to horse power about then, but it couldn't be helped. The poor woman was up in the basket for about two hours. And they say she turned the air blue when they finally got her down."

"I should hope so."

Jody came back to the edge of the gully after exploring the ruins. "There's a sign over there that says 'Beware. High Cliffs and Strong Winds.' Are you being careful?"

Matthew lifted her easily and set her on his shoulders. "Let's use you as a weather vane and see if we need to worry."

Jody squealed in delight, and they walked back to the wagon that way.

The road continued, hugging the cliff's edge until they reached the most important reason for coming to this section of the park for their picnic.

"Remarkable Rocks," Matthew said, switching off the ignition.

"Truly remarkable," Alexis agreed, while Jody oohed her admiration from the back seat. The rocks were massive granite, with lighter-colored quartz and feldspar bands, and they sat on a rock promontory overlooking the ocean like sculptures created by a master hand. Each rock—and there were over a dozen—had been weathered by erosion into graceful contours and designs. Some looked like fanciful blocks of Swiss cheese, others like elaborate climbing equipment for the lucky child of a giant.

They played in the rocks for an hour, hiding, laughing, sliding, until Jody declared she would die if they didn't eat. And when they finally set up their picnic in a nearby shelter, Alexis and Matthew ate as much as she did.

It was almost dark as they finished driving the winding road back to the rangers' homestead. There had been more to see, paths leading to quiet streams and an impressive waterfall, favorite spots for bird-watching and wildflower-naming. The day had been particularly special because there had been no tension. They had all set out to enjoy it, and it had been just that simple.

The park had been almost deserted, too. With the campgrounds closed for renovation and springtime grading, and repair work blocking parts of the main road leading into the park, few visitors had ventured into the Chase that day. "I feel like a pioneer," Alexis told Matthew, reaching across the gear shift to lay a seemingly innocent hand on his leg.

He wished simultaneously for a shorter distance to his house and a flying carpet ride for Jody to another sleepover. "A pioneer?"

Alexis smiled, turning her face to the window so he wouldn't see. His voice had been notes lower than usual. "Mmm.... I pretended...." She stopped, appalled at what she'd been about to reveal.

He ventured a glance into the back seat and saw that Jody's pioneer blood had given out. She was fast asleep. He covered Alexis's hand and moved it farther up his thigh. "Pretended what?"

She had pretended that the three of them were a family who had just come to homestead the land. There was something so untamed about the Chase, so vital yet desolate, that the fantasy had been hard to resist. Seventy-four thousand hectares, which meant over twice as many acres, and many of them had hardly known the tread of a human foot. The fantasy had been understandable but too intimate to share, because she knew it might scare Matthew away. He'd had a family, and he still grieved for them.

She rubbed her hand slowly back and forth. "I pretended I was a lighthouse keeper," she said, because that had been true, too. "I was out there, cut off from civilization...."

"I'm surprised that thought didn't send you screaming and fleeing back to the city."

"On the contrary, nature boy, it was a wonderful thought. You see, I also envisioned crates of good books and a warm man beside me." She gave a low laugh at his sudden change of expression, and her hand slipped farther up his thigh.

"The isolation would make you a crazy woman."

"If isolation could do that to me, I'd be crazy now." She laughed again. "Matthew, are you speeding up?"

"Be more precise with your questions. Do you want to know if *I'm* speeding up or if the car is?"

"Oh, I know what *you're* doing."

"There's a child in the back seat."

"A sleeping child, who, once asleep, will continue sleeping unless someone drops her on her head."

His eyes flicked to hers. "I hate to think of you having to take her all the way back to your house alone."

She lowered her eyelids, flirting unashamedly. "Then why don't you come and help?"

"I can't leave the Chase tonight. I'm on watch. Harry's going out."

She tried to hide her disappointment. "That's too bad, but really, I can manage Jody fine."

He sent her a smile that lodged her heart in the pit of her stomach before he turned his gaze back to the road. "I'm sure you can, but why should you, when my house is so near, and she could have the pleasure of waking up at the park tomorrow morning?"

Alexis hesitated. She wanted to spend the night with Matthew, and she was immensely pleased that he had asked. She hadn't expected him to want to share his bed with her. But Jody had to be considered.

Matthew understood what she was thinking. "I have three bedrooms, Alexis. Or, better yet, the room where we'll put Jody has a double bed. You can sleep with her tonight. *Late* tonight."

"Do you think I'm being silly?"

"I think you're being a good mother."

"Let's see if she wakes up when we put her to bed."

"You'll pardon me if I spend the rest of the trip muttering wishes."

"I won't hear them over mine."

Alexis had such a strong sense of their relationship taking a new turn that she was oblivious to anything else for the rest of the drive.

Matthew wasn't so lucky. He slowed the wagon well before he reached the homestead and flicked off the lights. Then, quietly, carefully, he pulled the car off the road into a grove of trees and turned off the engine.

"Isn't this a strange place to park?" she asked.

"Shh...." He gestured for silence.

She was alert now. Tensing, she listened closely, wondering what the problem could be. For a moment she had worried that he didn't want her wagon to be spotted if she and Jody stayed overnight. But now she realized that something different was at stake.

She heard noise in the distance, too. It was men's laughter. She didn't speak, but she turned her face to Matthew's profile, watching him. All traces of good humor had been wiped from his face. He was stone still, his expression ominous, with all his concentration focused on listening. Then one hand was on the door, opening it slowly, while his other hand threw the switch on the overhead light so it wouldn't come on. "Lock the doors after I get out," he whispered. "It's probably nothing, but I intend to find out."

She would have asked to come with him, but Jody still slept in the back seat.

"You'll be careful?" she pleaded.

He was already gone.

She locked the doors as he'd ordered, then forced herself to begin the wait. The night was clear, and a half moon shone in a sky bright with stars. But inside the shelter of the trees there was little light. She could see nothing, and the laughter subsided so that she could hear nothing, either. Jody's quiet breathing and the occasional cry of a more-pork owl were the only noises in a world gone suspiciously still.

She wasn't sure what Matthew feared. Although the campgrounds with toilets, showers and running water weren't in use, he had told her there were still campers using the bush camping areas, primitive campsites that were scattered throughout remote reaches of the park. And although he and Harry were the only staff who lived on the grounds, there were other park employees. The noise could be coming from any one of several possible sources, none of them threatening.

She felt threatened anyway. She wondered if she had lived with evil for so long that she had developed a sixth sense to detect it. Certainly the day she had shot at the poachers, she had sensed them somehow before hearing them or spotting their lights. Perhaps Matthew had developed his senses from the constant vigilance required of a park ranger.

The night was so still that when she finally heard a noise, it sounded like a cannon going off. The noise was nothing more than a pop, but it vibrated through the air for long moments afterward, accompanying the accelerated beat of her heart.

With unsteady hands Alexis grabbed the keys hanging in the ignition and slid them into her pocket. Then, with a glance to be sure Jody was still sleeping, she unlocked her door, opened it and slipped outside, locking the door behind her.

The air had turned cool, and she shivered, although she wasn't sure if it were from cold or fear. After creeping silently through the trees, she stopped at the edge of the grove. She could go no farther without jeopardizing Jody's safety. Her eyes adjusted slowly to the stronger light, and at first she couldn't detect anything out of the ordinary. Then she saw the figure of a man, bent low, darting from shadow to shadow in the yard of the rangers' homestead.

Her breath hissed softly in a warning the man couldn't hear. The man was Matthew, and she could see that he carried a rifle. The rifle confirmed her suspicion. Someone had fired a shot, and Matthew was going to be prepared for the next one.

The scene was a nightmare. She couldn't help; she couldn't even call out a warning. She could only watch and pray that he'd be all right. He disappeared around the side of the house, and she strained to see where he was going.

She wanted to keep her eyes on him, to somehow infuse him with caution just by staring at him, but he was out of sight for good. All she could do was listen.

She listened for minutes. She heard laughter again, one short raucous burst of it, then nothing. Just as she was about to go back to the car to check on Jody, she heard a gunshot and a shout. Even the distance couldn't shroud the words.

"Drop your bloody guns and raise your hands, or I'll pick you off like you've been picking off the bears!"

The poachers! Waiting in the dark, she had weighed the possibility, then dismissed it. No one, *no one*, could be stupid enough to venture right into the Chase and shoot koalas. But then she, of all people, should know that men could be capable of any act.

Her hands went to her mouth as she waited for an answer, another gunshot, sounds of a scuffle. There was silence for a full minute, then another shout.

"Alexis! Call the police."

She cupped her hands and shouted through them. "I'm coming."

"Bring the car."

She was turning to run back to get it when she saw a movement in the trees beside her. She caught a glimpse of a plaid jacket and long dark hair beating against it as a young woman ran past her. "Stop!" she yelled, taking after the woman herself. "Stop!"

The woman swung around just long enough to see how close Alexis was, then zigzagged through the trees, deeper into the forest. Alexis knew she didn't have a prayer of catching her. When she reached the car, she halted, out of breath and angry that she hadn't seen the woman in time. She had succeeded in one thing, however. She had gotten a good look at her face, and with the skill of someone who must catch and remember every detail so that she can someday use it in a book, she had recorded what she'd seen. Now she would know the woman anywhere. But, just as surely, the woman would know her.

Jody stirred on the back seat as Alexis turned the key and the wagon purred to life. "Mommy?"

"It's all right, sweetheart."

"Where are we?"

"At Matthew's. I think he just caught the poachers."

"Good," Jody mumbled. She snuggled against the seat cushions and promptly fell back to sleep.

Alexis pulled carefully onto the road and guided the wagon toward the homestead. She parked in front of Matthew's house and got out, following the sound of men's voices.

By the time she had followed the path to his back yard, Harry had already joined Matthew. Alexis caught a glimpse of the two poachers as Harry ushered them at gunpoint into a toolshed behind Matthew's house.

They were children—or almost. Even with just the pale light from Matthew's back porch illuminating them, she could see how young the two men were. One had the patchy complexion of an adolescent, the other the soft, thin wisps of a first mustache. Neither of them was as old as twenty.

"Why?" she demanded before she could stop herself. She was too angry to care whether she got between Harry's gun and the men. She stalked to the shed door, blocking their entrance.

"Alexis, stay back," Matthew warned.

She ignored him. "Why? Just tell me why!"

The first man swayed on his feet. He smiled benignly and opened his mouth as if he intended to answer. Then he frowned as he swayed again.

"They're both so drunk they can hardly stand," Matthew said, coming up to lead her away. "Even if they knew why they were doing it, they couldn't tell you now."

"Drunk?" She couldn't believe it. She shook off Matthew's arm. "Drunk? They killed those beautiful animals because they're drunk?"

Harry closed in, nodding at Alexis sympathetically. "They didn't kill anything tonight. They couldn't have hit the moon if it was sitting on the roof of my house. Now you've got to let me get them in the shed, darling. And Matthew's got to call the law."

She let Matthew lead her safely away. From yards distant, she watched the poachers stumble into the shed. Harry twisted a padlock into place. "Why?" she repeated, trying to understand.

Matthew didn't even want to tell Alexis what he suspected. The two young men who had maimed and murdered were probably not even selling the furs. He imagined the cops would find the pelts at their homes—nothing more than souvenirs. Their acts had been a rural version of a joy ride—something to do on boring spring nights on an island with few additional diversions. The acts of violence had been senseless and unusually cruel, but the men, who were hardly old enough to deserve that title, had probably thought of their poaching as nothing more than daring target practice.

"We may never know," he warned gently. "But at least the worst is over."

"How could they have come here? Into the park?"

Matthew put his arm around her to walk back to the car to get Jody. Harry stayed behind to guard the shed.

"I was away, and Harry was over at the office," he theorized. "With most of the campers gone, the place looked deserted. Who knows what they thought? Apparently the challenge appealed to them, and they were too drunk to consider the consequences if they were caught."

She suddenly thought of the young woman. "Or they were trying to impress someone." Briefly she told Matthew the story, adding a description as he opened the rear door of the car to lift a sleeping Jody into his arms.

She gave the same description to the police forty-five minutes later when they came to pick up the two young men. With Matthew's help they conducted a search of the nearby grounds, but, in the darkness, nothing was gained by it. The dark-haired young woman had disappeared.

"What's going to happen to them?" Alexis asked after the police had taken the men into custody and left. She and

Matthew were settled on the couch in his parlor, and Jody was sound asleep upstairs.

"They'll be taken to Adelaide to stand trial."

"What will happen then?"

"The Australian people don't take kindly to anyone caught shooting koalas. I doubt they'll get off easily."

Alexis sighed, and Matthew pulled her closer. "Does that bother you?"

"It does. That probably sounds silly, after everything. But they're just kids."

"And you think there's good in them?"

She didn't know how to answer that. At one time she had thought there was good in everyone. Then she'd met Charles. "Is there?" she asked, turning the question back to him. "I don't know what I think."

"I think we have to assume there is until it's proved otherwise."

"But there can be an otherwise?"

"Yes."

She cuddled tightly against him, needing his strength. "When I first met Charles," she said softly, "I thought he was good. I thought he was everything I needed. The thing that's so frightening is that he made me believe it. There were no signs of the man he really was inside."

"Or there were signs you chose to ignore."

"No signs," she said firmly. "And that's what's so horrible. That's why nobody I tried to talk to after our marriage believed me, except my lawyer. None of them had any hint who the real Charles Cahill was."

Knowing that, Matthew realized, knowing that sometimes it was impossible to tell who a person really was, she had still trusted *him*. Matthew felt humbled by that—and frightened. It bespoke more than trust. He wasn't ready for more—might never be ready.

But he wasn't ready to give up what they'd found together, either.

"Are you going to stay the night?" he whispered into her hair.

"Do you still want me to?"

"I think you should. There's a frantic young woman wandering the countryside, and we don't know if she's armed."

"She did get a look at my face. If she wants revenge, she'll know where to go for it."

"And you got a look at her," he reminded her. "If she has even a milligram more brains than her boyfriends, she'll go home, pack her bags and get off the island."

"Then it's perfectly safe for me to go home."

"I didn't say that."

She melted closer to him. "And why not?"

"Because I'll come after you if you do and drag you back here."

She dropped her hands lightly on his shoulders. "I respond much better to gentle coaxing and warm embraces."

He rested his palms against her cheeks and leaned to touch his lips to her forehead. "That's my first plan. Dragging you back is just my backup."

She stroked her hands up his neck and settled more fully against him. One finger began a slow trail to his lips. "You can discard your backup immediately. I guarantee you won't need to worry about it."

"No?"

"Your mind is going to be on something much more relaxing, Matthew."

Then neither of their minds was on anything at all.

Chapter 11

Is Jody an early riser?"

"She's not an anything. Sometimes she gets up at the crack of dawn. Sometimes she can't be dragged out of bed."

"I hate to bear the bad tidings, but it's almost the crack of dawn now."

Alexis curved her body into the warmth of Matthew's. "Why start the day with bad tidings?"

"Mmm...." He nuzzled her ear. "Is that how we started the day?"

They had started the day far differently. The night before they had fallen asleep in each other's arms after lovemaking that had taught them there were still new heights to climb. Then, hours before sunrise, Alexis had awakened to Matthew's hands stroking her body.

The sweetness of it, the tenderness of it, had almost been her undoing. She couldn't remember a time in her life when anyone had petted her that way. She had so often longed to be touched, but in her marriage, touching had been a fearful thing. Now it was pleasure-filled and mind-altering. She couldn't imagine any day that had begun like this one being anything but wonderful.

Matthew had awakened not in the midst of a nightmare but in the midst of an erotic dream of Alexis. And, once fully awake, he had found the woman more exciting than the dream. He didn't dare question why she felt so right beside him. He couldn't look at his own brash insistence that she share the bed he had slept in with Jeannie. He could only feel the rightness and push down all traces of guilt.

"I hate to say this, but I really should join Jody in her bed," Alexis said, moving just far enough away to see his eyes. "At least until the sun's up. Then I'll come downstairs, with her or without her."

"And you'll stay for breakfast?"

"Wouldn't miss it, but then I'll have to drive her to school."

"School." Matthew said the word as if he'd never thought of it.

"Yes, school. You know, that thing children do every day from eight-thirty until three. That thing that makes them elated one minute and comatose the next."

Matthew was silent, and Alexis realized who he was thinking of. She wished she hadn't been so flippant. "Matthew." She put her hand against his cheek. "You must miss your son terribly."

She watched the old frozen expression cover his face. "Don't," she whispered, trying to stroke it away. "You can tell me you don't want to talk about him, but don't shut me out completely."

"I don't want to talk about my family. Not now, not ever."

"Can talking hurt as much as not talking?"

"That isn't your affair."

His words hurt, but she knew he was absolutely right. She had no rights to his past, and he had given her no rights to his future. She had only the present, and she was quickly spoiling that. "I'm sorry," she said, leaning forward to brush his lips with hers. "The last thing I want to do is hurt you."

He relaxed a little. If she'd acted hurt or angry, he would have gotten out of the bed and left before she'd had a chance to leave herself. Instead she had shown him the ultimate respect: the right to his own feelings. He was filled with a vague sense of guilt that she could be so adult and he could be so much the hurt child. Resolutely he pushed the thought away. Jeannie and Todd were off-limits. She would have to understand that now.

"What are your plans for the day?" he asked gruffly.

Alexis tried to act as if nothing had happened. "I'm afraid I've got an unpleasant job ahead of me when I get back from taking Jody into school."

"What's that?"

"I'm going to have to check the property and see if the poachers were there before they came over to the Chase."

He hadn't thought about that possibility, but he knew she was right. If the poachers had gone to her house first, he didn't want Alexis to find the evidence. He remembered the night in the grove and her agony then. He wanted no repeats. "I'll check while you're taking Jody into town."

"You don't have to—"

He silenced her with a finger over her lips. "I do. It's my fault you have to make that long trip, isn't it? If you were home you could just pack her onto the bus."

"Fault?" She smiled warmly. "Fault isn't the right word."

"No?"

"Try wonderful idea."

"I'll admit there's a certain ring to that."

His expression had softened considerably. Alexis brushed another kiss across his lips, then went to join her daughter in the other bedroom.

Hours later, Matthew was standing in a grove of gum trees when an angry male voice sounded behind him. "And just what do you think you're doing?"

Matthew spun around, startled. He had parked his car on the road to Alexis's house and stopped to investigate the stand of trees where she had first seen the poachers. He had been so caught up in his investigation that he hadn't heard footsteps.

"I might ask you the same," he said, challenge a deadly light in his eyes.

"There are signs all over this land warning poachers to stay off it."

Matthew relaxed just a little. His first thought had been that the man was Charles. The accent was American, the man's expression cold and angry. But it made little sense that if Charles had discovered his ex-wife's whereabouts he would be worried about poachers. If he had come, it would be to torment her, not to ensure her safety. "I'm not a poacher."

"Then why are you here?"

"Just who are you to be asking me questions? This land doesn't belong to you."

"A friend of mine lives here."

"A friend of *mine* lives here."

The two men eyed each other cautiously, neither wanting to make a mistake, both hoping the other was telling the truth. Finally, Matthew stepped forward and extended his hand. Behind the anger, he had seen concern in the eyes of the other man. "Matthew Haley. I'm a ranger at the park down the road."

The man hesitated only briefly, then extended his own hand. "Gray Sheridan."

Alexis had told Matthew of the American who had helped her spirit Jody out of the U.S. Matthew clasped the other man's hand in relief. "Did Alexis know you were coming? She didn't say anything about it to me."

"She didn't know." Gray hesitated, then decided he could trust the other man with at least part of the truth. "She never wants to put anyone to any trouble. I was afraid that if I told her, she'd think we were checking on her."

"Are you?"

"Yes."

Matthew realized Gray had said "we." "Who's with you?"

"My wife and baby."

Matthew heard the quiet pride in the words. He nodded. "She'll be glad to see you. She should be back before too long."

"Is she all right? We got here yesterday after lunch, and she hasn't been home. We've been worried."

"Worried" seemed a mild word for the depth of concern in Gray's voice. Matthew knew Gray was aware of Alexis's story, since he had helped Jody disappear. He knew what Gray had envisioned.

"She and Jody were with me," he said simply.

Gray's eyes narrowed. Matthew's meaning was plain. "And she's all right?"

"Better than she was a few days ago. We've caught the poachers." He realized Gray didn't know the story. "Let me drive you up to the house. I'll tell you about it on the way."

At the house, Gray hesitated, as if he were embarrassed. "When Alexis and Jody didn't come home last night, we decided to stay here and wait for them. We have a hotel room in Kingscote, but. . . ."

"She'll be glad that you stayed here, but sorry she missed you. You didn't hear any gunshots last night, did you? Didn't see anyone prowling around the grounds?"

"I didn't, and I would have. I kept my eye on things."

"I'm glad. Apparently the poachers passed her by this time."

"She didn't need to have that worry."

"No, she didn't. She's a brave woman. I tried to get her to leave, but she refused."

"She's braver than you may know."

"I do know." Matthew gave Gray a reassuring nod. "She's told me her story and your part in it. I'm glad you were there to help her when she needed it."

"And I'm glad you're here now."

"Gray?" A lovely woman with long dark hair falling over her shoulders to her waist stepped out to the porch. "Is everything all right?"

"Julianna, meet Matthew Haley." Julianna descended the steps and held out her hand. "Matthew's a friend of Alexis's," he explained.

"Are she and Jody all right?"

"They're fine," Matthew reassured her. "And she should be back any time."

Julianna looked relieved. "Jody, too?"

"Jody's in school," Matthew explained. "She won't be home until late this afternoon."

Julianna looked disappointed, but the unmistakable wail of a baby in the house behind her interrupted any more questions she might have had. "I've got to feed Colly. She's just not going to wait another minute. Won't you come in, Matthew?" She hesitated. "Not that it's really my house to invite you into."

Matthew gave her a warm smile. "Alexis will be pleased to come home to all of us, I'm sure."

Inside, he followed Gray to the kitchen, while Julianna went down the hall to get their daughter. "How old's the baby?"

"Almost six months. She's gorgeous."

"Must take after her mother."

"I'm told she favors me."

"I think she was more wet than hungry." Julianna came into the room carrying a rosy-cheeked, chubby infant with just the faintest trace of golden hair. She held the baby out to Gray. "Here, Pops, hold her for me, would you?"

"How wet is she?" he asked, tilting his head in assessment.

"I changed her."

Gray held out his arms. "Of course I was going to offer to do it myself."

"Sure you were." Julianna gave her husband a smile that made Matthew feel distinctly like an outsider. "We *know* how much you love changing diapers."

"A man's gotta do what a man's gotta do."

Colly cooed and batted the air, as if she were trying to reach her father's face. Matthew had a sudden vision of a dark-haired baby boy who had often done the same. He looked away, and the banter continued without him.

"I nursed her not more than two hours ago. I think I'll see if she wants some applesauce."

"She's going to weigh more than I do if you keep stuffing her with food."

"I'll have you know that she's perfect. And if she's hungry, she's going to eat." Julianna blew Gray a kiss. "The apples and grinder are in the car. I'll be back in a minute."

"Apples and grinder?" Matthew asked, trying to push away his feelings.

"She makes Colly's baby food, even bakes whole-wheat teething biscuits for her. This is a very healthy baby."

Matthew forced a laugh. "This must be your first child."

Gray was quiet for a moment; then he shook his head. "No. We had another daughter, but she died. Colly means more to us because of Ellie's death. We don't take a minute with her for granted."

Matthew knew how much Gray hadn't said. He knew the grief, the despair, the simple words had covered. He knew them well. "And you found the courage to try again?"

"I'm glad we did."

Matthew wondered if he would ever find that kind of courage. He wanted to ask what they would have done if they had lost this child, too, or would do if they lost her still. But he didn't want to know, because suddenly it called his own courage into question. And he had never questioned it before.

"Nice, healthy apples. I got them from an old man in Penneshaw with an orchard. He promised me his trees had never been sprayed." Julianna came back into the kitchen and held out two apples which, if the small brown spots on them were any indication, were testimony to the orchard man's honesty.

"I think I heard a car out on the road as I was coming back in," Julianna went on. "I hope it's Alexis."

"I'll go see." Matthew pushed his chair away from the table. Suddenly the intimacy, the love and the courage in the kitchen were too much to bear.

Outside, he stood on the porch and waited. A minute later he spotted the red sheen of Alexis's wagon through the scrub that bordered the road. He was waiting to open her door when she got there.

"Hi, I didn't expect you to be waiting." Alexis smiled her pleasure as she got out. "Is someone with you?" She nodded toward Gray's rental car.

"Someone you'll be glad to see, I think."

"Someone I know?"

"Just go and see." He held her back as she started to move around him. "I've got to leave now. I'm due back at the Chase." It was true, although he could have been late with no repercussions. He didn't want to go back into the house to say goodbye to Julianna and Gray, though. He didn't want to think about courage and intimacy. He just wanted to go home. "Will you tell your friends goodbye for me?"

She was more puzzled than before. "Friends?"

"Will you?"

She was confused, but she nodded. "Certainly." When he started to walk away with no goodbye, she reached out and touched his arm. "Have a good day, Matthew. And thank you for last night."

He met her eyes. "My pleasure."

Her laugh was low and throaty. "Well, I hope it was your pleasure. It was certainly mine."

He wished he could laugh with her, but he couldn't. Even a smile was too much to manage. He lifted his hand and touched her cheek with his fingers. Then he turned and left her standing beside the car.

Alexis sat in her living room, the pleasant weight of a sleeping baby against her breast. Her hand rested on Colly's head, and from time to time she stroked the soft golden down that covered it. She had forgotten the pure pleasure of holding an infant. Her memories of Jody's early years were colored by fear. Now she just let herself enjoy.

"Colleen Jody Sheridan." She said the name with a lump in her throat. "Jody will be so pleased."

"Well, she's responsible for Colly's birth, in a way," Julianna said, a lump in her throat, too. "She helped make me realize what I was missing by being so frightened. When I think that I could still be alone, without Gray and without

Colly..." Julianna thought of the lonely years, the decade after she had run from Gray following their daughter's death. She was only glad that she'd been given another chance.

"I can't wait for Jody to see her."

Julianna frowned. "Well, there's a problem. Gray and I have to leave early tomorrow morning, so we won't have much time with her, I'm afraid. We're heading to Coober Pedy to see Dillon and Kelsey, then over to Cairns. A boutique there is having a showing of my new line on Friday."

"Islandwear in Australia?" Julianna was a successful fashion designer whose collections featured Hawaiian motifs. "When we were in New Zealand staying with Paige and Adam, I heard you'd been to Australia to get something started, but I didn't know it had worked out."

"Australia's an island, after all," Julianna teased. "But actually, my things are already selling quite well in Brisbane. So maybe you'll see more of us."

"That would be such a pleasure," Alexis said warmly. "I just wish Jody and I could come to Hawaii to visit you."

"Perhaps you can," Gray said from the doorway.

Alexis looked up and smiled sadly. "I don't think so. I'm afraid Honolulu's too full of tourists. I can't risk being seen by someone who might recognize me."

"Ron thinks you may be able to take that risk before too long." Gray came to sit beside her on the sofa. "That's one of the reasons we're here."

"Ron asked you to come?"

"No, we were coming anyway. But I let Ron know, and he asked me to talk to you."

"I think I'll put Colly on Jody's bed for her nap," Julianna said, rising to lift her daughter from Alexis's arms. "You two can finish this without me."

Gray watched her go. "I might as well tell you that Julianna knows about this, but she thinks Ron and I are being premature. She may be right, Alexis, but you'll have to be the one to decide."

"Decide what?"

"Decide if you want to come out of hiding."

Alexis stared at him, her mind whirling.

Gray sensed her turmoil. "I'll start at the beginning. Ron says he wrote telling you that Cahill might be marrying, and that he was about to get a major promotion."

"He did."

"Cahill and his bride-to-be set the date about two weeks ago. It's going to be a huge society affair in January. The promotion's in his pocket, and the man has a lot to lose if he keeps after you."

Alexis tried to suppress the hope welling inside her. "What no one understands is that Charles believes he's infallible. *We* may think he has a lot to lose, but Charles doesn't think that way. He thinks he can get away with anything at any time."

"And that's why Ron went to him on your behalf."

She stared at him, appalled. "He didn't!"

"He didn't tell him where you were, Alexis. He went to recite a few facts of life."

"What facts?"

"He just reminded Cahill that he had some paperwork that the media should find interesting. If Cahill touches you, or if *anything* happens to you, regardless of whether it can be linked to Cahill or not, Ron wanted him to know that he was going to send copies to Cahill's fiancée, the chairman of the board of his company and all the major wire services and news networks."

Alexis tried to imagine that meeting. "Ron's told him that before."

"But Cahill didn't have anything to lose then," Gray repeated patiently. "Now he does. And he knows what it's like to be a loser. When your book came out, he lost just about everything. He must know the same thing can happen to him again if he's not careful."

"But Gray, he's so clever. Not one thing he did after the divorce could be traced to him. If we'd gone to the press then, they'd have characterized me as a hysteric, or a vengeful wife. No one would have believed Charles had anything to do with my accident, or that he'd broken into my apartment under the noses of two security guards—"

"Cahill told Ron that he no longer cares where you are or what you do. He told him to tell you to stay out of his way and he'll stay out of yours."

"And Ron believes him?"

"Ron believes the detective who's been trailing Cahill."

"Detective?"

"Ron hired someone to see if he could find out if Cahill's still searching for you. The guy's top-notch, apparently. He can tell you what Cahill's done every minute of every day for the last month. There's absolutely no indication that he's looking for you now."

"How can he know that for sure?"

Gray grinned. "Don't ask, honey. Not all of it was legal."

"I'm afraid to believe it," Alexis said at last.

"Ron doesn't feel you should suddenly reappear on Charles's doorstep or do a round of talk shows, but he does think you can breathe easier. At least you can begin to make a home for yourself without constantly looking over your shoulder."

"And I could come to visit you?"

"By Christmas, probably. Julianna and I want to have a reunion of everyone who weathered Hurricane Eve together. It wouldn't be the same without you and Jody. By then we should know more about how safe you really are."

"Safe." She said the word like the dream it was.

Gray put his arm around her shoulder and pulled her to rest against him. "I think the worst is over," he said, giving her an encouraging hug. "There's a very good chance you can begin planning your life again."

Chapter 12

Planning her life. It seemed much too good to be true.

Alexis sat on her front porch and listened to the noises of a Kangaroo Island night. Jody had returned and with complete delight accepted an offer from Gray and Julianna to spend the night at their hotel in Kingscote. Since spring holiday was right around the corner and school for the restless children more of a formality than a challenge, Alexis had agreed to let her go. She would drive into Kingscote the next morning and pick Jody up before the Sheridans' plane left; then they would spend the rest of the day shopping. It would be a welcome break for both of them.

Alone now, Alexis wondered what Gray's news really meant to her. She had lived with Charles Cahill for six years, but she couldn't guess whether he had told Ron the truth or if he was just trying to make her careless. Ron seemed to believe him, and that, as much as anything, made her hope, although hope could be dangerous.

She didn't believe Charles had repented or reformed. She knew him too well to believe that either would ever be a possibility. It was possible, though, that in his own self-interest, Charles had decided to stop the chase. There was nothing in it for him except revenge. And perhaps revenge was less important to him now than his own self-aggrandizement. If so, she thanked God for his greed.

If it were true that she could stop looking over her shoulder, she wondered what that would mean for her life. If she didn't have to stay hidden in this remote foreign land, should she pack her suitcases and move somewhere more like home? Somewhere urban enough that there were schools for children with Jody's abilities, and culture at her fingertips? Should she forget what she and Jody had found here? And Matthew. What about Matthew?

She would have liked to share Gray's news with Matthew, but when she had called to invite him for dinner, telling him that she was alone for the night, he'd refused. There had been no explanation why, only a perfunctory no. She had felt somehow chastened and more than a little hurt. She'd had the undeniable feeling that Matthew was putting the brakes on their relationship without telling her. Since there had been no brakes last night, she could only assume it was because of something that had happened today. She remembered his withdrawal when she had pressed him to talk about his son. Now she wondered if he feared she was getting too close.

When she'd first met Matthew, Alexis would have said that the seven miles between their houses was too close. They were both too wounded, too frightened, for intimacy. But their relationship had blossomed despite, or because of, the pain they had both suffered. Oddly their plan had been for opposite reasons. Hers because her marriage had been so horrible, his because his marriage had been so good.

She wondered if taking her to the bed he had shared with his wife had reminded him of his marriage, if he now suffered guilt that he had brought another woman there.

In the past twenty-four hours the fears she had been living with had begun to ease. The poachers had been caught in the act and were no longer a threat. And Charles? Charles might have found enough revenge in just making her leave the country.

But as those fears receded she was left with a new one. The intimacy and joy she had found with Matthew might be ending. Perhaps his feelings had been based on nothing more than concern for her safety. Now he could retreat again, become the man who never smiled, who never laughed and who kept the memories of his wife and son inviolate.

The farmhouse seemed achingly empty when she went inside to go to bed. She locked it with her usual caution and left a night-light burning in the bathroom. But the rooms that usually cheered her with their whispered memories of family love seemed bleak and desolate tonight. Afraid that she might not sleep, she fixed herself a toddy, drinking it with little pleasure. When the whiskey finally began to work its magic, she fell asleep hoping that morning would come soon.

Midnight came, then half-past, before Matthew gave up the pretense of working. He was filling out forms, the endless lengthy forms for requisitioning supplies and accounting for park expenditures, but the forms weren't due for a fortnight. He was making work for himself to forget that Alexis was alone at her house and that he could be there making love to her.

He wondered what she'd thought of his refusal. No emotion had showed in her voice. She had repeated a few pleasantries, then said goodbye. He wondered if she'd had the same sense of parting that he had.

He had been haunted since morning by voices from his past. He had toiled for three years to silence those voices, yet today just a question about Todd and a short conversation with the Sheridans had activated them again. Perhaps the pain was always there, hiding just below the surface, but he'd learned how to suppress it.

Until Alexis and Jody had come into his life.

Now the warmth flowing back into his soul brought with it memories of other days filled with warmth. A little boy who talked to animals and knew they understood, a woman who gave far more than she would ever take, those brief, shining moments when he had been a part of something greater than himself.

Like blood returning to a sleeping limb, the warmth brought excruciating pain. He was coming back to life, but the pain was more terrible than he could bear. He had thought of himself as a man with courage; there was little he was afraid of, and nothing that had ever stopped him from doing and having what he wanted.

Except memories that he couldn't face.

He slammed down the top of the desk in his study and stood to stretch. He knew what had caused the tension in his body and what he had to do about it. Either he had to go to Alexis or make a decision never to go to her again. He was suspended between desire and fear, and every muscle in his body felt the stress.

A sharp rapping at his front door brought him upright. Late-night visitors meant trouble. Injury to a camper, the destruction of property, some other emergency that he would have to assist with. He was almost glad for the distraction as he strode to the door to throw it open.

Harry stood on the porch. There were no preliminaries. "One of the bush campers spotted a red glow in the sky to the east, over toward Hanson Bay. I've called in a fire alarm, but I'm on my way to check it out now. I've already called Teleford and Whitney and told them to come. We'll need every man."

A bush fire was always a danger to forest and animals alike in the Chase. All the rangers, whether they lived at the park like Matthew and Harry, or in the vicinity, like Sam Teleford and Hugh Whitney, were constantly alert to potential danger. But spring, with all its storms, was not the time of year when they were most alert. Particularly not this spring, which had been wetter than usual.

"Alexis!" Matthew felt a knot of fear coiling in his gut.

"Ring her and see what you can find out. Then meet me at the bay."

Matthew was already dialing the telephone.

* * *

The whiskey had hit her harder than she'd expected. Somewhere in the farthest reaches of consciousness, Alexis struggled to wake and blamed that struggle on the toddy. But each time she struggled, she sank farther back into sleep. Sleep? This drugged lethargy couldn't be sleep.

Then there were no more words in her mind, only the struggle and finally the surrender.

Smoke filled the room, but if part of her knew the danger, the greater part of her didn't. She was pulled down deeper and deeper into unconsciousness, filling her oxygen-deprived lungs with gases that were slowly choking her.

Pulling her farther and farther. . . .

There was a ringing somewhere. The microscopic part of her that still registered reality could hear the ringing. She wanted to shut it out, to surrender completely to the lethargy, but the ringing continued. Over and over and over. . . .

She stirred, as if to try to shut out the sound, but there was no way to do so. She stirred again, then coughed. She had coughed before, but this cough racked her body; as the ringing continued, her mind cleared fractionally. An instinct, not a conscious thought, forced her eyelids open.

She stared into the darkness as another cough shook her. She was neither awake nor asleep but in some sinister in-between. And then, as she gasped for air to fill her lungs, she found there was little air to breathe.

Smoke! She battled for consciousness. She forced herself upright, then bent forward as another cough sent her lungs into spasms. *The house was on fire.* Her mind was so foggy that she could only think that she had to get to Jody before the house burned down around them.

She slid to the side of the bed and tried to stand, but her legs gave way, and she tumbled to the floor.

There was air there, purer, nourishing air that helped clear her lungs and her mind enough for her to realize what she must do. She crawled toward her bedroom door, keeping her face low to the ground. Once there, she put her hands against the wood. It was cool to the touch, and she rose on her knees to open it.

The smoke in the hallway wasn't as thick. She stumbled to her feet, keeping her head low, and staggered toward Jody's room. She pushed the door open and stared through the darkness. The room was empty.

Jody was with Gray and Julianna. The relief that filled her wiped the last cobwebs from her brain. Jody was safe. She had to save herself now.

Turning, she stumbled through the hallway toward the kitchen. The source of the smoke seemed to be at the front of the house near her bedroom. Her best escape lay through the kitchen door. She reached the kitchen in seconds, stopping only once as her smoke-filled lungs rebelled and she doubled over in agony.

The air in the kitchen was clearer than that in the hallway. The stench of smoke filled the room, but breathing was easier here. She tried the light switch, but there was no response. She fumbled her way toward the back door, wanting nothing more than to escape into the night.

Her hand grasped the doorknob, and she twisted the dead bolt. Then she pulled. Nothing happened. She was aware that she still wasn't functioning at full capacity. Smoke, not whiskey, had dulled her senses and drained her strength. She pushed, sure she'd made a mistake and tried to open the door in the wrong direction. But the door wouldn't budge. She tried again and again, frantic now to get outside. She turned the key until she was satisfied that the dead bolt wasn't the problem and kicked weakly. Her head began to swim and she was forced to stop and draw several deep breaths.

The night was eerily dark, and without light from the kitchen to illuminate the porch, she couldn't tell if something was blocking the door from the outside. With rising panic, she only knew that the door was useless as an escape.

She felt her way to the windows and labored to lift one. They had been painted shut by the man who had helped ready the house for her arrival, and she grappled with it for a full minute before it responded. Once it was open she peered down to the ground below. Since the house was built on a hillside there was a drop of eight feet to the ground, which sloped sharply beyond the house. The space beneath the kitchen was a root cellar that could only be reached from an outside door; she couldn't get there from the house. Her choice was to jump from the windows and risk tumbling down the rock-strewn hill, or to find a side window that would allow an easier escape.

Her dizziness retreated as the fresh air from the open window reached her aching lungs. She drew a sobbing breath; then, with her choice made, she swung her feet over the window ledge and, holding tightly, lowered herself out the window.

Matthew listened for the wail of a siren as he raced down the road toward Alexis's house. Apparently no one had called the fire brigade before Harry, because there was no sign of them. With distances what they were and the roads in poor condition, they wouldn't arrive quickly.

As he neared Hanson Bay, he was sure that the smoke that was plainly visible from the road was coming from Alexis's house. The forest was too lush, too saturated, to burn. Later in the year, when the sun turned the scrub and forest floor to tinder, the oil-rich eucalyptus and ti trees would be in danger and there would be days of total fire bans. But for now the forests were relatively safe, unless someone deliberately set and fueled a blaze.

Deliberately set and fueled a blaze.

Still straining to hear a siren, he made the turn onto the dirt track that led to the farmhouse. He drove the road as if it weren't night and the road weren't rutted, taking chances no sane man would take.

He arrived at the farmhouse clearing to find the house ablaze.

"Over here."

Through a thick wall of smoke Matthew could see a small cluster of men beating the flaming shrubs with blankets and canvas tarps. He jumped down from his ute and sprinted toward them. Harry was there, along with Hugh Whitney and several men who Matthew recognized as having homes off the South Coast Road. Harry came to his side, pulling down a bandanna he'd tied around his mouth and nose.

"It's mostly the scrub and the porch so far." Harry filled him in without greeting. "Stay back," he commanded, clamping his fingers on Matthew's arm. "The smoke is tremendous up closer. That's the worst of it."

"Alexis?"

"Teleford and a mate got inside through the back door. There's nobody inside."

"Then where is she?"

"They're searching the grounds in the back right now looking for her. There was a window open in the kitchen. She and the little girl may have jumped."

Matthew didn't wait to hear more. He was almost to the back of the house when Sam Teleford materialized out of the thick smoke carrying Alexis in his arms. Matthew reached out for her, lifting her against his chest. "Is she breathing?"

"Yes. Fitfully. She's gotten quite a dose of smoke, I think. I would have gone right past her, but I heard a wheezing sound. Get her down to the beach where the air is clearer." Sam coughed as if to make a point. "We'll see what we can do about finding the little girl."

"She's not here. She's with friends."

Sam clapped him on the back and turned toward the house.

Alexis felt dangerously light in Matthew's arms, as if some part of her had already given up the fight to survive. Realistically he knew she was going to be fine. Her breathing was harsh but even, and his fingers had already found and measured a steady pulse. He turned and hurried away from the fire, searching for pure air to help speed her recovery. At the bottom of the hill he took a sandy path that veered toward the ocean. The air was clear and salty, laden with moisture to help ease her breathing. He lowered himself to the beach and sat her upright against him, rubbing her back.

Her eyelids fluttered open and she began to cough. He spoke encouraging words into her hair, not even aware of what he was saying, and he rocked her gently against him as she struggled for more air.

"You're going to be fine, dear one. Just cough out all that smoke. There's plenty of air here for you to breathe."

She alternately coughed and gulped until at last she was breathing more normally. She wasn't sure how she had ended up on the beach in Matthew's arms, but she had the good sense not to ask him now.

"I thought I'd lost you," he murmured, still rocking her. "I thought I'd lost you."

She began to remember events. She had swung herself out the window, then dropped the distance to the ground. She had fallen on rocks and lurched backward, just catching herself with her hands. But the impact had thrown her off balance, and she had rolled, scraping against rocks and clumps of vegetation, until she had come to rest at the base of stunted mallee.

She remembered nothing else.

"The house," she croaked. The words set off another coughing spell, and Matthew weathered it with her until she was silent once more.

The wail of a siren answered before he could. "I don't know more than what Harry told me," he said, holding her so that she wouldn't try to rise. "He thinks that it's mostly just the porch and the bush in front of the house that are burning. Now that the brigade is here, they should be able to put it out without further problem. But you're staying here. They don't need your help."

Alexis thought of the few personal belongings she and Jody had inside. Somehow the sparseness of their existence made the loss they would suffer worse. They had both chosen only the possessions they couldn't live without when they had packed to leave the States. On their travels, they had picked up souvenirs to brighten their new home as best they could. They had so little, and now they were losing that, too. She tried to suppress her tears, but they fell anyway, rolling down her cheeks to dampen Matthew's shirt-front.

"Don't cry." Matthew rocked her harder. "Don't cry, Alexis. They'll get the fire out quickly."

"My book."

"We can buy you more copies."

She shook her head. "The one I'm writing now."

He understood then. His arms clasped her tighter. "Where is it?"

"In my study. On computer diskettes." She tried to stand, but he wouldn't let her. "I've got to see if I can get back in and get it." The long sentence exhausted her, and she coughed again.

"The brigade won't let you in. I'd try for you, but they won't let me in, either. You'll have to wait until the fire is out."

"Why, Matthew?"

He knew she wasn't asking why she had to wait. She was asking why this had happened to her. After everything, why this, too?

The problem was that he didn't know. He had a terrible suspicion that it had been no accident, but until he spoke to the fire chief, there was no point in worrying her.

"I don't know," he said, soothing her still. "A spark from the porch light, perhaps."

"The light wasn't on. And Peter Bartow had all the wiring reworked before Jody and I moved in."

"Mistakes can be made."

"No." Her own questions had led her to the glimmer of an answer. She shied away from it, but it was too obvious to ignore. "Someone set the fire," she said after another spell of coughing.

"You don't know that."

"I do."

Since he suspected the same thing, he couldn't continue to argue. "We'll have to wait and see. I know the fire chief. He'll get to the root of this."

They heard someone coming down the path to the beach. "Matthew?"

"Over here, Harry." When Alexis tried to move to the sand beside him, he just held her tight. He wasn't about to let go of her. She might not need the intimacy of his lap, but he needed her there. He had meant what he'd said to her. He had thought he'd lost her. And he wasn't going to lose her again.

"How's she doing?"

"Better," Alexis answered for herself.

"Good on ya." Harry stood over them, watching the protective way Matthew held Alexis against him. "Is he letting you take a breath now and then, darling?"

"Now and then."

"I reckon he was right worried about you."

"I reckon," Matthew said, warning Harry with his tone that he'd said enough.

"The chief wants to see you when you're ready, Matthew. I'll stay with Miss Whitham."

"I'm coming, too." Alexis succeeded in wrenching free of Matthew's embrace. She stood on legs that threatened to give way but didn't. "I want to hear whatever he has to say."

She saw the men exchange glances, but in the darkness she couldn't tell what they were thinking. "Damn it, it's my house that's burning."

"It's about out," Harry assured her. "The damage isn't as extensive as you've probably thought. Most of the house is untouched, but the porch won't be the same for a long while."

She couldn't ask for particulars. She was afraid to hope that her meager belongings and precious diskettes were safe.

"Can you walk?" Matthew asked.

"I can manage."

Matthew put his arm around her waist, and they started up the path, with him doing most of the work for both of them.

Smoke still drifted to the sky, but the flames were out by the time Alexis and Matthew reached the clearing. He guided her to his ute and lifted her to sit on the hood, away from the smoke.

"Stay here and I'll get the chief."

She nodded, saving her breath.

The chief arrived quickly. He was about Harry's age, and obviously weary, but he was still every inch a man in charge. "We're going to have one of our men check you over," he said, motioning for a firefighter. "He's trained. If he sees any problem, we'll have you into the hospital in Kingscote."

"I'll be fine." She waved off the man who was gathering a kit of medical supplies. "He can check me later. I want to know about the fire."

The chief didn't look as if he liked having his decisions questioned, but he nodded. "All right. There's extensive damage to the porch, and both of the rooms in front have some smoke and water damage, but most of your possessions can probably be salvaged. The fire commenced in the shrubs at the front of the house and spread to the porch. It we hadn't been called so quickly, and if the rangers hadn't gotten here first to beat out what they could, the house would have gone up, too. It's old enough that, once engaged, it would have gone quickly."

She drew a deep breath and tried to forget that her life could have been lost, too. "The fire started in the shrubs? How?"

The fire chief was silent.

"I want to know," she insisted.

"Do you make a habit of wiring your back door closed?"

Alexis was taken aback, but she understood immediately what he must mean. "No," she said softly, wishing that she were back on the beach in Matthew's arms.

"Someone else wired it, then."

"The same person who set the fire."

The chief didn't answer.

"Do you have any clues who?" Matthew asked, trying to keep his rage from his voice. "Or how?"

"We'll have a better idea in the morning how it was done. I was hoping you or Miss Whitham might know who. I know about the poaching. And I know that one of the poachers wasn't caught."

"A young woman," Alexis said. "I saw her face, and she saw mine."

"I just had a chat with the police over my radio. They say the two men they took into custody wouldn't give any information about the woman. And the men hadn't been on the island long enough for anyone to remember seeing them with anyone. Isaac Bates up near Castle Hill had hired them to help him on his land, but Isaac didn't know anything about a woman."

"You think it was revenge?" Matthew asked.

"It's possible."

"Alexis?"

She shrugged hopelessly. It was certainly possible. Anything was. It was even possible that the man she had once vowed to love, honor and obey had just tried to kill her again.

"We'll have our man check you over now," the chief told her when she didn't respond. She nodded, too tired suddenly to protest. "Then we'll take you into town and find you a place to stay."

"She'll be staying with me," Matthew said. "Until the house is repaired."

Alexis waited until the chief had gone to find his medic before she objected. "I'm not going to put you out, Matthew. Jody's with Julianna and Gray in Kingscote. I'll get a room at their hotel."

"You're coming with me."

She shook her head. "You made it clear tonight that I was getting too close. How will you feel with me underfoot? You know I can afford a hotel room for as long as I need one."

"That's not the issue."

She shook her head again. She hadn't had time to make plans, but one formed as she spoke. "I'm not going to take any chances with Jody's safety. Julianna and Gray are going to visit a friend of ours tomorrow. I'll take Jody and go with them. We can stay there while the house is rebuilt. Then, if it looks safe, we'll come back. If it doesn't...."

"What happened to the woman who wasn't going to run away?"

"I didn't think Jody's safety was at stake!"

"Then send Jody with Julianna and Gray to wait it out."
He stepped forward and held her head still, a palm on each
cheek so that she couldn't shake it again. "Stay here with
me. I'll protect you. Let Jody visit your friends. School
holiday is almost here, anyway. By the time it ends, we
should know who's done this, and we'll know better what
to do to keep both of you safe."

"Why should I stay?" Her eyes rose slowly to his. She
was afraid of what she might see *and* what she might not.

"Because I want you to."

She stared at him, trying to fathom his feelings.

"I want *you*," he said.

"You didn't earlier."

He rested his cheek on the top of her head, aware that he
was going to have to tell her the truth. The words were hard
to push from his throat. "I was afraid. I still am. But I
found out tonight that I'm more afraid of losing you than
of having you. Stay with me until we're certain you're safe.
Let me take care of you."

Alexis could feel the tension in his body. She knew,
somehow, that this was the first time in Matthew's life that
he had ever admitted to fear. Her arms went around his
waist. She didn't know what to say.

"Will you stay?" he asked at last.

"I'll stay."

"Jody's welcome, too, if you don't want to send her with
Julianna and Gray."

Alexis considered her choices. She could hear the steady
beat of Matthew's heart against her ear and feel the strength
of his arms around her. Suddenly she was very, very glad to
be held by him. She never wanted him to let her go.

"I'll call the hotel tomorrow morning early and talk to
Gray," she said at last. "If he agrees, I'll send Jody with
them. I trust you to help protect us, but I want her out of
here. You can't be everywhere at once. If Charles has found
where we've gone...."

"Do you think it was Charles?"

She didn't know what she thought. She would talk to
Gray about that, too. Ron should be alerted.

"It could have been," she said as footsteps came closer. "But it's not his style. If Charles had done this, no one would have thought it was anything but an accident." She looked up to see the young medic, equipment ready. "I'm fine now," she told him.

"We'll just see." The young man lifted a stethoscope to his ears. "I'll have a quick listen."

"I'm going inside to see if your study was damaged," Matthew told her. "And to get your diskettes."

"And computer."

He nodded. "Anything else?"

"Jody's baby pictures."

He thought of everything else she could have asked for, but her request didn't surprise him. He would have expected exactly that. "Where are they?"

"They're in a lockbox under my bed."

"I'll bring some clothes, too."

"Don't bring too much. Surely it'll be safe for me to move back soon."

He wondered if the show of optimism was for his sake or hers.

He knew neither of them believed it.

Chapter 13

Jody hugged her mother, fitting her body to Alexis's as if she never wanted to let her go.

"You be good," Alexis said, blinking back tears.

"You come, too, Mommy."

"This is best for now." Alexis held Jody at arm's length and forced her to look up. "Dillon and Kelsey are thrilled that you're coming. Kelsey says you can be in her karate class, and Dillon says he'll teach you to mine opals."

"I want to stay here with you."

"You can't."

Gray stepped forward, as if on cue. "We'll have a good time on the trip, shrimp. You'll be staying in an underground house, and that'll be something to tell your mother about."

Alexis appreciated Gray's support, especially since she knew he had his own doubts about the wisdom of her remaining behind. Even more, she appreciated the support of the man who put his hand on her shoulder and spoke next.

"Jody, I'm going to take good care of your mother. Nothing will happen to her." Matthew left his hand on Alexis's shoulder, a physical sign of the claim he'd made.

"And when you come back, the house will be all fixed up again."

But it was Julianna who knew best what had to be done. She walked toward them from the ticket counter, holding Colly over one shoulder. "Jody, I'm going to have to have some help with Colly on the plane, and Gray's got some reading he has to do. You sit beside me and once we're up in the air, maybe you can take Colly on your lap for a while. You're so good with her."

Jody looked like a child who knew she'd been had, but couldn't figure out what to do about it. "All right," she said, giving her mother one last, tearful glance. Then she turned and followed a chattering Julianna.

"Don't worry. She'll be fine." Gray gave Alexis an encouraging smile. "You're the one I'm worried about."

"No worries about that." Matthew pulled Alexis into the crook of his arm.

Gray assessed the other man silently; then he nodded. "You'll take care of her."

Alexis's laugh was throaty with tears. "You fine gentlemen might remember that I've done quite a bit of taking care of myself."

"More than anyone should have to." Gray leaned over and kissed Alexis's cheek. "Just keep up the good work." He turned and followed the others.

Matthew had been fighting his own struggles with emotion. Now the fight began to overwhelm him. "There's nothing more we can do here, Alexis. Let's go."

"I want to see them take off." Alexis broke free from his grasp and went to the windows overlooking the small airfield. Seeing that the takeoff went well was less important than just needing to make a transition. Watching Jody's plane disappear would help her prepare for the days ahead when her daughter was no longer there to touch and hold.

Matthew didn't join her, but she was so engrossed in her own battle with tears, that she didn't think why. She only knew that he wasn't there, but he didn't understand what she was feeling. She pressed her nose to the glass, glad that it was cool, because her cheeks were flushed with her effort not to cry.

The ferry plane was small. Jody had never flown in a small plane before. They had taken the car ferry to the island. Alexis wondered how she felt, if she would be too sad to enjoy it, or if the lure of holding Colly would make her forget. She wondered if the plane would be buffeted by the wind. The day was clear, and Alexis guessed the ride would be smooth. The planes flew frequently, in good weather and bad, and the crossing was short, only forty minutes, so there was nothing to really be concerned about. Accidents were so rare they were almost unheard of.

Except that Matthew's wife and child had died on one such plane.

Alexis whirled and found that Matthew had come up behind her. His face was pale, and there were beads of sweat on his forehead. but he was standing there, waiting for her. As though his wife and child hadn't died the last time he had seen them off in this airport. As though he weren't in agony.

"I didn't think," she said, slipping her arms around his waist.

He didn't ask what she meant, because he knew. He couldn't answer, either. He looked down at her hair, watched the way the pale gold strands reflected the sunshine streaming in through the window. He could not watch the plane take off, but he could look at her hair and hold her.

Alexis waited for him to say something, but when he didn't, she squeezed him in silent commiseration. "Let's go."

"I can wait."

She pushed away from him. "There's no need. I've said goodbye. Staying won't change the fact that Jody's leaving."

"She'll be back."

This time Alexis couldn't answer.

* * *

Matthew had the rest of the day off, so they lingered in town, shopping together, then having a quiet morning tea in a quaintly attractive tearoom before they headed to the Hanson Bay farmhouse to survey the damage.

By day the damage didn't seem sinister, only pathetic. The house, which for half a century had proudly held a loving family, now seemed like an old woman, abandoned and alone, with not so much as a good memory left to warm her last days.

"We brought evil to the house," Alexis said, looking away to compose herself.

Matthew turned off the engine and gathered her close. "You brought love and laughter again. Someone else brought evil. We'll find out who and make them pay for what they've done here."

"If we can," she said, not at all sure it would be possible.

"We will."

Outside, the air still smelled of smoke despite the strong breeze from the bay. They walked around the skeletal remains of the shrubbery and up the walkway to the back of the house, climbing the stairs with reluctance.

They entered through the back door, which swung mournfully on its hinges, damaged by the men who had frantically sought entrance to find Alexis and Jody. The kitchen itself was undamaged, smoky and smudgy, but otherwise untouched.

"So far, so good," Matthew said, trying to cheer a very pale Alexis.

"The kitchen is the heart of this house. Sometimes I used to feel the love that was here."

"If the heart is healthy, the rest of the house can be healed."

She flashed him a weary smile. "If Peter wants it healed. He only keeps the land as investment property. I'm sure eventually he'll sell, and the house will be torn down to make way for something more modern. He may not want this expense."

"Did he say that when you spoke with him this morning?"

Alexis thought of the telephone call. Peter had been distressed over the fire, much more because of the danger to Alexis than because of property loss. He had assured her that he would have the damage repaired, and that he would fly in on the weekend to survey it and make arrangements for work to begin immediately.

Alexis wondered just how long she could continue to accept the goodwill of others. What was it costing the people who had so willingly given of themselves to help her? Time, money, security?

Matthew could almost read her thoughts. "Bartow said he was going to fix up the house, didn't he?"

She nodded.

"Then he will. Don't forget, this might have happened even if you hadn't been here."

Her look told him what she thought of that theory.

He put his arms around her and pulled her back against his chest. "Don't forget that one real possibility is that this was done as revenge for catching the poachers. And catching them was something Bartow approved of, I'm certain."

"Do you really think that's what happened here?"

"I think it's a good possibility. We'll talk to the fire chief and the police this afternoon and see what they've found."

They stood without making any attempt to move. Matthew wanted to infuse Alexis with new strength and hope. She wanted to stay in the shelter of his arms and forget about the rest of the house.

Suddenly his arms tightened spasmodically, then relaxed. She couldn't ignore it. "Matthew?"

He tried to make light of the tremor that had shaken him. "What is it they say? Someone just walked over my grave?" The moment the words were out he wished he'd kept them to himself.

She turned and searched his eyes. "You feel it, too, don't you? The evil?"

"A house can't be good or evil. It's boards and nails and roofing shingles."

"Someone tried to kill me here."

"I don't think so."

"The back door was wired shut."

"To confuse you and frighten you. But the windows weren't tampered with. All you had to do was open one or smash one and you were outside. Just what happened."

"And what if I hadn't awakened?"

He smoothed his hand over her hair. He found the silky fall against his palm and fingertips oddly reassuring. He hoped it reassured her, too. "Even in the midst of the ruckus last night, the fire chief could see that the blaze started in the shrubbery. Anyone who'd really wanted the house to go up swiftly enough that you couldn't escape would have set several fires, and set them directly on the porch, or inside, perhaps."

"Then why?"

"Childish revenge. I think the chief will find it was really an amateur's job. Flammables poured on damp shrubbery, causing more smoldering than flames, at least at first."

"So that I'd have time to get out?"

"Exactly."

Alexis considered his theory. If it were true, and if the woman she had seen with the poachers was the arsonist, then perhaps she had succeeded in getting what she'd wanted. Revenge. The satisfaction of knowing she had terrified Alexis and damaged her home. Perhaps it was all she needed.

If the woman was the arsonist.

"Ah, dear one," Matthew said, watching emotions pass so clearly across her face. "You don't need any more worries right now. I'll come back later and get everything. Let's get you to the park."

"Kiss me."

He had wanted to kiss her, to touch her, to make lengthy, mind-numbing love to her, since he had seen her unconscious in Sam Teleford's arms the night before. But she had been in shock. He had held her gently through the remainder of the night while his flesh grew taut with need and his need became an agony. Today he had still been afraid to touch her, except in comfort. What right did he have to make demands when the world was falling apart around her?

He leaned forward to touch her lips with his own. In comfort. In a promise that he would protect her.

Suddenly she wanted no comfort, no promises. She wanted to know that she wasn't a child to be cared for but a woman he cared about. She wanted to know that the greatest reason for Matthew's wanting to protect her was because he didn't want to live without her.

"Why did you want me to stay?" she asked when he drew away. Everything began to rise inside her and overflow. Despair. Anguish. Fear. All were being driven up and out. She was nothing. She was no one. No one except a woman whose sole reason for living was to inspire compassion in those around her.

Matthew sensed her swift change, but he didn't know what was causing it. "I told you last night."

"Last night you told me you wanted me. What's the real reason?"

He suppressed another shudder, but this time the cold he felt didn't come from some amorphous sense of evil. It came from deep inside him. He went very still, and his eyes narrowed as his arms fell to his sides. "Suppose you tell me?"

"You want to protect me. You're a good man, and good men don't like to see women or children hurt."

"Is there something wrong with that?"

"You couldn't protect your wife and son." She didn't say the words cruelly, just as a statement of fact.

He said nothing.

"Perhaps Jody and I are your second chance."

His breath hissed out in fury. "You think so little of me that you believe I'm playing out some warped scene from my past? Do you think I'm trying to come out with a different ending?"

She shook her head slowly. "I think so much of you that I know what kind of man you are. A good one. One of the best. When you lost your wife and son, it almost killed you. You've let down some of your guard with me, Matthew, because circumstances have demanded it. And now you feel responsible." She turned, folding her arms over her chest. "I shouldn't have stayed, and you shouldn't have asked me to."

"Last night my wanting you to stay was enough!"

"Last night your wanting *me* was enough. But you didn't really want me then, and you don't want me now. You want to take care of me and keep me safe."

His hand was like a steel vise on her shoulder, forcing her to turn and face him. "You need words, Alexis? Words I can never say again?"

"I'm not talking about love!" She pushed away the realization that she had just uttered a lie. "I'm talking about wanting me!"

Through his anger he saw her desolation. He understood, finally, what she meant. She saw herself as the object of his pity, simply because he had tried so diligently not to overwhelm her or intrude when she was still suffering from the fire. With a groan he pulled her to him and fastened his mouth on hers.

She struggled, horrified that she had forced him into a display of desire he couldn't possibly feel. Then she stopped struggling, slowly, as she began to see that his desire was as real as the bulge against her belly.

"You little idiot," he muttered at last, when he had compelled himself to break away. He kissed her cheek, her forehead, her eyelids, murmuring against them, "I'm nobody's benefactor, least of all yours."

"Then why—"

"Because I care about you. I thought your needs—"

"I needed you."

"Needed?"

"Need."

"A bloody fine place to make the announcement." He pulled her so tightly against him that she thought they would merge right there.

"Jody's bed—"

"No." His hands moved over her, lingering, tantalizing, demanding. His mouth silenced her protests. Finally he broke away long enough to pull her toward the back door.

"Where are we going?"

He didn't answer. At the windows he stopped, sinking down to the thick rug in front of them and taking her with him. She felt as if she were in a dream, as if she had no control over what was happening. And because she trusted Matthew, the sensation was heady.

He lay back, pulling her on top of him and taking her mouth with his all in the same movement. This was not the man she thought she had known. Even in the height of passion he was always controlled and careful, as if he were afraid of hurting both of them. Now his control seemed to be gone.

When his hands found her breasts, her control disappeared, too. She had wanted to be needed this way. Wanted. Needed. Desired for the woman she was. She had wanted to have the need drawn from her, discovered like a cherished secret and used for their mutual pleasure.

His pleasure was apparent. Matthew groaned as if all boundaries had been breached and nothing except sensation ruled him. He pushed her clothes away in seconds, forcing buttons from holes, wrenching her zipper free, until enough of her was bare to satisfy him. His mouth followed the path of his hands, as if he needed to fill all his senses with her, to taste as well as touch, to absorb her wildflower scent, to listen to the low murmur in her throat as all her doubts fell away.

Alexis tried to do the same, but Matthew wouldn't let her go long enough to create the space she needed. She had to content herself with reaching what she could, taking what she could.

His skin was fevered; the pulse in his neck slammed frantically beneath her lips. His muscles bunched at her touch, and he groaned with pleasure.

It wasn't enough. She couldn't get or give enough. She felt as if she were turning slowly inside out, giving up everything she'd ever felt, ever dreamed, to his keeping. And it wasn't enough. He was returning what she gave, reaching far inside himself to bare his heart, his soul, and it wasn't enough.

He rolled her to the rug, and she yanked the clasp of his trousers free, parting the zipper. He was hot and throbbing against her, already seeking what she was trying desperately to give him. With her hands against his flesh she struggled to work the trousers down, until, impatiently, he helped her, kicking them off at last so that he was free.

There were no more preliminaries, no more words. He thrust into her, searching, seeking, reaching for more than he had ever asked for.

She gave a low cry as he filled all the emptiness inside her. She moved beneath him, the answer to his search. Pulling him deeper still, she demanded more. He gave it willingly, his body so attuned to hers that even in the mindless depths of passion, he knew her needs and made them his. Then there was nothing for either of them except the white-hot inferno of sensation and the absence of thoughts.

And, finally, sensation was enough.

When sanity returned, when their kisses had become tender once more and their hands had touched and soothed and apologized, they stood, helping each other dress in silence.

"No, you didn't hurt me," she said in answer to the question in his eyes.

He frowned a little, like a man who can't explain where he's been and what he's been doing for the last minutes. "You're certain you're all right?"

She touched his forehead, soothing away the frown with her fingertips. She didn't know how to tell him that she had a whole new sense of herself. His lovemaking, his passion, were filling the chasms Charles had carved in her self-confidence. "I feel reborn," she said at last.

He pulled her close. He couldn't remember a time when his passions had been so uncontrolled. And she had gone willingly with him every step of the way. He wasn't ready to think what that said about their relationship. He just held her tight.

"Let's go back to my house."

She shook her head and forced herself to step out of his arms. "I want to see the rest of the damage."

He was reluctant. He felt curiously vulnerable, as if parts of him had been laid open that had never been exposed before. He knew she must feel the same. "Are you certain? We could wait for a better time."

She took a deep breath. "Yes. I'm certain."

He took her hand, hoping to ease the shock. Then he led her through the house, room by room. They spoke as little as possible, each sadly taking in the destruction, but realizing, at the same time, just how much worse it could have been.

"Most of it can be cleaned and repaired," Alexis said at last, when they were back in the kitchen. "What can't be fixed can be replaced."

He thought she had more courage than anyone he'd ever known. She asked for no sympathy; she just kept going as if she had the faith that, someday, her life would be filled with more than crisis and tragedy.

"Even when we've found out who did this, will you be able to live here again?" he asked gently.

Alexis knew he was referring to the lingering chill of evil. She considered his question, then, with dawning recognition, nodded. "Something's changed since we've been here, Matthew. I don't feel it anymore."

"It?"

She didn't want to name the feeling again. "There's warmth here now. We brought it back."

"Did we?"

She heard his skepticism, but he reached for her, enclosing her in arms that were definitely not soothing. "We did." She laid her palms against his cheeks. "Thank you."

"No one's ever thanked me for doing exactly what I wanted."

"It's a wondrous thing when two people need and take and still manage to give at the same time."

"A wondrous thing," he agreed, finding her lips to give and take and begin to build a need in both of them once more.

Chapter 14

The fire chief was a man who saw a fire on his island as a personal affront. A fire set on purpose was tantamount to a declaration of war. Hours were spent combing the Hanson Bay property for clues to the identity of the arsonist, and the fire chief was present for every one of them.

But it was the police who finally turned up the best clue.

Matthew came home from the park office six days after the fire to find Alexis baking brownies. She was bending over the oven when he walked in, and when she turned, her cheeks were glowing from the heat.

"That's a smell I haven't enjoyed for a decade," he said appreciatively.

She lifted an eyebrow, moving toward him to wave the brownies under his nose. "No?"

"They're not popular here. You never see them. But since we lived in the States so long, my mother learned to make them. I think I was the only kid in Australia who brought brownies in my school lunch. I used to sell them to the highest bidder."

She laughed. "Jody couldn't live without them." The laughter died abruptly.

He saw the worry, the regret. "She'll be back to enjoy another batch soon."

"I'll have to do something, Matthew. I can't leave her in Coober Pedy indefinitely. She needs me."

"I have some news."

She met his eyes, then nodded. "Sit down and I'll cut these. They'll crumble, because they're supposed to cool, but you don't care, do you?" She realized she was chattering because she was afraid to hear what he was going to say.

"I don't care."

She went to the cupboard and got two glasses, then poured milk. He cut the brownies while he waited.

Alexis sat down and passed his milk across the table. "Well?"

"There's no way to trace the fire to anyone. There's just no evidence."

"I didn't think there would be." She lowered her gaze to her plate. She didn't want to burden Matthew with her disappointment.

"But the police think the poachers were responsible."

She looked up. "How could they be? They're in jail."

"There were three poachers, Alexis, besides the woman. More than we thought. The two that were caught are loyal, but not clever. It seems they've been overheard talking late at night. I suppose they've got nothing better to do until they come to trial."

"Talking about what?"

"A mate and their lady friend. To get right to the heart of it, another man got away that night, and neither you nor I caught sight of him."

"Did the poachers give a name?"

Matthew shook his head. "But the police know something else. The two in custody have been heard to laugh about what their mate will do to get even with us."

"Us?"

"The ranger and his woman," he repeated bluntly.

She wasn't sure how she should feel. One thing was clear. She was still in danger.

"There's more," Matthew continued. "It seems the police have a good clue who the other poacher is. Now that they know another man is involved, they've questioned Isaac Bates up at Castle Hill again. He remembers a local lad, Donald Carson, hanging around the farm. And Carson has a sister. She's had a spot of trouble, parents tossed her out once, then relented and let her come home again. She fits your general description."

"If she's the one, I'd recognize her."

"I told the police you would. They're going to do some investigating and find a time when you can see her informally at the pub. If you identify her, they'll take her and her brother in for questioning."

Alexis realized she had crumbled her brownie into a hundred pieces. "My attorney says that Charles hasn't left the country in the last month."

"He's certain?"

"As certain as anyone can be about Charles."

"And he has no indication that Cahill's found where you are?"

"None. And none that he's still searching."

Matthew reached across the table and stopped the hundred crumbs from becoming a thousand. "Then I'd say we're in reach of having this over with."

She desperately wanted it to be over. She missed her daughter. She missed having her own things around her, missed the study overlooking the silver-tipped surf of Hanson Bay. But there was another reason for wanting the waiting to end.

Living with Matthew was too painfully bittersweet to continue.

She woke up each morning in his arms. And a day hadn't yet started without that early morning cuddling turning into slow, glorious lovemaking. She bathed while he shaved, and witnessing the supremely masculine ritual always warmed her to the core. Then, while he showered, she made their breakfast. Matthew had protested at first, perhaps because it seemed too domestic, or perhaps just because he didn't want her to feel she had to. But she had insisted, enjoying the chance to spoil him a little and give back some of what she was getting.

He left for work soon afterward, and she worked in her makeshift study in his spare bedroom. Neither her computer nor her diskettes had been damaged, and the book was progressing, if slowly. As she worked, the knowledge that he was coming home for lunch stayed with her, building to excitement as noon drew nearer. When he finally arrived, he always seemed as pleased to see her as she was to see him. He was often late going back, a development that apparently none of the other staff commented on, since for the last three years he had worked like a man possessed.

She usually quit writing in mid-afternoon, sometimes to bake a treat for their dinner as she had done today, sometimes just to dream. And sometimes to worry.

Matthew had learned to read her so well that he always seemed to know which it had been. Just as now he seemed to know what she was thinking.

"This hasn't been easy," he said, reaching for her hand.

"For you as well as me."

He thought of their evenings together. Of watching darkness steal through the Chase, of sitting on his porch, arms entwined, or walking through the menagerie of animals who lived near the rangers' homestead. Of relaxed silences, animated conversations, of finding that their values were remarkably similar although their lives had been so different.

Of finding that she was the last thought in his head as he fell asleep after making love to her and the first thought in his head each morning.

Of finding that she possessed his dreams as surely as Jeannie once had.

Now he didn't know what to say. She was right; it hadn't been easy having her live with him. He was filled with conflicting feelings and sure of little. But he *was* sure of one thing. Bittersweet though their time together had been, he wasn't ready for it to end.

"I'm glad you've been here." He turned her hand palm up and pressed a kiss into it. "But I'll be pleased when we don't have to worry about your safety."

She wondered if that day would ever come. Part of her knew that, despite everything she had said, it was time to run again. Except that now she had so much to lose if she did.

"When am I supposed to identify the girl?"

"The police will ring us if she goes to the pub. There'll likely be a crowd, and the police will just wait for you to point her out if you see her."

"Couldn't that take days?"

"They don't think so. We've been asked to stay close to the telephone tonight. Apparently she spends a bit of time there."

Alexis slid her hands from his. "I think I've just spoiled our dinner, feeding you brownies in the middle of the afternoon. These were supposed to be for dessert." She stood, gathering their plates.

"I'll be back about half-past five, and I'll cook tonight."

"I've already started a roast."

"You don't have to work so hard." He stood, holding her back as she passed to head toward the sink. "You don't have to pay me back for having you here. I *like* having you here."

She started to let his comment pass, but she couldn't. "I do things for you because I like to," she said. "Don't you know how I feel by now?"

He was afraid he did. He was afraid that in spite of everything her marriage had been, she was falling in love with him. And in spite of his obsession with her, he knew he would never fall in love again.

"I think what you feel is gratitude," he said carefully. "And I think you do things for me because you're a warm, generous person and because we've become good friends. Just don't work so hard that being my friend becomes drudgery."

"Friend" was such a lukewarm word for what she felt that for a moment she could only stare. "Gray and Julianna are my friends, Matthew. Harry is becoming a friend," she said at last.

He knew exactly what she meant. He also knew that talking any more could ruin what they did have. "Sometimes words can't say enough." He bent and kissed her lightly, then dropped her arm. "I've got to get back to work. I'll be over at the campground if you need me."

Alexis watched him go, or rather, she watched him run away.

Matthew wasn't ready for even the smallest commitment to her. She had known his reluctance, yet the truth had never been brought home to her more clearly. He cared about her, and he desired her. Sometimes he looked at her as if he couldn't live without her. But deep down, where commitments grow—where love itself grows—Matthew was empty.

Or perhaps he was still full. She sank back down to her chair and gazed around the room. As much as she enjoyed cooking for him, she did not like his kitchen. It was bare—barren—empty of everything except the most utilitarian items. She didn't feel like an interloper here because there was nothing of his wife left in it. Jeannie and Todd had been so thoroughly cleared from this house that it was as if they had never lived.

Except that they lived deep inside him where he had never been able to say goodbye. There was nothing of them left to see, but there was everything of them in Matthew. He couldn't bear, even after three years, to say their names. He couldn't bear to face any reminder of them because he had never been able to let them go.

Until he did, there was no real place for her or for Jody in his life.

She hadn't faced the truth before. Now she did. Matthew would never tell her that he loved her because he couldn't love her. He was in love with a woman who would never return his love again.

She fought back tears. He had never led her to believe otherwise. What kind of fool was she that she had once again fallen in love with a man who couldn't love her back? Charles, too, had been incapable of love, although for very different reasons. Charles had been the antithesis of love. Matthew was everything warm and human.

But his warmth, his humanity, made it impossible for him to break free of the love he had already given. She should have known he couldn't give himself to her. And she shouldn't have given herself to him.

The tears fell anyway. She cried for an empty kitchen, an empty house and the agony of a man who had loved as few men can.

She cried for herself.

The silence had gone on so long that Matthew had become uncomfortable. He turned his head to reassure himself that Alexis was still beside him. "You don't need to be frightened," he said when he saw that she was.

"I'm not frightened." She stared out the window at the swiftly passing scenery. "I'm just looking forward to this being over with."

"Can't blame you for that." Matthew began to talk about his day, trying to take Alexis's mind off what was to happen.

Alexis listened to the rich, liquid-Australian cadence of his voice and wished that she could spend a lifetime listening to it. But in a short time—if everything went as it was supposed to—she wouldn't be listening to it at all.

The call had come, as expected, almost immediately after supper. They were on their way to Parndana to the Community Club to see if Alexis could identify Yvonne Carson as the young woman who had been with the poachers the night Matthew had caught them.

"You're not listening, are you?"

Alexis smiled ruefully. "Not as closely as I should."

"What can I do to make you relax?"

"In a car going forty miles an hour?"

The look he shot her should have burned up the air between them. "Another comment like that one and I'll turn around and take you back home."

She wished he could. She wanted desperately to hold him. She wanted to cling. But she wouldn't. When this had ended, she would pack her suitcases and go back to Hanson Bay. The repairs there were far from being completed, but the house was liveable again, even without a front porch. Once she was no longer underfoot it would be Matthew's decision how far their relationship evolved, and she had no false hopes about what that would mean.

They entered the little town of Parndana. It was set in the midst of farmland, and it was a picturesque, sleepy burg with little more than a post office and a shop or two. The Community Club had a dining room, a beer garden and a playground for children. It was a friendly, family place, hardly the sort of atmosphere Alexis would have chosen for police work. But then, she hadn't been given a choice.

Matthew parked the wagon a distance from the club and came around to open her door. He held out a hand. "I'll be right beside you."

She wanted to tell him that this worried her less than what would happen to them when it was over. But that, like most of her thoughts and feelings, was not to be spoken. "I'm fine," she said instead.

"I know. You've more than your share of courage." He touched her cheek briefly, then turned, tucking her arm under his. "When we get inside, we'll take a table on the fringes. Just take your time and look around."

"It seems crowded tonight."

He guided her around a tree. "It's crowded every night. But if you can identify your mystery woman in the midst of so many people, we'll be sure you have the right person."

"If she's here, I'll know it."

He squeezed her arm in answer.

Inside, the taped blare of midnight oil greeted them just before a chorus of voices hailed Matthew.

He gave a careless wave, turning Alexis toward a darkened corner before anyone could stop them. Once she was seated, he positioned himself so that she wasn't readily seen from the rest of the room. "What would you like?" he asked.

"Whatever you're having."

"Will you be all right while I go up to the counter?"

She nodded. "No one's going to burn the pub down around me. I think I'm relatively safe with thirty-odd people milling about."

One corner of his mouth lifted in a reluctant smile. If he'd been in her place, he wasn't certain he could have joked. "Then I'll be right back. Keep your eye on the door. If your young woman is here, she may be trying to leave any moment now."

She wanted to ask if he knew whether Yvonne Carson was in the room, but she realized it might influence her identification. "I won't let her past me."

After he'd gone, she nonchalantly studied the faces of the people closest to the door. There were several young women, even one with long dark hair, but she knew immediately that none of them was the woman she had seen in the grove. That woman's features were indelibly imprinted in her memory. If she were here, Alexis would recognize her.

Matthew returned, taking up the seat in front of her again. He pushed a beer across the table. "Anyone leave?"

"An old man. Do you suppose she's wearing a disguise?"

He just smiled. "I'll watch the door now. You go ahead and look around. See if you can find her."

Alexis adjusted her chair so that she was gazing toward the other end of the room. She examined two groups of young people and dismissed them. She passed over two older couples and one hard-bitten cowboy—or stockman, as they were called in Australia. Then she focused on a young woman in the far corner entertaining two young men just out of their adolescence. The woman was dressed in an emerald green blouse and pants, but it didn't matter. She might as well have been wearing red plaid. She might as well have been fleeing through a eucalyptus forest.

"She's over in the corner with the two young fellows wearing hats. She's wearing green." Alexis turned back to Matthew.

"You're certain? You can tell from this distance?"

She had no doubts. "Is that Yvonne Carson?"

Matthew didn't even look. He knew. "Yes."

"Then you know her."

"Not well. Her mother was a friend of . . . Jeannie's."

She felt strangely chastised. "I'm sorry I'll be bringing her mother unhappiness."

Matthew shrugged. "Not you. Yvonne's done that. Who knows? Perhaps this will be the thing that straightens her out." He stood and made eye contact with the stockman. Matthew nodded. The other man rose and started toward the corner. Another man from the other side of the room started after him.

Alexis watched, bewildered. "Matthew?"

"They're going to take her in to be questioned now that you've identified her. They'll pick up her brother, too, and then I suppose they'll search their home for koala skins."

"They're policemen?"

Matthew sat down. "Yes. They're taking care of it now."

Alexis didn't want to watch, but her eyes were drawn to the scene in the corner anyway. The policeman in stockman's clothes approached the trio of young people and began to speak quietly to them. His partner came to stand behind him. Yvonne registered shock, then fury. Her head swiveled, and she looked straight at Alexis. Alexis didn't avert her eyes, but she felt the chill of the other woman's anger.

"They're bringing her this way," Alexis said softly.

Matthew muttered a succinct, profane reply. He moved his chair closer to Alexis. "You don't have to say anything."

The trio wove its way between tables. Alexis realized that the policemen were giving her one last chance to change her mind about the girl's identification. But the closer they got, the more certain she was. Right before the table, the policemen turned to guide Yvonne through the door, but Yvonne had a different idea.

"You should have minded your own business, Yank," she shouted at Alexis.

Alexis held the woman's gaze but didn't speak.

"It would have been safer!"

One of the two policemen gave Alexis an apologetic grimace, then forcibly escorted Yvonne from the room.

The club was as quiet as it could be with rock music still blaring. Alexis had never felt so humiliated, nor so alone.

"I'd like to leave," she said, looking down at her beer.

Matthew covered her hand with his. "You did what you had to."

"Miss Whitham?"

Alexis looked up to see one of the women from the next table. She wasn't sure how the woman knew her name, but her smile was assurance enough that she didn't intend to follow Yvonne's lead. "She's a troubled girl. She's always been troubled. Don't worry about what she said. We're glad to have you on the island. You're welcome here."

A man rose to echo the woman's sentiments, and then another. Before Matthew and Alexis could leave, half the club had come to introduce themselves and tell her they were sorry she'd had so many problems. By the time she was out the door, her throat had an unmistakable lump in it.

"We're a friendly sort," Matthew told her, taking her hand as they walked to the car. "But we don't take to everybody. Those people in there took to you. Now you'll be asked to be on every committee on this end of the island."

She smiled, but her mind was on something more vital. "You believe Yvonne set the fire, don't you?"

He helped her into the car before he answered. "It seems as if she may know who did, even if she didn't. It could very well have been her brother."

They were halfway home before Alexis spoke again. "Do you suppose one of them will admit it?"

He wished he could reassure her, but honesty seemed more important. "Would you, if you were in her place?"

"I don't suppose Australian cops use Third World interrogation techniques, do they?"

"No more often than American cops do."

"Then we'll probably never know for sure who set the fire."

"The police will do everything they can to find out."
Matthew glanced at Alexis and saw the tension on her face.
"You're still worried it might have been Cahill."

She thought about the possibilities. She had Ron's assur-
ances about Charles, and Yvonne's last words strongly im-
plicated her in the fire.

Alexis had stayed alive this long because she had developed finely tuned survival instincts. The problem was that
those instincts could border on paranoia. The line between
was nearly invisible. Survival instincts could save her life
again; paranoia could ruin it.

"I don't know what to think for sure," she said, miles
later. "But it does seem that it was probably Yvonne or her
brother who set the fire."

Matthew was assaulted by conflicting emotions. He knew
that she would run if she believed she and Jody were still in
danger here. He wanted her safe. He wanted her nearby. But
there was a part of him that was confused and inarticulate
and frightened, and that part of him wanted her gone.

"You have time to decide what to do." He turned her
wagon onto the road leading to the Chase. "You're welcome to stay with me for as long as you need."

She wondered how welcome she was. Earlier today she
had wept for both of them. Since then she had sensed that
their relationship was approaching another crisis. It could
not stay the same. A change was in the wind.

"I'd like to stay with you tonight," she said as he pulled
into the parking space in front of the homestead.

"Of course. I hadn't expected anything different."

"Tomorrow I'll decide what I have to do."

"Don't rush things."

"We both know I have to." She wondered how much
more she could say without Matthew closing down all com-
munication. "Whatever I decide..." She realized she
couldn't go on. She had wanted to tell him that she loved
him, but she knew what that would do to him. "Whatever
I decide, I want you to know how much I've appreciated
your hospitality." They were cold, stupid words, words she
would have used with any acquaintance who had offered her

a meal or a bed for a night. Words that didn't even begin to touch what she was feeling.

Matthew didn't know how to answer. He had heard the words she hadn't spoken. He didn't even want her to think them. He got out of the car and came around to open her door, but she had gotten out already.

"Look at those stars." Alexis hugged herself for warmth. In the darkness her hair was a pale halo against a face as white as moonlight. Matthew found his hand entangled in the silky strands.

"Come inside."

She blinked back tears, furious that she would cry now. "I think I'll stay outside for a few minutes and look at the sky."

"You're shivering."

She shrugged.

He was awash in feelings that he couldn't isolate. The only thing he knew for certain was that he had never wanted her more. "Come inside."

Alexis heard the demand. She turned her head to his, and her eyes glistened. "This is so hard, Matthew."

He didn't need an explanation. He bent to kiss her. Then he drew away. "Come inside."

She sighed. "Just tell me. Is it hard for you, too?"

Even that was asking for more than he wanted to give. Yet he couldn't refuse. He knew he owed her what part of the truth he could recognize. "Harder than I can say."

She searched his eyes, then, finally, nodded.

His hand dropped to his side. "Now, will you come inside?"

"For tonight." She leaned against him as his arm slid around her waist. Framing his face with her hands, she fitted her body against his. "Make love to me, Matthew."

His breath caught. "Here? Now?"

"Now and later."

He clasped her close and kissed her with the desperation he had heard in her voice.

Chapter 15

Matthew was gone. Alexis knew it without opening her eyes. She could feel the empty space beside her without stretching out her arms. She could hear the stillness, taste the loneliness.

She turned from her side to her back and forced her eyelids open to stare at the ceiling. She didn't know what time it was, but she knew it was late by the intensity of the sunshine beaming in through the window.

She had missed the chance to share their morning ritual one last time.

The night before had been long and passion-filled, and they had gotten little sleep. They had made love without words, made love and made memories, and each time they had tried to part, they had joined once more as a talisman against the solitude neither of them wanted.

When she had finally fallen asleep, she had slept deeply, dreamlessly. She wondered if Matthew had slept at all.

She missed him, but she was glad he was gone. Leaving would be hard enough without having him there. Now she could pack and go. At the house on Hanson Bay she could make her decision about the future.

She sat up slowly, vaguely aware of new aches in a body satiated from Matthew's lovemaking. She was tired and sore, but so much more weary inside that she hardly noticed.

In the bathroom she showered quickly and changed into the skirt and blouse she had worn the day they had visited the lighthouse and Remarkable Rocks with Jody. She remembered that day and the feeling she'd had that they were a family.

They would never be a family, because Matthew couldn't accept the fact that his wife and son were gone. She could have borne his refusal to let Jeannie and Todd go if she hadn't believed that he loved her, too. But last night had proved to her, beyond any doubt, that Matthew did love her, although he would never say the words. He needed her, although he would never admit it.

Her weariness was pierced with a slim shard of anger. Who was the woman who held such sway over Matthew's heart that three years after her death he still couldn't say goodbye? She had no way of knowing, because there was nothing of Jeannie Haley left in the house.

Soon there would be nothing left of her, either.

She had never really unpacked, living out of a suitcase for the last week, although Matthew had offered to give her space in his dresser. Now she gathered up the few articles she had left in the bathroom and took them back in the bedroom to pack. She found the shoes she had worn yesterday and put them in the suitcase, along with a magazine she'd been reading and her hairbrush.

In the bedroom she'd used as a study she gathered up her diskettes and a handful of reference books and took them back to pack them. Then she closed the suitcase and flipped the locks to carry it downstairs. She made another trip for the computer and one more for the lockbox that held Jody's baby pictures and other precious mementos.

She had packed the car before she remembered the two boxes in the attic. Matthew had made a trip to the house immediately after they had toured the wreckage and gathered and boxed everything that seemed valuable. He had done it without telling her, and she had been grateful for his thoughtfulness. But now those boxes were in the attic, and unless she removed them and took them home, Matthew would have to do it.

She wanted to give him no excuses to come after her. If he did come, it had to be because he wanted to. Not because he was worried about her, not because he felt responsible for things she had left.

The steps to the attic were narrow and steep. As she climbed them she wondered why he had stored the boxes here instead of in a spare bedroom. The only answer she could think of seemed too optimistic. He had expected, or hoped, that she would stay.

If that were true, why hadn't he asked her to? He had offered his home as a refuge, but he hadn't asked her to live with him. The two were very different.

In the attic she was momentarily confused by the number of neatly stacked boxes lining the walls. On closer examination she saw that they were covered with heavy dust, while hers were closer to the center and dust-free. Her boxes were heavy, but not unmanageable, and she had carried them one at a time to the doorway before curiosity overwhelmed her.

What was stored in the boxes lining the low walls? What was so important that it occupied so much of the attic's space, yet so unimportant that it hadn't been touched in what appeared to be years?

She had no right to find out. Matthew had given her no rights in his life. She was a guest, both in his home and in his heart.

But "guest" wasn't the status she wanted. She wanted more.

What was stored in the boxes? A suspicion began to form. What would a man pack away so meticulously, then never return to examine? Matthew wasn't a collector, a pack rat; the sparseness of his furnishings and the absence of any personal memorabilia attested to that. What would he have stored here except memories?

The dust was three years thick.

Suddenly, finding out about Matthew's family was vital. How could she fight for him if she didn't understand?

Fight for Matthew. She thought about what those words meant. She had never been a fighter, but slowly, through the years, she had learned to stand up for what she was entitled to.

In the early days of her marriage she had taken Charles's abuse; she had been sure, on the most basic level, that something she had done had caused it. Her parents had taught her to be responsible, until she had grown to believe she was responsible for everything that happened around her. Responsible for Charles's anger, his violence, his sadism. Responsible for trying to make the marriage work, and when she had matured enough to realize it never would, responsible for trying to end it.

It was then that she had begun to stand up for herself. The process had been slow but steady. There had been no one but Ron to help, no one to applaud. She had simply had to stand up or lie down forever.

What had she learned? That things would take care of themselves if given time? Or that she had to take care of things herself? In the most important sense she had finally learned to *be* responsible, not just to *feel* that way.

She stooped to accommodate the sloping roof and made her way to the nearest pile of boxes. The tops were carefully overlapped to seal them, but there was no tape, no string and no labels.

She had no right to violate Matthew's privacy. She opened the top box anyway, because she had decided she was going to fight. She would not lose Matthew to ghosts.

Dust clouded the air, and her still-weakened lungs were racked by a spasm of coughing. The dust settled slowly, and the coughing stopped. She stared into a box of trophies before picking up the two on the top.

"Todd Haley. Junior Park Ranger," she read. The first trophy was a brass-plated kangaroo. The second was a traditional loving cup. Todd had apparently been on a tennis team.

Tears filled her eyes. She hadn't expected to cry. She was fighting for Matthew, but she held a little boy's triumphs in her hands, a little boy who would never triumph again. How had Matthew lived through the agony of his son's death?

She rummaged carefully through the remainder of the box. There were more trophies and a pile of certificates and progress reports from school. He had been a bright child, and his teachers had praised his attitude. He had been a son to be proud of.

She remembered that he had talked to animals, just like Jody.

The last trophy was carefully wrapped in what looked like a tattered baby blanket. She unwrapped it slowly, knowing instinctively that the blanket had once been Todd's most precious possession. The trophy itself was simple, another loving cup. Inscribed on it were the words, Todd Haley. World's Best Son.

She cried in earnest now, the cup against her heart.

It was minutes before she could bear to wrap the trophy once more and return it to the box. She wasn't sure she could go on with her search, but, more than ever, she knew she needed to. What she was learning about Matthew's family was important, but perhaps what she was learning about his grief was even more so.

The next box was filled with toys. There was a train set, a miniature village, a football, a stamp collecting kit. The next box held more of the same, and so did the last box in the stack. Todd had been a child who liked a variety of things to do. His stamp album was almost half filled with neatly pasted stamps, all labeled with his carefully crafted script. The football looked as if it had been the center of myriad exuberant games.

The next stack of boxes was Todd's, too. One was full of stuffed animals, a well-loved koala gracing the very top. Another held books. He had been partial to the Hardy Boys and British children's classics. There were several books about a girl named Dot that were distinctly Australian. The third box held fading artwork, pictures that ranged from finger paintings to more complicated watercolors. There were ashtrays made from modeling clay and a well-done wooden carving of a possum.

He had lived and grown and thrived here in Flinders Chase. He had played and worked and done his homework. He had been loved by his parents and loved them in return.

When Alexis had closed the last box in the stack, she knew Todd Haley. And she loved him, too.

The next stack was separated by several yards. Alexis approached it with uneasiness. It had been one thing to find out about Todd; it was another to find out about Jeannie.

This was the woman who Matthew had loved, who still held him as surely as if she were alive and her arms enclosed him. Alexis hesitated at the first box, but she was fighting for Matthew. Her hands were unsteady as she pulled the flaps open.

Photograph albums. Four of them. Dust had seeped through the box, and she had to wipe the top one clean before she opened it.

The title page showed a smiling bride and groom in formal wedding clothes. The groom was unmistakably a younger Matthew. The bride had to be Jeannie.

She was tall and slender, not really pretty, because her features were too strong for classic beauty, but vibrant and very much alive. Her dark hair was chin-length, thick and curly around a square face, and her eyes shone with love for the man beside her.

Matthew's eyes shone with love, too. In many ways his face had remained unchanged through the years, but the Matthew in the picture had never known sorrow. He hadn't learned to hide his feelings, to gaze with chilling blankness at those around him. There were no lines carved around his eyes and mouth, no tension in the way he held his body. He was a man about to begin a new life, and he was clearly eager to be alone with his bride.

Alexis turned the page. There were more photographs. Matthew and Jeannie, hands clasped, cutting their wedding cake. Jeannie alone, her face softened for that moment into radiance. Matthew with friends. Both of them with people who were obviously family.

She turned the page again, then again. The next photographs were labeled. They had gone to Fiji on their honeymoon, and there were pictures to document it. They looked happy, relaxed and totally wrapped up in each other. Alexis skimmed the photos quickly, feeling as though she were trespassing on something she shouldn't share.

There were miscellaneous photographs after that, pictures of houses and people she couldn't identify, and places they had been.

The next photograph album held the pictures of Todd.

Unquestionably they had wanted their son. In all the photographs both Jeannie and Matthew looked as if they had just been handed a miracle wrapped up in rainbows. There were countless photos of Todd as he developed from infant into toddler, his loving parents attending each step of his progress with smiles and encouragement.

The third album was devoted to his preschool days, and there were more family portraits. They had been at the Chase by then, and interspersed with shots of Todd climbing trees and chasing kangaroos were shots of the house where Alexis now sat in the attic.

The fourth and final album was Todd's school years. He was a handsome sturdy boy, resembling his mother more than his father, but Alexis could see Matthew in Todd's eyes. There were pictures of the whole family, too. Jeannie's hair was shorter, but her smile had grown wider. Matthew looked like a man content.

And then the photographs stopped.

She felt a shudder of loss. Everything had ended so suddenly for the Haleys. One moment there had been family and love, the next a dark, anguished void.

She understood Matthew's grief better.

Alexis replaced the albums and refolded the flaps on the box. She didn't have to see any more to know what he had suffered and why Jeannie and Todd still had such a hold on him. He had packed them away, both here and in his heart. Until he could take them out once more and openly feel the love he would always have for them, he would never be able to give his love to anyone else.

She started to stand, defeated. She wasn't fighting Jeannie and Todd. She already cared for them both because they were part of Matthew. She knew instinctively that Jeannie would be appalled at Matthew's continuing grief. She had been a vital, enthusiastic woman, and she would not have wanted Matthew to suffer endlessly. She would have wanted him to love again.

She wasn't fighting Jeannie and Todd; she was fighting Matthew. Until he faced his past....

A new thought, half-formed, began to tug at her. Matthew would not talk about his past; he could hardly bear to utter Jeannie and Todd's names. But his past was here, waiting to be rediscovered. Below her was a house devoid of any hint of his previous life and any particle of warmth. But the attic held all the warmth he needed to have breathed back into him.

If she had the courage to do it.

Alexis settled back on the floor. Her hands were shaking harder as she drew the next box to her, but by the time she had finished going through all the boxes in the attic, her hands were steady once more. And, strangely enough, she had the undeniable feeling that the spirit of a warm-hearted, dark-haired woman was giving her the courage she needed.

At lunchtime Matthew was surprised to see Alexis's car still parked at his house. He had expected her to be gone; she had made it clear yesterday that she would be leaving.

He didn't know what he should feel; he only knew what he felt. Gratitude that she was still there. Fear. Shame that he was afraid.

He knew one other thing. Before Alexis had come into his life he had let himself feel nothing.

He paused on the front doorstep, realizing immediately that something was different. It took him seconds to figure out what it was and seconds longer to understand that Alexis had breached his privacy.

Under his feet was the reed doormat that Jeannie had bought on their honeymoon trip to Fiji. It was worn where years of muddy feet had been relentlessly wiped against it, but the inscription was still clear enough to read. Peace to Those Who Enter Here.

He felt something akin to nausea wash through him. The last time he had seen the mat, it had been at the bottom of a box of household goods he had packed away after Jeannie's death.

His hand gripped the doorknob, and he threw the door open. "Alexis!"

There was no answer. He strode into the hallway. The walls that had been bare were now covered with framed photographs. He could not avert his eyes because they were everywhere: Jeannie in her wedding dress; Todd at his first cricket game; their first Christmas as a family; Matthew himself with one arm draped around an emu's neck.

"Alexis!"

She wasn't in the parlor, but mementos of his marriage were. There was the ashtray that Todd had proudly made in his second year of school, although no one in the family had smoked. There was the possum Todd had carved in Scouts, a watercolor of Remarkable Rocks that Jeannie had painted, their wedding photograph album on the table beside his favorite chair.

In the dining room he found his wedding china in the cabinet that had held nothing for three years except simple crockery. In the kitchen he gazed at walls crowded with the tiles and tea towels Jeannie had collected everywhere she'd gone. He gazed at the familiar blue enamel kettle and red enamel canisters. He gazed through blurry eyes at the red and blue plaid rug that lay in front of the sink, just where Jeannie had always placed it.

Bile rose in his throat, and he forced it down. He didn't even call Alexis's name; he just started back through the hall to the stairs.

He bypassed the two spare bedrooms and went immediately to his own. He threw the door open, remaining on the threshold. Alexis sat quietly, waiting for him on the hand-crocheted coverlet that had been a Christmas gift from Jeannie's Scots grandmother.

"Get out."

She had expected anything, even this. She stood, carefully brushing her skirt over her knees. "You had a beautiful family, Matthew."

"My family is none of your bloody business!"

She nodded sadly. "I know. But I made them my business anyway."

"What gave you the right?"

"Loving you." She lifted her chin. She was not cowed by his anger. "I'm not the first to love you. Jeannie loved you, and Todd loved you, too. You had them for just a short time, but they can live in your memories still, if you'll let them."

"Get out. I didn't ask you into my life."

She nodded gravely. "You'll shut me out, just as you've shut them out. Then you'll have nothing and no one, Matthew. Is that what you want?"

"I want you to leave."

"I'm packed." She walked toward him. "It's funny. Now I think I know Jeannie better than you did. She was a woman who would be appalled at your guilt and your suffering. You've wallowed in it for three years, when you could have been warmed by what you once had."

He raised his hands to her shoulders and shook her. "What do you know about suffering?" he demanded through clenched teeth. "What do you know about loss?"

Her head fell back, but even in his rage she wasn't afraid of him. He hadn't hurt her, and she knew he wouldn't. The only bruises he would leave would be on her soul.

"More than enough about both," she said when his hands dropped to his sides. "I would give my blood and bones to have been loved for even one day the way you were."

All signs of anger disappeared. He became the Matthew she had first met, the man with nothing inside him. She spoke again before he could. "I'm leaving."

He stepped aside, encouraging her. She paused on the threshold and her hand dropped to the nightstand beside his bed. On it she had placed a framed photograph of Matthew, Jeannie and Todd. She suspected it was the last one that had been taken before the crash.

She touched it tenderly. "If you're ever able to tell them goodbye, tell them I said goodbye, too. And tell them that I've mourned for them today." She lifted her eyes to Matthew's. "I'll mourn for you, too."

His eyes didn't flicker, and he didn't move.

"Goodbye, dear one," she whispered. Then she turned and started down the stairs.

Chapter 16

The wind off Hanson Bay held the chill of ice-capped mountain ranges two thousand miles away. With a cup of fresh coffee to warm her, Alexis sat on the makeshift steps where her porch had once been and watched twilight thicken into night. On the beach below, surf lapped in a hypnotic rhythm against the shore. The only other sound disturbing the deep evening stillness was the occasional soft grunt of the koala roosting in the gum tree closest to the house. He had been there to greet her when she had returned from Matthew's, shaken and drained. Somehow his presence had made it possible to go into the house and unpack.

She had been preparing a dinner she wasn't hungry for when she decided to come outside instead. The steps were uneven and rough, but the moon was rising, threatening a sunshine brightness, and she didn't want it to rise without her. She missed the front porch, but Peter was going to have it replaced. In time the house would look much as it had before the fire.

Only nothing would really be the same.

Nothing would be the same in her life, either. She had gambled for Matthew's love, and she had lost. In the process she had caused them both untold pain. Strangely, she had no regrets. She had done what she had to do. They could not have remained occasional lovers. Now they wouldn't be friends, but perhaps that was more honest. And kinder.

She had spent the afternoon since leaving Matthew's planning the next months of her life. Running had been a temptation. She could fly to Coober Pedy and pick up Jody, then begin the long journey to nowhere again. She owed Jody more than that, though. Just as she had fought for Matthew, now she knew she must fight for the right to stay on the island.

In a way that nowhere else had ever been, the Hanson Bay house was home. Two days before, when she had discussed the progress of the repairs with Peter, he had told her that when she was ready to make a decision about putting down permanent roots, he would sell her the property if she wanted it.

She wanted to stay, although the prospect of sometimes seeing Matthew was enough to make her want to run. But she was bone weary of the race. She had been running for a year. Now the pursued had turned to wait for the pursuer. And he was no longer there.

She told herself that Charles was no longer there. She told herself that he had balanced revenge and greed and chosen the latter. She was free of him as long as she stayed out of sight.

Charles wasn't there, but Matthew was. Now it was love, not hate, that tempted her to run. And she had decided that she wouldn't run from either.

A small surge of warmth spread through a body chilled from more than the cold Antarctic wind. She was becoming the woman she had so often longed to be. But why, if she had finally gotten the courage she had needed for so long, hadn't happiness come with it?

She heard no answer in the wind, only the faint rumble of an engine. She listened intently, surprised the sound would carry so many miles from the main road. As she listened, the sound grew louder, and she realized that the vehicle wasn't on the main road, but on the track leading up to her house.

She was going to have a visitor.

Matthew had come. Whether to hold or revile her she didn't know. But he had come; he had not erased her from his life as she had feared. He had come, and perhaps now they could begin again.

She wondered what he would see when he drove up. Would he see the woman who had cried for his family today? The woman who had cried for him? Her hand went to her hair, and she felt a pang of self-consciousness. Her hair was tangled from the wind, her cheeks and eyes reddened. She had changed into faded jeans and an old yellow sweater, and there wasn't time to do anything about that. But she could comb her hair and wash her face.

She stood and went into the house. When she lifted the brush to her hair, she saw, dispassionately, that her hand trembled.

She was ready in a minute. She was afraid to take longer because she wanted to greet Matthew on the steps. She didn't want to give him a chance to change his mind about seeing her.

She opened the new front door and peered out into the darkness. Her eyes took seconds to adjust and seconds more to see that there was no ute parked in front of the house. She listened intently, but there was no longer the sound of an engine on the wind. There was only the lapping of the surf.

Disappointment filled her. Either she had imagined the sound or her visitor, whoever it had been, had turned around and gone. She had been a fool once again. She had believed that, after everything, Matthew would seek her out tonight. When would she learn to be a realist? When would she stop believing in happy endings?

She descended the steps and gazed into the darkness. She'd believed she'd cried every tear inside her that day, but, surprisingly, tears clouded her eyes once more.

She was the very worst kind of fool, the kind who had let herself cry over two men. She was not going to cry again. The time for tears was done.

There was a faint rustling noise at the edge of the clearing, near the gum tree that held her koala friend. She knew that if she went inside she wouldn't find the strength to fight off her grief. She needed to be outside, face to the wind, watching the moon rise. The rustling grew louder. She knew that koalas moved along the ground after dark. She wondered if she could approach silently enough to see the koala scurrying to another tree. Forcing herself to try, she walked carefully across the clearing, past her car, to the gum tree.

The light of the rising moon diffused through the tree branches. A dim silhouette was outlined against the sky, but she couldn't tell if the silhouette was a koala or an intersection of branches. There were no soft grunts to guide her, only a peculiar stillness, as if the night creatures were listening intently.

The stillness seemed suddenly ominous. The moon was rising, yet even the insects seemed to keep their counsel, as if they were waiting for another signal before they began their evening song. Alexis felt a chill run down her spine. The day had been too emotion-laden. The last months had been too emotion-laden. She was so completely alone now that she was imagining danger when for the first time danger seemed behind her.

Yet it was just such a sense of foreboding that had told her the poachers were on her land the night she had warned them away with a gunshot.

She listened intently, searching the areas nearest her for movement. The rustling she had heard could have been anything, the koala, a wallaby, possums. It could even have been a gust of wind rattling branches. But if so, why was her alarm growing? Was she overwrought, emotionally exhausted from the events of the day, or was a sixth sense telling her to beware?

The house was yards behind her, and so was the gun locked securely in her bedside drawer. She had left the house's sanctuary to fight off her grief. Now grief seemed preferable to the fear that was rapidly growing inside her.

She started to cross the clearing and go inside before what courage she had left was gone completely.

"A remote, desolate spot for a woman afraid of dying, Dana."

Alexis whirled, searching for the voice. But even before the man materialized from the edge of the clearing at the side of the house, she knew who she would see. The voice was the substance of her nightmares.

"Charles." The name was said through a throat constricted with horror.

"Dana," he said, taunting her by using the same tone.

She stared at him, horror growing. In the moonlight his brown hair shone with silver. The time since she had last seen him had left hardly a mark. He was trim and fit, and if his hair was grayer, his face was still unlined and youthful. Like Dorian Gray, nothing of the man inside showed.

"Aren't you going to ask me why I've come?" He advanced slowly toward her.

More than anything in the world she wanted to retreat. But she stood her ground. As he had begun to move, she'd seen moonlight reflect off the barrel of a revolver. If she turned to run, she would be dead in seconds. Charles would shoot her in the back without a second thought.

Frantically she searched for a way to escape, but her face showed none of her desperation.

He raised one eyebrow, and she knew he was surprised that she hadn't dissolved at his feet. He had always counted on her fear to make him strong. She had no time to reflect on what was happening, but she did know that she wasn't going to let him see she was afraid. If she died tonight, she wouldn't give him the satisfaction of knowing she'd been terrified. It would be her revenge.

"I can guess why you've come," she answered at last.

"Then your memory serves you well."

"How did you find me?"

"I've known where you were since the day you arrived."

She didn't doubt him, but his answer drained off more of her courage. Nothing she had done had fooled him. He couldn't be beaten.

"Don't you want to know how?" he continued. His voice was as silky, as warm as a lover's, except that Charles had never had a drop of love inside him.

She nodded, not because she wanted an answer, but because she wanted to keep him talking. As long as he talked, he needed an audience—a living one.

"Did you think I wouldn't check out every name in Bartow's address book, every contact he made in the last year and a half?"

"I couldn't run far enough, could I?"

"No."

She made herself look into his eyes. "We knew you'd quit searching. We just didn't know why."

"You underestimated me." He had moved close enough that he could touch her now. He stretched out his hand to brush a lock of hair off her face. He was surprisingly gentle, but she knew he was always most gentle right before he struck.

"No," she said softly, forcing herself not to flinch. "I never doubted you could find me. I only hoped you wouldn't want to bother."

"Ah, Dana." He shook his head sadly. "I told you I would kill you."

"Why, Charles? What will you gain?"

He smiled a little. "The memory of your blood turning cold and the breath leaving your body."

Horror threatened to overwhelm her. She pushed through it. "That's very little. You have so much to lose. If you leave now we can both forget you were ever here. You can have a real life, not a sadistic memory—"

His fingertips caressed her cheek before he slapped her. Alexis's head spun, and her knees buckled. She stumbled backward, catching herself just before she fell.

His eyes lit with pleasure at what he saw as a retreat. "Are you going to run from me, Dana?"

Involuntarily her hand covered her cheek. "So you can shoot me in the back?"

He held the gun in front of his chest, aimed directly at her. "Go ahead. I'll give you a head start."

"There are people here who know my story. You'll be the first one they suspect if my body's found riddled with bullet holes."

He smiled a little. "There's a big, beautiful ocean out there."

"With tides that wash back in to the island."

"Not if I take you out deep enough."

She knew reasoning with him was a waste of time. His mind was so twisted, his hatred so extraordinary, his intellect so powerful. He was right, and they both knew it. He would commit this crime, and he would get away with it.

"When your house almost burned down around you, did you think of me?" Charles lowered the gun just a fraction.

"When anything evil happens I think of you!"

He nodded, almost as if he admired the courage her answer had taken. "I hired someone to do it."

That was a possibility she hadn't considered, but then, she'd believed that Charles hadn't found her, too. She had a brief flash of sympathy for Yvonne Carson and her brother. "I'm sure you have the connections."

"That piece of trash you wrote was even more realistic than you'd thought. My *connections* are extensive."

"The fire fizzled."

"It was meant to. I was hoping the fire would make you run somewhere where no one knew you. It would have made this easier for me, and I would have liked to see you run again."

"Why didn't your friend just finish me off?"

"Because I wanted that pleasure myself."

She couldn't listen to any more. The courage that had carried her this far was almost used up. He was playing with her; his sadism had never been more apparent. He wanted her to cry, to grovel, to plead. But no matter what she did, she was going to die.

Unless she took him by surprise.

He was already surprised at her courage. She had seen just the faintest trace of admiration cross his features. It was the same quality of emotion a snake probably felt before it devoured a valiantly resisting mouse, as much emotion as he was capable of. She had become a worthy opponent. But he would relish killing her just the same.

Unless she took him by surprise. Completely by surprise.

She moved toward him until they were within touching distance again. She could not bear to continue talking as if they were old friends exchanging a year's worth of chit-chat. She knew that in moments he would begin to talk about his plans for Jody, and she would cry. She wouldn't die with tears on her cheeks.

She delivered her surprise with no emotion. "Then take your pleasure, Charles." She forced herself to stare into his soulless brown eyes. "I'm not afraid of you anymore."

For a split second his eyes showed confusion. Then the hand holding the gun lifted, as if to strike her down for her disrespect. She tensed, ready to spring forward.

A shrill grunting wheeze filled the stillness. Above them the koala was calling for a mate. Charles faltered, his head snapping back to look up in the tree. Alexis dove for the arm holding the gun. Astoundingly, she caught him off balance. He slipped backward, and as he fell, the gun flew through the air, disappearing into the dense scrub that hadn't burned in the fire. She knew that his fall had given her only a second's advantage, but she took it, stumbling, then running full-speed toward her wagon.

He didn't follow immediately, screaming curses instead as she ran away. She couldn't risk a glance behind her, but she suspected he was searching for his gun. She expected any moment to hear the whine, to feel the shattering impact of a bullet. She was inside the wagon, turning the key she always left in the ignition before she dared to breathe.

She was escaping. Somehow, she was escaping Charles. Her tires screeched as they spun in the loose dirt, but the four-wheel-drive vehicle was made for moments like this, and in seconds she was speeding down the track. She switched on her lights just in time to see a car blocking her path. Charles had parked his rental car squarely in the middle, as insurance against anyone coming or going. But he hadn't taken into account her terror-fueled daring. She swerved into the mallee lining the track and listened to it being ground under her wheels. Miraculously the wagon kept moving, gathering speed when she was once more on the road.

She was escaping! Alexis focused on her driving, taking the track at a speed she would never have dared for any other reason. She had the advantage of knowing the road, and with a concentration born of her will to survive, she skirted potholes and ruts, taking the jolts of those she couldn't avoid by bracing herself against the steering wheel.

She was almost out to the main road before she saw lights behind her. They were diffused and weak, indicating that Charles was coming, but still a distance behind.

Charles was coming. She shot onto the main road and instinctively turned left toward Flinders Chase. Parndana was thirty-five miles away, and although there were houses and farms set back from the road before the town, there was no one she knew, no one who would understand the danger before she could take the time to tell them. Somewhere along the track out to the road she had realized that she was going to have to run to Matthew.

She switched off her lights and prayed that Charles would think she had taken the route toward town. She floored the accelerator, frantically searching the moon-shadowed road for ruts and crevices. The steering wheel jerked from her hand as she bounced into a deep hole she hadn't seen. She was barely able to keep the car on the road, but she didn't slow down because she knew she was racing death.

She had taken Charles completely by surprise. It was the only thing that had saved her life. He had expected terror, expected her to plead and cower. Instead she had stood up to him, and when she'd had the chance, she had defended herself. Still, she wouldn't have expected to escape him, not in her wildest, most hopeful fantasies.

She was not going to let him kill her now. She would fight with everything inside her.

A mile had flown by before she knew that he was still following her. She couldn't risk a glance in her rearview mirror because of the speed she was traveling, but she could see the reflection of lights on her windshield. She had hoped to outsmart him, but he had second-guessed her. She realized then that if he'd been keeping track of her, he knew about Matthew. He had guessed correctly that she would flee to her lover.

The head start was still hers. She had the better car; she knew the roads. He might be fueled by hatred and a need for revenge, but she was fueled by the desire to live. She was going to live.

She swerved around a deep crater, brushing tree limbs on the roadside. She heard the sound of shattering glass and wood gouging metal but ignored it. Broken windows were nothing.

The car jumped a rut so deep that she knew if she'd hit it wrong, she would have stalled. The rut didn't matter. Nothing mattered except living. She was going to live.

The reflected lights seemed brighter, but her only response was to try to coax more speed from the wagon for the last mile before Flinders Chase. When she entered the park, she was forced to slow down and switch on her lights. The road here was narrower, although well-graded. A more important consideration was the park's tame kangaroos and emus, which wandered back and forth across the roadway looking for tourists to feed them. If she hit a kangaroo at high speed, she would be killed as surely as it would.

As she slowed she risked a glance in her mirror. There were no lights visible, but she doubted her luck would hold. False hope was an emotion she couldn't afford. Charles would come, and unless she found a haven at Matthew's, he would kill her.

Matthew. For the first time she doubted whether he would open his door to her. He had been coldly furious; he had looked at her as if he never wanted to see her again. Now she would be pleading for his help. She had needed his help before, and he had given it, although he hadn't wanted her in his life then, either. Surely he wouldn't turn her away now.

He wouldn't. No matter what she had done, he wouldn't turn her away. He would take her in, shelter her, call the police. She would be safe there until....

Until Charles came for her again.

For the first time Alexis felt threads of panic take root. She might succeed in eluding Charles this time, but he would be back. Even if she ran, he would find her. And next time she wouldn't be able to surprise him. She would never be safe.

She realized there was nothing she could do about the future. She had to take the present one moment at a time. And right now her task was to survive this encounter. There would be time to plan for the next.

She sped up onto a grassy plain leading into the rangers' homestead. Her headlights illuminated the two houses sitting on the edge of the sugar gum grove.

No lights were on in Matthew's house. Nor was his ute parked in front.

She couldn't believe he was gone. He had to be there. She leaned on the horn once, then again. There was no response.

Alexis slammed on her brakes. There was a steadily intensifying glow from the road behind her. Charles hadn't given up. Perhaps he had known from the start that Matthew wasn't there.

But the park wouldn't be deserted. One of the rangers was always there. She calculated the time it would take Charles to reach her. With the engine still running she threw open her door and jumped down. At Matthew's door she pounded and shouted. There was still no response. She willed him to be home; she pleaded with him to be home. He wasn't. She rattled his doorknob, but his door was locked.

From Matthew's porch she could see one light upstairs at Harry's. She had honked and shouted, but there had been no response from his house, either. The light on the road behind her was growing brighter.

Caught between the possibility of not rousing Harry and taking her chances on the road through the park, she gambled on the latter. The Chase was a maze of tracks. She knew many of them now. She could lose Charles.

She fled back to her car and pulled out on the road. In moments she had picked up speed, careening past wide-eyed animals. She narrowly missed a kangaroo, praying that no more would block her way. In a minute she was deep in the woods. So well did the trees hide her view that she didn't know Charles was there until she dipped into a small clearing. The headlights fifty yards behind her were a shock. She had lost precious time banging on Matthew's door.

She realized in a flash how foolish she had been to leave the homestead. There would be no chance to drive off the main road and hide. Charles was right behind her. She had no choice now but to follow the road toward the lighthouse. It made a wide loop just before the cape. If she followed it and Charles followed her she would eventually end up at the homestead again. Then she could decide what to do.

Her gaze dropped momentarily to the gas gauge. She had enough gas because she had filled up recently at the tiny station between the Chase and Hanson Bay. If even the slightest bit of luck was hers, Charles's gas would be getting low. If he had rented the car in Kingscote or Penneshaw, he had traveled many miles to reach her. If she was lucky. . . .

She forced all her concentration back to the road in front of her. She was gaining a little on Charles. She knew what to expect from the road because she'd been on it before. Charles didn't. She silently, fleetingly blessed Peter Bartow for advising her to get a four-wheel-drive wagon. It was made for the roughest terrain, and it was getting the test of its life. It was performing magnificently.

She swerved around curves, applying the brake judiciously, speeding up once more. Her hands were slick with perspiration, but she couldn't lift them off the wheel to dry them. She gripped it harder until her knuckles were white.

Minutes passed, and she made more gains. Charles's headlights were still visible, but dimmer. She was just beginning to believe that she might escape him when a crater the size of a small canyon loomed before her. She spun the wheel and hit the brake, trying desperately to avoid it, but her right front tire went over the edge. The car rocked dangerously, then found purchase on the edge of the crater. In a moment all four wheels were on smoother road again, but a fierce grinding noise sounded from the right side of the car as she picked up momentum.

Even without the ominous grinding, she knew she was in trouble. The steering was no longer responsive to the slightest twist or turn of the wheel, and although she pressed the accelerator to the floor, the car couldn't regain most of the speed it had lost.

She had gone half a mile before the engine began to miss. She didn't have to check the mirror to find that Charles was closer.

The landscape was bleaker. They had long ago left the forest and now traveled along limestone ridges adorned by nothing taller than heath and mallee. In the distance she could see the night-shattering glare of the lighthouse. There was no place to pull off, no place to hide if she left the car on the road. And clearly, the car was not going to take her back along the road to the rangers' homestead.

There was no time for despair. The engine missed, sputtered and, for a terrifying second, nearly died. Alexis eased up on the accelerator and hurled a prayer into the darkness. The engine caught, and she continued at a slower speed.

She knew there would be no place to hide at the lighthouse. For a moment she considered running to the cliff's edge there and descending the steps to Admiral's Arch. But Charles would surely find her, and there would be no escaping him when he did.

The only other possibility was Weirs Cove. She remembered the limestone ruins of the storehouses where the lighthouse keepers had stored supplies. It was little enough shelter, but shelter it was. The engine missed once more, and her decision was made. She flicked off her lights and concentrated on driving the short distance to the parking lot.

The engine missed one last time, then died just before she could pull into the lot. She guided the rolling car to a spot sheltered by brush.

She was out in seconds, running with the wind.

Chapter 17

She wasn't home.

Disappointment and concern warred in Matthew's head. Concern won. He hadn't passed her car on the road from Parndana, yet Alexis wasn't home; her car was gone, and there were two lights on in the house with an almost-full cup of cold coffee sitting on the front steps.

She was too well-organized to overlook either detail unless she had left in a hurry.

Or unless she had just been too upset to think clearly.

Not for the first time that day, he felt a sickening pang of regret at the way he had treated her. Because she loved him, she had forced him to look at himself.

Because he loved her, he had been able to.

Now he had come to tell her what he had found, but she wasn't here.

She wasn't here. Silently, Matthew apologized, then pulled out a credit card to jimmy the lock on the front door. He twisted the knob as he slid the card between the door and the frame, and the door came open in his hand. She hadn't locked it.

He strode inside, giving each room a cursory investigation. In the kitchen he found more reasons for concern. A lone lamb chop sat in a pan on the stove, uncooked. Beside it was an opened tin of corn. Another pan held cubed raw potatoes in several inches of water. And the coffee-maker was still on, keeping most of a pot warm.

She had left in the middle of preparations for the evening meal. She had left without putting anything away, and despite her experience with fire, without turning off the coffee-maker. If she lived in a city, the signs would tell him that he could expect her to be coming right back. But she didn't. She lived on one of the remotest spots on a remote island a hemisphere away from her home. There was no place to run out for another liter of milk, another kilo of sugar.

Concern was replaced by fear.

Where was she?

He was dredging up possibilities and rejecting them when the telephone rang. He gave no thought to not answering it. The call might just provide him with a clue.

"Matthew?"

The voice on the other end sounded quizzical, as if Matthew were not the person the man had expected to find. Matthew recognized it immediately.

"Is that you, Gray?"

"Yeah. I was calling for Alexis, but you're even better. Look, I've got bad news, and she shouldn't hear it over the phone."

Matthew leaned against the telephone table. "What is it?"

"I just spoke to Ron Bartow, her attorney. He tried to call her a little while ago, but he didn't get an answer there or at your house. So he called me. Julianna and I are still here in Cairns, so I told him I'd keep trying until she answered."

"What is it?" Matthew repeated.

"Her ex-husband's left the U.S. He's supposed to be in Frankfort, at a convention, but the investigator who's been watching him dug a little deeper. Cahill put in an appearance at the convention, covered all his bases, then vanished. It took the investigator most of a day to find out that he wasn't there anymore, because everything is operating as if he still is. It looks as if he's establishing an alibi.''

"Can you tell where he went?"

Gray didn't hesitate, but it was clear he wished the news were different. "It's not certain yet, but it looks as if he might have taken a flight to Australia by way of Singapore."

Matthew clutched the receiver.

"Matthew? Are you there?"

"What about Jody?" Matthew asked, the muscles in his throat as tight as his fist.

"She's still in Coober Pedy. I've alerted Dillon. He and Kelsey won't let anything happen to her. It's Alexis we're worried about. Can you tell her what's happening and get her out of there until we're sure she's safe?"

"She's not here, but I bloody well intend to find her."

"You don't know where she is?"

Matthew ran a hand through his hair. Guilt and fear were a seething pit inside him. With the poachers in jail he had let down his guard and submerged himself in grief without thinking of the danger Alexis could still be in. He had sent her back here alone.

"Matthew, where the hell is she?" Gray asked angrily.

Matthew knew that Gray would be no help pacing the floor for the next hours. He decided not to share his own fears. "She's probably in town. Give me a number where I can reach you." He listened as Gray recited the number of his hotel in Cairns and committed it to memory. "I'll be back in touch as soon as I find her."

Gray didn't waste any time on additional questions or information. "She's no match for Cahill," he said tersely. "He's the devil incarnate."

"If he comes after Alexis," Matthew said, "I'll be sure he's a dead devil." He replaced the receiver and headed for the door.

Outside, he cupped his hands and shouted through them. "Alexis!" He didn't expect an answer, but he listened intently. More shouts produced the same lack of response.

Since her car was gone, Matthew knew better than to waste any more time here. He pushed away the vision of Alexis lying somewhere nearby, wounded or worse. He had to trust his intuition. Her car was gone. *She* was gone. Now he only had to find where.

He was a hundred yards down the track when his headlights illuminated mangled brush to his left. He stopped, jumping out to investigate. Branches dangled from damaged limbs. One small mallee had been uprooted. The destruction was recent; sap still oozed like fresh blood.

What would have caused Alexis or anyone to drive off the road and through the scrub? An animal? Then why wouldn't she just have slammed on her brakes? She never drove the road to her house—or any road, for that matter—at high speed. She was cautious behind the wheel.

But caution could be easily discarded if there were danger.

He jumped back into his ute and continued on. Tensely he watched for more damage, more signs that would help him piece together what had happened. By the time he had reached the main road his frustration was building right along with his fear.

The island didn't seem small now that he was trying to find Alexis. It loomed before him, ninety-six miles long and thirty miles wide. His chances of finding her were infinitesimal unless he could successfully guess what had happened. Had she gone to Parndana or one of the two larger towns, as he'd assured Gray? And if she had, why?

When was more obvious. She had left sometime after she had begun dinner preparations. And that answered at least one other question. She hadn't gone to Parndana, because he had come back from that direction himself, and he hadn't seen her wagon. He had driven aimlessly for hours through an endless afternoon, drawn to the road because his house and the Chase itself had been brutally painful reminders of both Jeannie and Alexis. He had driven, stopping once for petrol and once to walk a deserted beach.

While he'd been searching his soul and heart, what had happened to Alexis? He slammed his palm against the steering wheel. She hadn't gone to Parndana. And she wouldn't take off for Kingscote or Penneshaw in the middle of making dinner. Then where in the hell had she gone?

Gone at high speed. Gone without locking her doors. Gone as if she were being pursued. He shut his eyes and imagined her careening down the track, dragging the remains of twisted mallee with her. Someone had been after her. *Before I Sleep* told him who.

If she hadn't fled toward Parndana, there was only one other place she could have gone. She had gone for help to the one man on the island who knew her story.

And he hadn't been there!

Matthew gunned his engine and pulled onto the main road, gaining speed quickly. Halfway to the park, shards of glass glinted at the outside perimeter of his headlights. He pulled closer and jumped out to examine them. The glass could have been from anyone's windows, but the flecks of paint still clinging to the limbs that had done the damage were dark red, the color of Alexis's wagon.

He was back on the road in seconds. In minutes he was at the rangers' homestead. There was no wagon parked in front of his house, no sign of Alexis or anyone else.

Where had she gone?

"Matthew?" Harry's front porch light was a sudden glare. Shielding his eyes, Matthew jumped down from the ute. Harry closed the front door behind him, threading a belt through his trousers. "We've got some sort of trouble."

"Have you seen Alexis?"

Harry descended the steps. "I haven't seen anyone. I was upstairs taking a quick shower. I had me box off." He pointed to his hearing aid. "I thought I heard honking, but I couldn't be certain. By the time I got out and threw on me dressing gown, there wasn't anyone out here, but I saw lights going south on the Shackle Track."

"Lights?"

"Two cars, I think. Might have been more, but that's all I saw. Probably some local blokes out for a good time. I'm going to go see."

"How long ago was this?"

Harry screwed up his face in thought. "Seven, eight minutes? I had to dress and—"

"Get your rifle."

Harry didn't even ask why. He turned and took the steps back up two at a time while Matthew ran to get in the ute and pull it closer. Harry was beside him in moments, shouting, "Go!"

Matthew knew he was going to have to tell Harry Alexis's story. Luckily she had made that simple. He took the road too fast, aware that he was gambling that the park wildlife was prowling or sleeping somewhere else. He was out of the woods and on a clearer section of the track before he spoke. "You know that book, *Before I Sleep*?"

"She wrote it, didn't she?"

Matthew didn't ask how Harry had known. He had asked Harry about the book when he was adding up the facts himself, and Harry wasn't a man to let anything past him. "She wrote it," he acknowledged. "She lived it. Now she may be living the ending."

"You think it's Alexis in one of those cars?"

"I pray to God it's not."

Harry sat back, bracing himself. He began to mutter softly.

"What are you doing?" Matthew snapped.

"Praying in earnest."

With nothing to frustrate it for miles unending, the wind swept across the cape and out to sea with the scream of a space-age jet. Alexis bent low against it, moving as if in slow-motion. She'd had dreams where she was running from Charles, running as fast as she could but barely moving, while he steadily closed in on her.

She didn't know what kind of progress he was making now, but the wind was like a giant's hands holding her back from her goal. By the time she reached the ruins she was exhausted, as if she had already fought Charles and lost.

There was shelter from the wind against the crumbling limestone walls, but the wind still whipped away all other sound. She could tell nothing about where Charles was, and there were no headlights to guide her. Apparently he had turned his off right after she had. The cat was using the mouse's own stratagem.

Not only was the wind her enemy, but the moon, which had guided her this far, was now her enemy, too. The sky was too clear, too bright with stars, to offer any hope of cloud cover. She flattened herself against one end of an interior wall of the storehouse, one of the few parts of the structure that still stood, and prayed that its shadow would camouflage her.

There was a chance, a faint one, that Charles hadn't seen her turn off at the ruins. He might have believed she would follow the road to the lighthouse. He might have continued on himself. If he had, his mistake would cost him precious minutes. Frantically she tried to think of a way to make use of them, but she couldn't. She had no weapon to use against him; there was no place to run to that would be safer. The most she could hope for was that Charles would somehow overlook her.

She might as well hope that he would have a last-minute change of heart. There had been a shortage of miracles in her life.

Except Jody. And Matthew.

She knew that thinking of them now was a way of preparing herself for the worst, but the timing seemed right. She had once told Matthew that as tragic as his wife and son's death had been, at least they had died knowing they were loved. Now she knew the same was true for her. Jody loved her with the unqualified love that only a child can give. Matthew loved her, too, although his love was more complex, more difficult to admit.

Her death would devastate them both.

She tried not to dwell on that. She wasn't dead yet, and she wasn't going to give up. Her resources were meager, but she would use them all. Her eyesight and hearing were keen. She was in good physical condition. And she wanted to live more than Charles wanted to kill her—if that were possible.

She wondered what would happen if she left the ruins, crawled through the stunted heath and mallee away from the roadside and along the steep cliff. She tried to remember if the loop road leading back to the homestead followed the cliff. It seemed to her that it did, potentially making her a target for Charles's headlights.

The only other possibility was to cross the peninsula and follow the other coastline, a coastline with no road beside it. But if she remembered the terrain correctly, the peninsula was half a mile wide or wider, and the bush wasn't tall enough to conceal her as she crossed. She couldn't crawl that far, and even if she did, edging along the cliffside was suicidal. The long drop to the sea and the rocks below would mean certain death.

"Dana!"

She shuddered. She couldn't tell which direction the shout had come from because of the wind. She only knew that Charles was frighteningly near.

She flattened herself tighter against the wall.

"Let's get this over with!"

Had she ever been such a coward that this kind of bullying would have succeeded? Anger cut through her fear. Charles was underestimating her. Perhaps it might work in her favor. She had taken him by surprise once, knocking the gun from his hand. She could do it again.

There was a large chunk of limestone at her feet. She bent and lifted it against her chest.

His next shout was closer. "You're prolonging my fun!"

She alternately watched both ends of the wall, tensed and waiting for his shadow to appear. If he came around the corner where she stood, she would be ready with the rock. If he came around the other, she would run.

She heard a noise before she saw a shadow—rocks rolling, soft cursing just to her right. She had no time to weigh her action. She jumped toward the noise, limestone lifted. Charles was only feet away, down on one knee where he had stumbled. Alexis slammed the limestone sharply against the back of his head.

He fell to the ground with a grunt. In a moment she was running toward the place where she had parked her wagon. She was gambling that he had parked near her and left his keys in the ignition. If not, she had no choice but to chance the run across the peninsula.

The wagon's windows glinted in the moonlight. Fifty yards behind it was Charles's car. She was running with the wind now, and she reached the car in seconds. Frantically she jerked on the door handle. But the door was locked.

She turned to start across the road, but the figure of a man blocked her way. He held a revolver in front of him, aimed directly at her heart. His other hand cradled the back of his head.

"Going somewhere, Dana?"

"The lighthouse or the ruins?" Matthew asked tersely.

"We've got no choice but to try the ruins first, since they're on the way."

"And if she's at the lighthouse?"

"Then we've wasted precious time," Harry conceded.

Matthew knew Harry was right, but it horrified him that they might make the wrong choice. Alexis could die because of it. "I'm going to turn off my lights. We'll do a turn through the car park at the cove. If we don't see anything we'll go on."

"Right-o." Harry punctuated the word with the click of the rifle as he snapped it apart to load it.

"I want the gun," Matthew told him, accelerating around a turn. "When we stop, hand it to me."

"No."

"I won't argue about it, Harry. I'll take it from you."

"Half deaf I may be, mate, but I'm strong as an ox. You go for me gun I'll slam it into your belly." The rifle clicked as he snapped it back together. "If there's any shooting to be done, it'll be me doing it."

"This is my fight!"

"This is the law's fight. I'm the senior here, and I'm as much of the law as we have in this park."

Matthew cursed and spun the wheel once more. The lighthouse shone in the distance.

"Ease up or you'll take us over the cliff." Harry braced himself as Matthew made the turn toward Weirs Cove. "There's a car!"

Matthew had seen it, too. It wasn't Alexis's, but he slammed on his brakes anyway. In a moment he and Harry were both out of the ute.

The wind howled along the track, covering any trace of voices. Harry put his fingers to his lips. He moved close to Matthew and whispered, "You'll have to be me ears."

Matthew listened intently. At first there was nothing; then just the faintest murmur was carried over the wind. He pointed toward the cliff. Stooping, they skirted the brush edging the path down to the cove where the supplies had once been hauled up the narrow man-made gorge to the storehouses above. They had gone fifty yards before they got a clear view.

There were two silhouettes at the guardrail. Matthew recognized Alexis immediately, but he was too far away to help. He touched Matthew's arm. "Alexis, on the left," he mouthed. Harry nodded. "Cover me," Matthew mouthed again.

Matthew ran beside the bush as far as it extended. Harry followed close behind.

"You're going to save me the trouble of shooting you." Charles rubbed the back of his neck, as if he still couldn't quite believe Alexis had hit him. "I'm just going to back you off this cliff."

"I planned it this way." Alexis struggled to sound calm. "If my body is found at the base of this cliff, they'll know it was murder."

Charles stepped closer, forcing her backward a pace. She had slowly been moving toward the cliff's edge for the last few minutes. "Between the surf and the rocks, there won't be enough of you to identify."

"There'll be enough. And my car will be here. You can't drive it out. It won't run."

"You never understood, did you? I can't be beaten." His eyes glittered with madness. "I can do anything I want. I can do anything to you that I want." Charles lifted his gun and motioned her over the metal guardrail that protected tourists.

She turned her shoulder toward the wind, praying it wouldn't sweep her over the cliff before she had the chance to lunge for Charles. If she was going to die here at the cliff's edge, he would die with her. She put one leg over the rail. "You can't make me afraid of you."

"No?" He cocked his revolver.

The guardrail was between them. She gripped it as the wind tore at her. "You're a coward, Charles," she taunted. "You're too much of a coward to get close enough to see if I'm afraid. You've put a fence between us."

Smiling benignly he stepped over the rail. "One step backward, Dana. Just one, maybe two. Look at me and tell me you're ready to die."

"Alexis!"

Charles raised his gun, and an explosion rocked him backward. He screamed, and the gun fell from his hand. He lunged toward Alexis.

"Get under the rail!"

Alexis dove under the guardrail as another explosion sounded. She knew the voice issuing the command. It had been Matthew's. The explosion could only have been a gun. She waited for a jolt of pain, waited for the world to go black.

Behind her Charles was screaming curses. She struggled to crawl toward Matthew; he was beside her in a second, kneeling to embrace her. She felt no jolt except relief.

"You're all right," he said, rocking her back and forth. "Oh God, tell me you're all right."

She threw her arms around him, unable to speak.

"Matthew!"

Alexis looked up to see Harry standing beside them, a rifle pointed toward the cliffside. Matthew kissed her forehead, then thrust her aside as he stood. She turned and saw Charles rising from the ground.

"Just step over the rail nice and easy," Harry shouted.

Matthew started toward Charles.

"Stay back, Matthew," Harry warned.

Matthew ignored him.

Alexis found her voice. "Matthew! No! You'll go to prison!"

Harry cocked the rifle. "I'm warning you, Matthew," he shouted.

Matthew stopped just short of the rail. The tensed lines of his body proclaimed his struggle. Then he stepped back. "Over the rail, Cahill." He motioned to the ground in front of him. "Try anything at all and I'll take pleasure in finishing you off."

Charles clutched his bleeding arm. "This is your fault, Dana!" he screamed. He backed away from Matthew toward the cliff's edge, one step, then two. For a moment he teetered there, fighting the wind as if his mind wasn't made up. Then he turned and plunged to the surf and rocks below.

Chapter 18

Alexis stood on the deck of the ferry, her arm lightly draped around Jody's shoulders.

"I remember the first time we came to the island," Jody said, watching the ferry glide up to the dock. "That was before my father died. When we were still running away."

Alexis didn't doubt that in the future Jody would have more questions, more doubts, about Charles and the "accident" that had taken his life. But for now the little girl seemed to understand and accept the facts as she knew them. Her father had come to Kangaroo Island looking for them. He had gone sightseeing and fallen from a cliff. His body had been recovered the next day.

With Matthew, Harry and Alexis as witnesses to Charles's jump from the cliff, there had been no problems with the Australian or American authorities. Officially the death was listed as accidental and the case closed. Alexis felt that "accident" was a fair assessment. Gripped by insanity, Charles had believed he was invincible. He had not committed suicide. She knew that he had jumped believing that he could not die.

The day after his death, Alexis had gone to Adelaide to begin the long bureaucratic procedure to fly the body back to Michigan. She and Jody had flown back, too, so that Jody could put this chapter of her life to rest.

Charles's death hadn't been so much a loss for Jody as a gain. Both his family and Alexis's had missed the child who had disappeared so precipitously from their lives, and they had welcomed her with an affection that had soothed her sorrow.

Alexis knew that Jody mourned a father she had never had, but she let Jody mourn, just as she let her parents try to alter the mistakes they had made so long ago by showing their granddaughter a warmer, more accepting part of themselves than Alexis had ever seen. The trip had been a healing one for the little girl.

"We aren't running anymore." Jody lifted a hand to wave to the strangers at the dock.

They weren't running anymore. In the month they had been in Michigan, Alexis had wondered if she would ever get used to not looking over her shoulder. She was free now, free to go anywhere she wanted, to live anywhere she wanted, to be anyone she chose to be.

"No, we aren't." Alexis squeezed Jody's shoulder. They had come back to Kangaroo Island *because* they weren't running anymore. They might not stay, but if they didn't, it wouldn't be because they had run again.

Jody looked up at Alexis. "I wonder if anybody missed me?"

"I'm sure your friends did."

"Do you think Matthew missed me?"

Alexis tried to smile reassuringly. "Of course he did."

"Can I still go to school this afternoon?"

Alexis nodded. She had called the school officials from Adelaide that morning to make the arrangements. "I've got to drop off the rental car and pick up our wagon in Parndana, anyway. You can ride the school bus back to our house."

There was a thud as the ferry docked; then Alexis led Jody by the hand to the area where their suitcases were stored. In a short time they were in the rental car they had reserved and on their way toward Parndana.

The trip from Michigan had been an exhausting one, even though they had stopped for several days to rest and sightsee in Sydney. Now, with the adaptability that had gotten her through the last months, Jody closed her eyes and fell instantly asleep. Alexis wished she could do the same, but even if she hadn't been driving, she knew sleep would elude her.

She was going to see Matthew. Today, while Jody was in school. The last time she had seen him was a month before, the day after Charles had leaped off the cliff. That morning he had accompanied her to the Kingscote hospital to identify Charles's body, and he had held her hand as she made the identification. There had been no time to talk about their relationship, nor had the timing been right. He had comforted her, just as he had so often done, but there had been no words of love.

There had been no words of love the night before, either. After Charles had jumped to a certain death, Matthew and Harry had taken her directly to Kingscote, where they had spent the remainder of the night telling the whole story to the police. Then she had fallen into a bed at the Queenscliffe Hotel in the early hours of the morning and slept until Matthew had called to tell her that the body had been recovered.

There had been few words at the airport after the identification had been completed. Matthew had held her as if he didn't want to let her go, and she had clung to him. "Come back," he had said. "If you don't, I'll come for you."

Now, a month later, she still didn't know what he had meant. She had heard nothing from him, and her confidence was shaken.

Jody was ravenous when she woke up from her nap. They picnicked by the side of the road on meat pies they had bought in Penneshaw, then continued on to Parndana.

As they came to a stop at the school, Jody gazed out the window, as if she were assessing the building. Then she turned to her mother. She spoke as if she were telling a secret. "Grandma took me back to the Academy one day. She wanted me to stay in Michigan and go to school there again."

"I know. She told me." Alexis could almost hear her mother's voice droning on and on about duty. Just as clearly, she could hear her own answer. She had gently but firmly explained that she would tolerate no interference in her life, and she would never again listen to any discussion designed to make her feel guilty. There had been a shocked moment of silence, then a brief nod. In the years to come they might fight the same battle again, but after everything Alexis had been through, she knew she would score the victory.

"I liked the Academy," Jody said, looking back out the window.

"I know you did."

"But I like it here, too."

"You can like both places."

"Here I can just be me. There, I was *special*. I didn't like being special."

"All kids are special."

"But here I'm special because I'm Jody, not just because I'm smart."

Alexis gazed past Jody's head to the school where the little girl might spend the rest of her formative years. It wasn't new, and it wasn't large. It didn't incorporate the latest in educational philosophy or design, but it was a comfortable place, filled with laughter and the murmur of childish voices as they learned the things they needed to equip them for a changing world. "I'd say this is a pretty good place."

"Yeah." Jody turned to give her mother a hug. Her eyes twinkled. "G'day, mate."

"G'day." Alexis watched Jody open the door and run up the sidewalk. If speed were any indication, Jody was glad to be back.

At the garage in town she traded the rental car for her wagon, pleased to see that all the damage had been repaired. The ride to the house on Hanson Bay seemed uncomfortably silent. Silence gave Alexis time to think—and to admit she was afraid. She drove the final miles down the track to the house, and she remembered the last time she had traveled this road. She had been frightened then, frightened that she might die. Now she was frightened again. In less than an hour she would drive to the park to see Matthew. And then she would know what the future held for both of them.

She could tell the moment she pulled into the clearing that the repairs had been completed. There was a new porch, wider and more ornate than the one that had burned. More surprisingly, now it wrapped around the side of the house facing Hanson Bay. There were even wooden rocking chairs with bright plaid cushions and a table covered with a cloth of the same plaid.

The burned skeletons of the shrubbery had been replaced by a garden of bushes and blooming summer annuals. She parked and opened the door to stare. New grass had been sown and a stone walkway installed.

Peter Bartow had promised repairs; he hadn't promised a face-lift. Alexis got slowly out of the car and noted more changes. There were shutters on the windows, forest green shutters surrounding windows with new burgundy trim. The house was newly painted, too. It was a white so bright she wanted to blink.

Then she did blink, because tears had suddenly filled her eyes. The house spelled welcome. It told her she had come home, and there was nothing she wanted more. She was afraid to hope it could be true.

The front door creaked, and she saw Matthew standing in the doorway. For a moment she wasn't sure he was real. He seemed part of the dream, a fantasy that only her deepest, most secret desires could have created. Then he started toward her, and she knew he was flesh and blood.

"How did you know I'd come today?" she asked when he was only an arm's length away.

"Peter rang me this morning."

"Peter called you?"

"I suppose he was tired of me ringing him."

She tried to smile, but there were too many fears, too many unanswered questions, in the way. "So you've been getting reports?"

He extended his hand. "Come inside."

She wasn't sure she was ready to go with him. She had believed she had another hour to prepare for this meeting. "Have you had anything to do with all these changes, Matthew?"

He smiled, a warm, natural smile that blasted away her hesitancy. "Come inside."

She slipped her hand inside his. Immediately she knew that touching him was a mistake. She wasn't sure she would ever find the strength to let him go again. His palm caressed hers; their fingers intertwined. The sense of homecoming overwhelmed her.

He led her up the porch steps. They were bedecked by pots of blooming red and white begonias. "You planted the garden and the pots, didn't you?"

He gave her the same, heart-stopping smile. "Will you let me answer all your questions in my own way?"

She nodded.

Matthew pulled her over the threshold. The wooden floors in the hallway had been refinished, and they gleamed like satin. The hall itself was freshly painted and decorated with photographs. Alexis recognized many of them. There were Jody's baby pictures, framed now in dark wood frames. There were other pictures of her family, too, that had been in her lockbox, and some of her as a child. Interspersed with them were similarly framed photographs of Matthew and, more touching, photographs of Todd that she had unpacked from Matthew's attic and placed on his walls. The photograph that she had placed at Matthew's bedside, the last photograph that had been taken of the Haley family, was on the wall with the others.

She couldn't speak. But Matthew was able to.

He cleared his throat and began. "I remember when Jeannie tried to take this photograph of Todd." He pointed out one of a chubby, frowning baby. "He had just gotten up from a nap. He was always a happy little boy, but that day she couldn't get a smile out of him. She said she took this to remind us he had a darker side when we started feeling too smug." He touched the frame. "Later all we had to do to get him to laugh was show it to him."

Alexis swallowed. She knew what the explanation had cost him. "He was beautiful, even when he was angry."

He nodded. "Yes, he was." He was silent for a moment; then he pointed to another photograph. "This was his first day of school. And this—" he pointed to another "—was the first time he rode a horse. We loved him dearly. We wanted more children, but Jeannie wasn't able to have them, so we poured all our love into Todd. I suppose we spoiled him a bit, but he didn't show it. He was a son to be proud of."

"World's best son," she said softly.

He smiled a little. "Yes."

"Matthew—"

He squeezed her hand. "Tell me about this." He pointed to a photograph of Jody. "Why is she sticking her tongue out?"

She had to push her words past the lump in her throat. "She was two. That was the year her tongue was out of her mouth more than it was in. I finally threatened to put pepper on it if it passed her lips again." She tried to laugh. The sound was more like a sob. "When we stayed in New Zealand before coming here, we visited a Maori meeting house. Some traditional Maori carvings have images of men with their tongues out to scare away enemies. Jody asked me if I had my pepper with me. She still remembered."

"She's not an easy child, just a wonderful one."

"World's best daughter."

He squeezed her hand again and began to lead her through the hallway. He bypassed her bedroom and the study. Both doors were closed. Instead he stopped at Jody's room. That door was open.

"I've been assured that this bedroom is every little girl's dream. Her friend Annie gave her approval." He stepped aside so Alexis could see. The room had been wallpapered in a delicate print of rose and apple green. The trim was painted rose, and the green was picked up in both a large plush throw rug and a rose and green flowered comforter and matching canopy on the bed in the corner. The bed was pine, and there were a pine desk and dresser to match. Todd's carving of the possum sat on the dresser top, along with Jody's own possessions.

"Matthew. . . ." Alexis didn't know what else to say.

"Come on."

She couldn't resist him. She let him lead her down the hallway. She got a glimpse of new furniture in the living room; some she recognized from Matthew's house. But it was the kitchen where he finally stopped.

"What do you think?"

She couldn't think at all. She could only feel, feel the love that had always been present here magnified one hundred-fold. With a soft cry, she flung herself into his arms.

He clutched her as if he would never let her go. "Anything you don't like, we can change. I just had to show you. . . ." He buried his face in her hair.

"That you love me."

"I love you." Matthew turned her face to his. "So much that I'll never be able to tell you how much." He kissed her, and they didn't part until they were both breathless. He turned her so that she was snugly against him, crossing his arms around her waist. "Do you like it?"

The kitchen had been remodeled with tender care. The slate floor had been scrubbed and polished to a bright shine. The window trim had been stripped and refinished until it now glowed a warm honey-gold. All the cabinets had been given the same careful treatment and adorned with new enamel hardware. The walls had been primed, but not painted, as if they were waiting for final approval. But no one had waited for approval on the appliances. They were all new and almond-colored, selected to complement the unadorned simplicity of the huge room. The only touches of color were the rug they had once made love on and Jeannie's red enamel canisters and blue teakettle.

Best of all, the table she had hoped to refinish someday had been done for her. And gracing it, as if they had always stood there, were four dining room chairs from Matthew's house.

She turned and touched his cheeks with her fingertips. "It's the most beautiful room in the world."

"Will you let me share it with you?"

"The room, the house, Jody, everything I have."

Not until relief showed plainly on his face did she know he'd been afraid she was going to say no. "I don't know how you can still want me," he said.

"I don't know how you could believe otherwise."

"You had so much courage, and I had so little."

She thought of the times he had risked his life for her and shown courage any man would envy. But she knew Matthew meant something different—the courage of the heart. She tried to tell him it didn't matter. "You love fiercely and forever. It wasn't cowardice, it was grief that made you afraid to love again."

It was a long time before he stopped kissing her. "You gave me back Jeannie and Todd," he said against her cheek. "I can let them go now. We can pack away the memories and make our own."

"You don't have to forget them," she said earnestly. "I love them, too. They were part of you once. They still are. Leave their pictures on the wall. Leave pieces of them here with us. If we have children together, we'll want them to know about their brother, and they'll be curious about Jeannie. Let's teach them that even when love hurts, it's worth giving."

He crushed her against him; then he lifted her and carried her back through the hallway. She had no time to notice the changes he had made in the bedroom. She only noticed the firm mattress under her back and the man she loved against her.

They made love as if they had never been apart. Each caress was a reawakening; each kiss kindled a flame that had never died. Their clothes disappeared as if by magic, as if the mere mechanics of making love again could be ignored. No one led, and no one followed. They moved together, pleasing each other as they pleased themselves. Finally, restraint was a punishment.

Alexis clung to Matthew as he took the pleasure he had given her seconds before. Later she clung to him still when he tried to leave her. She wasn't ready to be without him. She didn't think she ever would be.

His smile was lazy and warm enough to reignite the embers they had just banked together. "Won't I be crushing you like this?"

"I'll take my chances."

He kissed her forehead, then turned them both to their sides so that they were still facing.

"Thinking of you here, like this, was the only way I got through the last month." He stroked her hair, letting it slide through his fingers.

"Would you really have come for me?"

"I told myself I'd wait until the house was done. I knew you needed time."

"I needed you."

"You needed to know you were safe. *I* needed to know that you wanted me anyway."

She frowned. "Did you think I wouldn't? I didn't love you because you helped me when I was in danger."

"Both of us had to be certain that was true."

She wanted to protest, but she knew he was right. They had been thrown together by circumstance. The month apart had shown them that circumstance had nothing to do with the feelings they had for each other.

And more. "Did you need time to know Jeannie and Todd again?"

He nodded, relieved that she understood. "I had to say goodbye."

She stroked his cheek in silent sympathy.

He kissed her palm. "Can you live here? You came to the island because it was so remote. Will that bother you now?"

"You're here." She traced the line of his jaw with a fingertip.

"That won't always be enough."

"I have my work. I have Jody. After the island, the rest of the world seemed frantic and unreal. I'm glad to be back."

"Then you'll marry me?"

Her finger slid to a stop. "Someday, when I have a starry-eyed teenage daughter, she's going to ask me how you proposed. What'll I tell her?"

"Tell her that I kissed you. Like this." He demonstrated. "And then I asked if you'd be my wife. Tell her it was right here in this very . . . house."

"And I'll tell her I said yes without a second thought."

"Several teenage daughters." He drew the meandering fingertip to his mouth and kissed it. "I'd like Jody to have a sister. Will that be all right?"

"And a brother." She saw the answer in his eyes and knew that he was really healed.

"Todd would have liked a brother. I'd like another son," he said as he pulled her closer.

They fell asleep together then, dreaming of the years ahead. Outside, in a lone gum tree at the edge of the clearing, the koala called for his mate.

And from deep in the forest, there was a rapturous answering cry.

Epilogue

Jody leaped into the arms stretched out to greet her. "Gray!"

"Merry Christmas, shrimp. You've grown again."

She snuggled close as Gray lifted her against his chest for a hug.

"Pass her around, Sheridan. I want a turn." Dillon Ward, a man who looked like the opal miner he was, reached for Jody, and she went into his arms for an embrace that equaled Gray's.

"Is everybody here?" Jody giggled as Dillon threw her into the air, then caught her and set her down. "Are they?"

"Why don't you go see?"

Jody started down the hallway. "Julianna! Kelsey! Paige!"

"If the baby was napping, she won't be now." Alexis stepped over the threshold, followed by Matthew. She hugged both men, then stood back to watch Gray introduce Matthew to Dillon. The two men looked each other over, then smiled.

Alexis slipped her arm through Matthew's with a new wife's pride. "Gray, the house is spectacular."

Gray beamed. "Do you like it? Dillon thought I should have built it underground, like his dugout in Coober Pedy."

"Gray said it would be a bloody aquarium if he did." Dillon clasped Gray's shoulder with affection.

A delicately lovely strawberry blonde came from the far end of the hall to greet them. She kissed Alexis on the cheek and offered her hand to Matthew. The strength of her handshake proved how delicate she wasn't. "I'm Kelsey Ward." She looked him over much as her husband had, then smiled.

"Don't let Outback Man here fool you, Gray," she said when the greetings were finished. "He's been lapping up these ocean breezes to remember when we're back of beyond again." She lowered her voice conspiratorially. "I saw him reading the real estate section in the paper."

Dillon threw up his hands in defeat. "For a summer cottage," he said, while everyone laughed. "A holiday spot."

"Kangaroo Island's closer," Alexis pointed out.

"And there's always New Zealand."

Everyone turned to stare at the raven-haired beauty framed in the open doorway. Then there was a rush to greet her and the dark-haired man and child behind her.

"Paige, you're pregnant! You didn't tell anybody." Gray hugged her first.

"I had no doubt you'd be able to tell for yourself," Paige said wryly. "Adam's thinking big. We're having twins. Just like most of our ewes." She reached down to lift the little boy into the middle of the greetings, but her husband shook his head and lifted him himself.

"You're not supposed to be lifting anything heavy," Adam scolded her.

"I'm not anything. I'm a little boy," five-year-old Jeremy informed his father.

"See?" Paige said, when the laughter died. She smoothed Jeremy's hair. "Don't worry, darling. When I sit down, you can sit on what lap I have left."

Jody came running down the hallway to greet the new guests, followed by Julianna carrying a Buddhalike Colly.

Another round of kisses and hugs was exchanged.

"We have a house," Julianna informed them all when there was a large enough lull to be heard. "Not just a foyer."

Laughing and talking, they slowly headed toward the living room and the lanai off it. An architect, Gray had designed the house on the coast of Windward Oahu, where he and Julianna now lived year round. It showed all his creative ability in its attention to line and integration with the landscape. It also showed all Julianna's wizardry with color and pattern. Now, in mid-December, it was decorated for Christmas and this very special reunion.

Jody lagged behind. Julianna had given her Colly to hold, and the baby was cooing delightedly. Jeremy wriggled free from his father's encircling arms and came back to join them. In a minute the three children were alone in the hallway.

Jeremy frowned his concern. "Colly still doesn't have any teeth."

Jody nodded wisely. "She will. These things take time."

Colly reached for Jeremy, grabbing a fistful of shiny black hair, which she tried to pull into her mouth. Jeremy slipped away, giggling. "I'm glad I'm not a baby!"

"Do you want to hold her?"

Jeremy considered his answer. "No," he said finally.

"But you ought to practice. You're going to be a big brother."

He frowned as if he wasn't sure he was looking forward to that. "I never had a brother or sister before."

Jody transferred Colly to one hip. She put her other arm around Jeremy's shoulder. "You've got me."

"But you don't live with me."

"My mother says family is something you make right here." She touched Jeremy's chest. "In your heart. Everybody here is my family. So you must be my brother. And Colly's our sister."

Jeremy nodded. The logic seemed good enough for him. "I still don't wanna hold her."

"Okay." Jody looked up and saw her mother standing in the doorway. Her new father stood behind her, his arms wrapped around her waist.

"Would you like me to take Colly so you and Jeremy can explore?" Alexis asked.

"Daddy can take her," Jody said, hoisting Colly off her hip to thrust her at Matthew. "He likes little girls, and he never got to hold me when I was a baby."

Matthew took Colly, then bent to give Jody a kiss. "But I get to hold you now, don't I?" As an afterthought he ruffled Jeremy's hair. "Family," he reminded the little boy. Jeremy grinned.

In a moment the two children had run off to play.

"Family is something you make right here," Matthew said, reaching down to touch Alexis's chest. His hand lingered as Colly teethed happily on the collar of his shirt. "Did you really tell her that?"

"I don't know, but if I didn't, I should have."

"You should put it in a book. You should put all this and everyone here in a book. All the love. All the stories, including ours." He gestured widely, encompassing the house and everyone in it.

"I just might." Alexis stood on tiptoe to kiss him; then she stepped back, smiling. "Do you think anyone would believe it?"

*   *   *   *   *

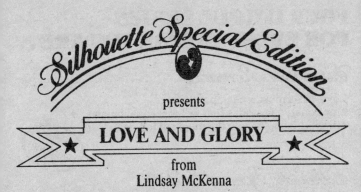

Silhouette Special Edition

presents

★ LOVE AND GLORY ★

from
Lindsay McKenna

Introducing a gripping new series celebrating our men—and women—in uniform. Meet the Trayherns, a military family as proud and colorful as the American flag, a family fighting the shadow of dishonor, a family determined to triumph—with **LOVE AND GLORY!**

June: A QUESTION OF HONOR (SE #529) leads the fast-paced excitement. When Coast Guard officer Noah Trayhern offers Kit Anderson a safe house, he unwittingly endangers his own guarded emotions.

July: NO SURRENDER (SE #535) Navy pilot Alyssa Trayhern's assignment with arrogant jet jockey Clay Cantrell threatens her career—and her heart—with a crash landing!

August: RETURN OF A HERO (SE #541) Strike up the band to welcome home a man whose top-secret reappearance will make headline news . . . with a delicate, daring woman by his side.

Three courageous siblings—
three consecutive months of

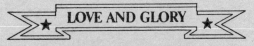

★ LOVE AND GLORY ★

Premiering in **June**, only in
Silhouette Special Edition.

FOUR UNIQUE SERIES
FOR EVERY WOMAN YOU ARE...

Silhouette Romance

Love, at its most tender, provocative,
emotional... in stories that will make you laugh and
cry while bringing you the magic of falling in love.

6 titles
per month

Silhouette Special Edition

Sophisticated, substantial and packed with
emotion, these powerful novels of life and love will
capture your imagination and steal your heart.

6 titles
per month

Silhouette Desire

Open the door to romance and passion. Humorous,
emotional, compelling—yet always a believable
and sensuous story—Silhouette Desire never
fails to deliver on the promise of love.

6 titles
per month

Silhouette Intimate Moments

Enter a world of excitement, of romance
heightened by suspense, adventure and the
passions every woman dreams of. Let us
sweep you away.

4 titles
per month

SILG-1R

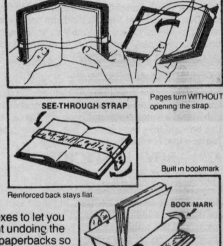

COMING NEXT MONTH

#289 TIGER DAWN—Kathleen Creighton

Zoologist Sarah Fairchild was one of the privileged, the elite, and Dan Cisco knew that his kind and hers didn't mix. But when poachers threatened Sarah and her orangutans he realized that society's rules could always be broken in the name of love.

#290 THE PRICE OF GLORY—
Lynn Bartlett

It was déjà vu for news bureau chief Seth Winter. Once terrorists had taken the lives of his wife and child; now they had kidnapped his star reporter, Cassandra Blake, the woman who had brought love back into his life. This time, he swore, justice—and the heart—would triumph.

#291 ABOVE SUSPICION—
Andrea Edwards

Trapped in a web of danger and deceit, Claire Haywood knew that only love could set her free. But if she told Jonathon Tyler the truth and admitted that she'd begun their relationship as a spy, would he be able to see the genuine love beneath the lies?

#292 LIAR'S MOON—Mary Anne Wilson

Michael Conti was a finder of missing people, and during his most recent assignment he'd discovered the love of his life. But his findings also suggested that Alexandria Thomas was a thief. And it was true—because he knew she'd stolen his heart.

AVAILABLE THIS MONTH: